TO SLIP
THE BONDS
OF EARTH

TO SLIP
THE BONDS
OF EARTH

Amanda
Flower

KENSINGTON
PUBLISHING CORP.

www.kensingtonbooks.com

KENSINGTON BOOKS are published by

Kensington Publishing Corp.
900 Third Avenue
New York, NY 10022

All Kensington titles, imprints and distributed lines are available at special quantity discounts for bulk purchases for sales promotion, premiums, fund-raising, educational or institutional use.

Special book excerpts or customized printings can also be created to fit specific needs. For details, write or phone the office of the Kensington Special Sales Manager: Kensington Publishing Corp., 900 Third Ave., New York, NY, 10022. Attn. Special Sales Department. Phone: 1-800-221-2647.

Library of Congress Control Number: 2023949943

The K with book logo Reg. U.S. Pat. & TM Off.

ISBN: 978-1-4967-4766-2
First Kensington Hardcover Edition: April 2024

ISBN: 978-1-4967-4767-9 (ebook)

10 9 8 7 6 5 4 3 2 1

Printed in the United States of America

For Katharine Wright and all the teachers
who change children's lives, including mine.

Acknowledgments

First and foremost, I have to thank Katharine Wright for living such an independent and amazing life. Without her, this book would not exist. Her brothers Wilbur and Orville may have been world famous, but she was equally as intelligent and industrious as they.

Thanks always to my fabulous agent, Nicole Resciniti, who continually pushes me to write things I never considered before.

Thanks, too, to my wonderful editor at Kensington, Alicia Condon, and the rest of the Kensington team, especially my publicist Larissa Ackerman. This is the first book I have written for you with no mention of Jethro the pig, but as you can see, I got his name in here anyway.

Gratitude to the late historian and author David McCullough for his definitive work *The Wright Brothers*. Of all the books I have read about the family, this is the most compelling and one I will read again and again. Gratitude also to the historical interpreters and park rangers at Carillon Historical Park and Dayton Aviation Heritage National Historical Park, who answered my countless questions about the Wrights, and in particular about Katharine. Walking in the places where the Wrights lived made all the difference for this novel.

Thanks to Kimra Bell for reading this manuscript, and thank you to all my wonderful readers, who read my mysteries no matter where or what time I take them to.

Love and gratitude to my husband, David Seymour, who had food delivered to me and encouraged me when I was in the last hours of turning in this book.

And finally, thanks to God in heaven for opening yet another door in a career I will never take for granted.

If I were giving a young man advice as to how he might succeed in life, I would say to him, pick out a good father and mother, and begin life in Ohio.

—Wilbur Wright

CHAPTER 1

How dare Bufford Lyons make such a fool of me at the teachers' meeting this afternoon? As we were coming to the end of the fall semester, I had made a formal request to teach Greek III in the spring. The language was one of my first loves and the reason I took my teaching position, but ever since I had begun teaching at Steele High School, I had been regulated to the introductory classes in languages. First-year Latin was a painful course to teach. Most of the students didn't want to be there and had no interest in learning any language, especially not a dead one.

I had thought with so many years teaching under my belt and the upcoming retirement of Mr. Wellings, the current Greek III teacher, I would be allowed to take on a more demanding course.

"We can't have a woman teaching upperclassmen," Bufford had said when I'd made the formal request in front of the faculty assembly. "The young men in these courses are far too close to Miss Wright's age. They won't take a young woman seriously, and they need to concentrate on their lessons, as our students of Greek are the most likely to go on to college. Steele High School has a reputation to uphold."

I stood up. "I studied Greek at Oberlin College and graduated with top honors in the course. I am more than cap—"

"You are still a *woman*." He said the word as if it was
some sort of slur.

I put my hands on my hips. "Should I be pointing out the
obvious, that you are an old man?"

The principal, Mr. Mellon, took his mallet and banged the
table in front of him. "Miss Wright, please calm yourself."

I balled my hands at my sides. Why was I asked to calm
myself, but Bufford wasn't? I knew why—because, as Bufford had pointed out, I was a woman. That was reason
enough for them to reprimand me, and that truth set my
teeth on edge.

"I do understand your educational background," Mr. Mellon went on. "But the school board has already decided it
would be best if the upperclassmen were taught by Mr. Lyons."

Bufford sat back down in his chair with a smug look on
his face.

"What?" I asked. "He doesn't know half the Greek I do."

Mr. Mellon held his gavel in his hand, as if he was con-
templating rapping it on the table again. "A veteran teacher
is best for the course. You are still early in your career."

"You mean a veteran *male* teacher," I corrected.

"Miss Wright," the elderly principal said, "the matter is
settled. Now we must move on to other topics of concern."

"Yes, Miss Wright," Bufford said. "You should stick to
selling Christmas trees. That's more appropriate for a female
teacher." He smiled at me, and his gray mustache twitched,
as if he was holding in a laugh.

"Excuse me for caring about the students and wanting
them to have access to an arts program while in high school.
I am willing to make that extra effort for my students rather
than sitting on my laurels and accepting positions I'm un-
qualified for simply because I am the oldest man in the room."

"Miss Wright," Mr. Mellon exclaimed in shock.

The smile had faded from Bufford's face. I had successfully hit my mark. He'd made me look like a fool, but he was the fool. He couldn't even conjugate in pig Latin.

At the end of the meeting, I stormed from the room. Typically, after school I went home, like the dutiful and obedient daughter and sister I was, but on that day, I was just too spitting mad to face the demands of my family.

It was a crisp December day, and a walk into town was just what I needed. Fresh snow dusted the lampposts and street signs, but it was not yet thick enough to stick to the ground. The shop windows were all done up for Christmas with evergreens, red ribbons, and toy trains.

I let out a sigh. I should be concentrating on my holiday shopping instead of what Bufford Lyons had said. His comment about the school fundraiser steamed me the most. I'd been working for weeks to make sure the Christmas tree sale and carol singing went off without a hitch, and it was set for the holiday break. All the proceeds would be going to the music department.

Even though music wasn't my specialty, I loved listening to it and knew it was an important part of a public education. I was working with the Parent-Teacher Association and association president Lenora Shaw to organize the fundraiser. The PTA was in its infancy, but I recognized what a vital partner it could be in achieving our fundraising goals. When I'd told Principal Mellon of my enthusiasm, he'd appointed me as the teacher liaison. It wasn't until later that I learned he'd chosen me because I was a woman, not because of my support of the group.

Bufford, Principal Mellon, and all the men in that building were the same. They believed I should be grateful I was allowed to be in the same room with them, and completely ignored the fact I had more common sense in my left pinkie than all of them combined.

I had to put the incident at school behind me, if only for a little while. Winter recess would be here soon, and I needed the break as much as my students did. This afternoon I hoped to visit the bookshop and find something new to read to take my mind off the ridiculous school rules I had to abide by as a female teacher. I might find a gift for my father and brothers as well.

A gentleman I recognized from town but could not name tipped his hat to me.

"Good afternoon, Miss Wright. We heard your brothers are at it again. What are they thinking? That they can fly like a bird? It goes against nature. If God wanted us to fly, he would have given us wings."

"Are you suggesting humans should not swim, because we do not have fins?"

He blinked at me, as if my retort was some sort of riddle he couldn't make heads or tails of. "I beg your pardon?"

I adjusted my spectacles on my nose. "If anyone can achieve flight in our lifetime, it will be my brothers Wilbur and Orville Wright."

"Two boys from Dayton?" he snorted. "That is as likely as Old Saint Nick walking down the street."

I lifted my chin. "Well, I suggest you make up for being on his naughty list, because I heard he is out on a stroll, checking off names." With that, I marched away.

I left him there and headed into the bookshop and browsed for a long while. There was nothing like books to put my mind at ease.

"Katie, I didn't see you there," a kind voice said. "You were so hunched over that book. What is it?"

I held up the tome in my hands to show my old school friend Agnes Osborne. "A history of Rome."

Agnes snorted. "I should have known you would be engrossed in something of that sort."

I smiled. "My interests have not changed, Ag."

"You're nothing if not consistent." She tugged on a lock of hair that had fallen from its hairpin. "Have you heard from your brothers? I would be interested to know how they are getting on in North Carolina."

"They write, of course, though not as often as I would like," I replied. "They write more often to Father than they do to me, but they seem to be getting on fine. They said they are very close to heavier-than-air powered flight."

She cocked her head. "Haven't they said that before?"

"A time or two," I admitted.

"Why aren't they happy with the bicycle shop? Why isn't that enough for them? Would they not be happier to settle down and marry? Don't they want children?"

I shook my head and said nothing. These were questions I received often in regard to my brothers, and I had tired of answering them after so many years. I was grateful when Agnes changed the subject.

"Will you be at the Shaws' party this Saturday?" she asked with sparkling blue eyes.

"I plan to go as long as Father doesn't need me. Lenora Shaw is hosting and inviting everyone on the Steele PTA."

"I heard of lot of young men will be coming home to see their families for Christmas and they'll be at the party. You know the Shaws' party is the real start of the holiday season in Dayton. This will be the first time I have had an opportunity to go."

"The presence of young men is of no concern to me. I'm far too busy with my teaching, caring for Father, and minding my brothers' bicycle shop to have time for such things."

She clicked her tongue. "You need to have a life of your own. You are too wrapped up in others' lives. Haven't you ever cared for a man who wasn't a family member? Have you thought about being in love?"

My friend gave a little swoon at the very idea, but Agnes

Osborne had been dreaming of love since we were in pigtails. I knew this because I had heard about it ad nauseum for the past twenty years.

I pressed my lips together. When I was in college, I had briefly been engaged. My family never knew about it, and I didn't love the man. It just seemed getting engaged was what senior men did, and as a sophomore, I'd gone along with the proposal. Thankfully, both of us had realized our foolishness before it was too late or before I made the mistake of telling Father or my brothers. They would never have forgiven me had I married. However, there had been another man, whom I'd cared for deeply. Unfortunately, he was now married to someone else.

I said none of this to Ag and was thankful she'd never visited me at Oberlin College, where I had attended school, so she knew nothing of either man. No one in Dayton knew of them. I looked at the small watch pin attached to the lapel of my coat. "I should be heading home. Father will be wondering where I have been so long."

"I hope I didn't upset you, Katie," Agnes said with a frown. "That wasn't my intention."

"I know." I smiled at her. "But I would appreciate it if you would not bring the idea of romance up again."

She didn't give me an answer one way or another as we said our goodbyes.

Taking the Roman history I had purchased at the shop, I made my way home to number 7 Hawthorn Street. The white house with green shutters came into view. I noted that some of the greenery and red bows I had wrapped around the posts on the wide front porch had come loose. I would need to fix those before I entered the house. Ever since my mother had died when I was fifteen, I had been determined to keep a nice home for my father and brothers. That went for both the inside and the outside. Everything had to be just so.

I stepped onto the wide porch and set my satchel on the white rocker, but before I could even pick up the first bow, the front door flew open.

"Miss Wright, you're home!" exclaimed Carrie Kayler, our seventeen-year-old maid. She wore her dark hair in a bun at the back of her head, and her attire consisted of a simple gray dress with a white apron. Her hazel eyes were the size of dinner plates.

"Carrie, what is wrong? Is Father all right?" Fear clawed at my chest. Had my father fallen ill?

"I'm fine," my father said in his booming bishop's voice. He stood in the foyer, holding a telegram. He kept looking down at it.

A new fear overtook me. Had something happened to my brothers? "Are the boys all right?"

He handed the Western Union telegram to me. What I read took my breath away.

SUCCESS FOUR FLIGHTS THURSDAY MORNING ALL AGAINST TWENTY ONE MILE WIND STARTED FROM LEVEL WITH ENGINE POWER ALONE AVERAGE SPEED THROUGH AIR THIRTY ONE MILES LONGEST 57 SECONDS INFORM PRESS HOME CHRISTMAS. OREVELLE WRIGHT.

The paper fell from my hands. It seemed that everything in the world was about to change.

CHAPTER 2

Istood on the front porch and stared at the telegram. I read it again. This time much more slowly. Then I held it in the air and cried, "They did it!"

I had known from the start that Wilbur and Orville would fly, and now I had the proof in my hands.

"Katharine," Father said. "Don't make such a spectacle of yourself."

As the bishop of the Church of the United Brethren in Christ, Old Constitution, my father was very much of the belief that our family must set an example. We did everything correctly and properly. Loud outbursts of delight were not condoned, but that didn't stop me in the least.

"This is the most wonderful news, and most welcome after such a dreadful day."

"Dreadful day? What has happened, daughter?" Father asked.

"It doesn't matter now. We have to celebrate. Does Lorin know?"

Lorin was one of my older brothers. He lived with his wife and children just a few blocks away.

The bishop shook his head. "You are the first person I have told."

"Rightly so," I said with all the confidence in the world. I should be the second to know after Father. Orville, Wilbur, and I were exceptionally close as siblings. Lorin, who was older, stood outside our triumvirate, and our eldest brother, Reuchlin, lived in Missouri, too far away to be part of our inner circle. "I'll go to Lorin now. Orville instructed us to tell the press. Lorin would be the best one to do that."

"It's growing late," the bishop said. "We can tell him in the morning. He will be tired after work and sitting down with his family for dinner."

I wrinkled my forehead. "You expect me to keep this bottled up all night? My head might burst if I do so."

Father shook his head. "Katie, you are too emotional at times. Everything doesn't have to be addressed the moment you learn of it. Let the reality settle before you act."

"Lorin deserves to know right away. Think of how he would feel if news of this got out before we told him. He would be beside himself."

My father shook his head. "I see your mind is made up and there is nothing that I can say to change it. Go take the telegram to Lorin, but be careful with it. I don't want it to get lost. Wilbur and Orville have solved the problem of human flight. I wish to keep this telegram as a memento."

With that pronouncement, Father went back into the house.

I turned to Carrie. "Hold off on dinner until I come back. If Father complains, give him a little something to tide him over until I return. Today is a day of celebration!"

Carrie rubbed her arms, as if to fight off the cold. "Now that the boys have conquered flight, I wonder if this will be the end of their tinkering. We have spent too many days tripping over bits of their flying machines scattered about the house."

"It won't be the end. It's just the beginning." I folded the telegram and tucked it into my coat pocket. I secured the button on the pocket to make sure it didn't fall out. I knew very well how valuable this piece of paper was. It was proof of a new era.

Lorin, his wife, Nette, and their four children would be as excited to hear the news as I was. I was sure of it. As I hurried down Hawthorn Street, I bumped into Herman Wheeler at the corner. Herman was an old classmate of Wilbur and Orville's. If I remembered correctly, he was now working for the Shaw family at their paper mill. Paper was a big business in Dayton, as five rivers converged in the city. The rivers provided plenty of power for the mills to make paper. At one time, Wilbur and Orville had run their own printing press and published a newspaper too. They still did some printing for faithful clients and for themselves, but when their cycle shop took off with the new bicycle craze, they'd reduced the printing business in size and volume.

Now they had moved on from bicycles to flying machines. My brothers never did anything by halves. If they chose to start a business, they did so with their full hearts and souls and did not stop until they accomplished their goals.

I didn't know where Herman lived, but I knew he wasn't a neighbor, and the Shaws weren't nearby either. The family lived on a grand estate in a much more affluent part of Dayton. I could see no reason at all for Herman to be on the corner of West Fourth and Hawthorn, but there he was.

"Miss Wright," Herman said formally, with the slightest bow. "I'm so sorry. I just about knocked you over."

That was a bit of an exaggeration, but I didn't correct him. I wasn't a delicate flower by any stretch. My father liked to say I wasn't too big or too small. I wasn't too pretty or too plain either. I was in the middle in every way. When I was younger, there had been times when I'd lamented—if only to myself—my unremarkable appearance, but now, as an adult, I found it served me well. Those who had been lulled by the relative dullness of my looks had been disarmed by the sharpness of my wit.

Herman was just an inch or two taller than I and painfully thin. If the December wind gusts picked up, there was a very good chance he'd blow over just like the first test glider my brothers had built for Kitty Hawk.

"It's quite all right," I said after a beat.

"You seem to be in a great rush. May I ask where you are off to in such a hurry?" He smiled at me, and I noticed for the first time how his two front teeth overlapped each other. It was a defect that would not be seen from afar, but close up, I found myself staring at it.

I took two large steps back. "This is my street, which is reason enough for me to be walking on it at any pace I should like," I said rather sharply. "I have every reason to be here. It's a crisp evening, and the cold air is refreshing. It would make much more sense for me to ask you what *you* are doing here, as you don't live in this neighborhood."

He forced a laugh. "I forgot how direct you can be. I suppose that comes from living in a house full of men. If your mother had lived long enough to teach you how to behave as a proper lady, you would not be at such a great disadvantage in life."

I balled my hands at my sides. *Disadvantage?* The nerve of this man! I had no disadvantages in life at all. This Neanderthal knew nothing about my mother. She was the one who'd taught Wilbur and Orville to build with their hands. It wasn't our father, who had been too preoccupied with sermons and church politics. And it was she who had taught me to stand on my own two feet. That was a much more valuable lesson than the feminine teachings that Herman thought I lacked by losing my mother so young.

"Perhaps you are in a hurry because of your brothers' success." He smiled.

"What do you mean?" I asked

"Is it not true that Wilbur and Orville flew?"

I stared at him. How did he know this when I had just heard of it?

"I would love to hear more about their flight if you have the time. As their sister, I am certain you are privy to many details. I have a great interest in it."

"I do not have the time. If you will excuse me," I said in a clipped tone, "I would like to continue on with my walk alone."

I brushed by him and didn't realize until I was stomping my way down Lorin's street that he never had told me what he was doing in my neighborhood that night. It would be many days before I learned the truth.

CHAPTER 3

By the time I reached Lorin's modest house with its wide front porch and cheerful Christmas greenery around the porch railing, I had calmed myself. My father had told me more times than I could count that I was a wrathy young woman. He said I had been worse as a child. Truth be told, my sharp temper served me well in the classroom. Even the worst of the boys in my first-year Latin classes quickly learned how far they could push me, and—as my father said—it was less than an inch.

I ran up the steps of Lorin's home, taking care to skip the step with the hole in it. Milton, Lorin's eldest, had stepped through the rotted board on that step and cut his leg. He had had to get four stitches. Lorin hadn't yet had the time to fix the board. If Wilbur or Orville were home, it would have been repaired by now. Actually, it would have been more than repaired; it would be better than new. The boys would have torn the stairs down to the studs and rebuilt them twice as strong.

I hoped that with their latest success, Wilbur and Orville wouldn't ignore all the small projects that the whole family had been saving for their return. I knew Lorin had many more projects than I did. Time and money were always tight for my second oldest brother. He was doing his very best to care for Nette and his four children and was in a constant state of agitation, trying to make them more comfortable. That meant he spent many extra hours laboring and not much time at home mending all the broken pieces of their house. Even so, I knew my brother and his family were happy, and there was little more that I could have asked for him. The children were all gems, and I loved them like my very own. Between being an aunt and a teacher, I did not have the maternal urge for children of my own. Not that I'd ever make that admission aloud. It would be far too shocking for some to digest.

The front door opened before I could even knock. Young Milton—named after my father, the bishop—stood on the other side of the entryway. His eyes lit up when he saw me standing on the porch. "Aunt Katie! What are you doing here? Mama didn't say you were coming."

"I hadn't planned to come," I told the youngster. "It was a last-minute decision."

His eyes went wide. "It must be important, then. You don't make last-minute decisions. Papa says that you sort everything out from the start."

I smiled at his statement.

This was true. I liked to have all my ducks and plans in a row. How else was I to teach and manage the house on Hawthorn Street? Keeping up the house wouldn't be possible without my gift for organization. That and Carrie. The young maid was a godsend. Even if she made a mistake with the ironing now and again, I was grateful for her. Hiring her was one of the best decisions I'd ever made.

"Is your father home from work?" I asked my nephew.

Before Milton could answer, Lorin's voice rang out. "I'm here, Sterchens!" He appeared in the doorway behind his son.

Sterchens was a nickname of sorts my brothers had derived from the German word *Schwesterchen*, meaning "baby sister." It was an endearment or a curse, depending on their mood. It was very bad news for me if Wilbur ever yelled it. Wilbur was even tempered, so it had happened only a handful of times. Each time, I'd fled the scene. His outbursts were typically caused by my bumping into one of the many models he had created when we were all young and consequently smashing it to pieces.

"Hello, Lorin. I have news, and I need your connections at the paper to share it."

The corners of his thick mustache dipped down as he noted my tone. Lorin Wright was very much a mix of Wilbur and Orville. Like Wilbur, he was quite tall and rather thin and had a gaunt face, but he had the impressive facial hair of Orville. Both Lorin and Orville groomed their mustaches with the same care high-society ladies gave to styling their coifs. Visits to the barber for expert maintenance were a must for them both.

Wilbur, conversely, was clean shaven and balding at a rapid pace. I had always thought he chose not to grow facial hair like his two brothers because he feared the top of his head would be jealous of his upper lip. All my brothers had long, prominent noses, and anyone who saw them together would know they were brothers without a doubt.

Lorin stepped back from the door. "Here, come inside before you catch your death of cold. Milton, you come in too. You don't even have a coat on. Your mother will get after me for that. You know how she worries over any of you children falling ill. She is in a constant state of anxiety about it, especially in the winter months."

Milton ducked back into the house.

Lorin ruffled his brown hair as he went. "Go on, you little scamp."

The wooden flooring of Lorin's home shone, not from

Nette's constant mopping but from the relentless shuffling of feet across the boards year after year. Now, I don't want to give the impression that Nette was a poor housekeeper in any way. The house and its modest furnishings were well cared for, just as the children were well loved.

"Who was at the door, Lorin?" Nette came out of the kitchen, wiping her damp hands on the edge of her white apron. The apron had tiny poinsettias embroidered onto it. Nette, who loved needlepoint, would have added the embellishments herself. She certainly had the skill and the patience to do it. I had neither.

My sister-in-law was a very handsome woman with dark curls and bright eyes. She wore her brown hair in a wave and pinned the remainder at the back of her head. It was very becoming. I would never attempt such a look. Day after day, I wore mine in a schoolmarm bun tethered to the back of my head, with no frills other than an occasional hair net to hold it in place if I was feeling especially clumsy with my fingers before school in the morning.

"Katie, what brings you here on a school night?" Nette asked with just the barest hint of alarm when she saw me standing inside the front door. "Is all well?"

"Very well," I said. "I have news about the boys."

Nette and Lorin didn't have to ask who the "boys" were. All of us in the family referred to the inseparable pair this way.

"Let's sit at the dining room table," Nette said. "I need to feed the youngest, or he will begin to wail. Katie, should I fix you up a plate of beef stew? I made more than enough."

I shook my head. "No, thank you. I won't be long, and I asked Carrie to hold dinner until I returned."

Lorin's thick brow wrinkled. "Father must be excited about this news, too, if he is willing to wait for his supper."

The children, Nette, Lorin, and I all sat at the table. Nette dished out stew for the children, but out of politeness, she didn't serve any to Lorin or to herself. Since I'd opted not to eat with them, she and Lorin would dine after I left.

"So what is it?" Lorin asked.

"It's best if you read this," I said as I unbuttoned my coat pocket, removed the telegram, and handed it to my second oldest brother.

He took it from my hand and then covered his mouth. "They did it!"

"What? What is it?" Nette asked.

Lorin handed the telegram to her, and she read it aloud to the children.

"What does that mean?" Milton asked as he poked at his stew. He had been a notoriously picky eater since the day he was born.

"They flew. That's what it means. They are the first in all the world to achieve flight in a heavier-than-air flying machine!" Lorin cried. "They cracked it. The boys cracked it, just as we all knew they would. Orville directs that we should inform the press. I have to do so now!" He jumped out of his seat.

"Lorin, what about your dinner?" Nette asked.

Lorin took the precious telegram from his wife's hand. "The newspapermen have to know. This must be plastered across the front page of every paper in the nation."

"Be careful with that telegram," I said with the same sternness my father had cautioned me. "I don't want it lost. It will be the first of many clippings I will be putting in a scrapbook about Will and Orv's many accomplishments."

"I will guard it with my life," he promised.

"But your meal," his wife complained.

"I'll eat when I return home," he declared. He kissed her on the top of the head and dashed out the door.

Nette picked up a tea towel and wiped gravy from toddler Horace's chin. "All of you are so proud of Will and Orv.

Lorin adores his brothers." She frowned and folded the towel on her lap. "But there are times when I wonder if Lorin believes that he missed his chance."

I was about to stand and leave myself, but her words stopped me in my tracks. "What do you mean?"

"If he hadn't married, would he be in North Carolina with the younger Wright boys and be part of this history we all have a front seat to watch? With a family to support, it is too difficult for him to leave home as Wilbur and Orville can. They walk away from their business, but you and Charlie Taylor do a fine job running it when they are away. Extra help for work can always be hired. One can't hire someone to be a husband and father, so Lorin is left behind to worry about practical things, like keeping a roof over our heads and our bellies full."

"Lorin loves you very much," I said. "I don't think he views it that way in the least. He chose to marry you and have a family because he loves you and the children. He's never had the interest in building and engineering that Will and Orv have."

She smoothed the tea towel with the back of her hand. "I hope very much you are right."

She stared out the kitchen window, as if she remained unsure, which put doubts in my own mind as well.

CHAPTER 4

The next morning I hurried down to breakfast. I was eager to see how the Dayton newspapers had covered the news of my brothers' miraculous feat. I could still hardly believe their flying machine had stayed aloft for nearly one minute.

Father was already in the dining room, sipping coffee. Carrie came in with a plate of eggs and bacon for him. He set his coffee aside and reached for the salt and pepper shakers. At his side were the crumpled remains of the newspapers. They were thrown about in a haphazard manner on the table.

I gathered up the pages and put them back into order as best I could. I began looking for any mention of my brothers, but there was nothing on the front pages or in the front sections at all.

"It won't do you much good trying to find anything in there about your brothers. I have looked at all three papers, and not a single one of them got it right," Father said. He held up the *Dayton Evening Herald*. "*The Herald* claims the boys flew an airship three miles! It's embarrassing and untrue. That is not what Lorin said. I can assure you of that. Even worse, the *Dayton Daily News* made the smallest mention of it. It's so small I doubt anyone will even read it! The

Journal wrote nothing at all. I don't believe you should read any of it, as it will rouse your temper."

I paid him no heed and read the dismissive articles. "This is outrageous! How can they be so belittling of all that Wilbur and Orville have done? What was Lorin thinking? Why didn't he make them write something more respectful of the boys' accomplishments and of our family?" I folded the papers and tucked them under my arm. "I plan to give Lorin a piece of my mind. How could he treat Will and Orv so poorly?"

"Don't," my father cautioned. "Lorin has already been here, and I can tell you he's eaten up over the whole situation. He said he showed the newspapermen the telegram, and their response was scoffing. Lorin pushed the editors to include the news, and now he feels the mocking tone is due to the fact that he pressed the issue."

"This is unacceptable. You know, if I had been the one to go down to the newspaper office and ask them to print the story with the facts, I would have demanded to read the copy before they went to press. Was Lorin just too much in a hurry to get back home to eat Nette's stew?"

"That is not fair to your brother, Katie. We have to tread lightly with the press on these affairs. We don't want to make enemies of the newspapermen. They are a vindictive bunch and will discredit your brothers if they are offended. The impartiality of the press is a ruse. It's clear there will be many more mentions of your brothers to come, and we must be future minded."

"Would you like breakfast, miss?" Carrie asked in her quiet voice.

"I'll just grab a piece of toast from the kitchen and fill my thermos with coffee before I head to school. It seems to me that I have to do some damage control. The newspapers really made a mess of things."

"Oh, Katie. Do not make a scene," my father warned. "I'm grateful my children are so close they will go to any lengths to defend each other's honor. I have seen it happen time and time again, but perhaps we are looking at this all wrong. The newspapers' ignoring the boys could be a very good thing."

"How can you say that?" I demanded.

"I don't know when the boys plan to show off their flying machine. You know how they are. Perhaps it would be better for them to keep quiet until the patent comes through. We can't have anyone trying to make off with their ideas. They've worked too long and too hard for that."

I shook the folded newspapers at him. "It could be months, if not years, before the patent office comes through. In the meantime, some crank will claim he is the first to fly and will steal their glory. I tell you I won't allow it. I just won't. I will do something about this myself."

"There are times I believe you are more difficult to debate than all the men in the church conference." My father sighed and dug into his eggs.

I tucked the folded up newspapers into my bag with the second-year Latin exams, which I had failed to mark up the night before. I'd been too excited over the news about Wilbur and Orville's flight. It was best if I arrived at school early so I could grade them before the school day began. Before I left the house, I kissed my father on the cheek as a goodbye and thanked Carrie for the toast.

It was Friday, and I was grateful that it was the last school before the Christmas holidays. My students would have their minds elsewhere on this day, but there was much they still had to learn today if we wanted to stay on schedule for the school year.

While other teachers might give them a Christmas party or time to catch up on missed assignments, it wasn't going to be that easy with me. Furthermore, I would be giving out assignments to complete over their two-week break. It was important not to slip back when learning a foreign language, and the study of Latin was very serious business.

I treated all my students the same. I didn't care if a student was the son of a wealthy industrialist or of a fishmonger in the market. All of them had to prove their proficiency before leaving my classroom.

By the final period of the school day, word had gotten around Steele High School that I wasn't going easy on any of my classes, and the seniors who came into my room for the last period were not happy about it.

"Miss Wright," Benny Shaw said, "you are the only teacher all day who has expected us to work, and now here we are in the final period. Can't you ease up? It's Christmas. Have a heart."

I narrowed my eyes at Benny. He was a tall football player with wavy blond hair and deep-set green eyes. I had noticed many of the girls in my classroom staring at him with dreamy looks on their faces. In my case, a young man's outward appearance had never swayed me in the least.

I put my hands on my hips. "Do you think they will take it easy on you in college? I can tell you that when I was a student at Oberlin, we worked up to the very last second of every class, and woe to any student who didn't turn in his assignments on time. The professor would have asked him to give a recitation in front of the entire class—in Latin no less. If he was unable to do that, he was asked to leave the room and not return."

"You're assuming that everyone in this room is going to college," Benny retorted. "I have no reason to. My future is set with the family business. I won't have a worry in the world as to my own success. Knowing Latin makes no difference at all to me or my family."

Whispering filled the classroom as the fifteen other students reacted to Benny's smart remark.

"Miss Wright is going to set him straight," I heard one of the girls whisper to a friend.

The pair of them laughed.

I shot them both a withering glance, and they dropped their eyes to their desks.

"Well, Benjamin," I began, purposely using his given name, because I knew how much he preferred Benny, "you can leave. If you are not interested in what we have to learn today, I see no reason for you to be here disturbing your classmates, who are willing to work."

His mouth fell open. "You can't be serious."

I picked up the ruler from my desk and smacked it on the palm of my hand. "I am very serious. Now, I suggest that you leave before I send one of your classmates down to the principal's office to have you physically removed."

When I said this, all the other students ducked their heads. It was clear that none of them wanted to be the one who was sent to the principal's office on such an errand. No one wanted to go against Benny, who was the most popular boy in the school. The social ramifications of such an act would be terrible. Even knowing this, I didn't back down. I refused to be disrespected by a student, especially in my own classroom.

Benny stood up. "You can't treat me like this. My father will have a word with you."

"I would be pleased to speak to him about your behavior when the time comes."

"My mother is your boss."

I scowled at him. "That is laughable. Your mother is the head of the PTA, but she is not above me in any way."

Benny glared at me. "I know you are on my family's guest list for the annual Christmas party. You're uninvited," he said in a surly tone.

I said nothing. I didn't mind missing the party if it garnered me respect in the classroom.

"I will tell my father *and* mother what you have done, how you have treated me, and you will never darken our door again," he continued at my silence.

"I think it's time for you to go," I replied calmly.

Without another word, he gathered up his things and stomped out of the classroom.

I looked at the remaining students. "Does anyone else have complaints about how we will spend the last fifty minutes of our school day before the break?"

Nary a student spoke.

CHAPTER 5

The final bell rang, and the students tripped over each other to escape the classroom. They couldn't leave our Latin verbs review fast enough.

Even though I took my time tidying up my classroom and calmly packing up my own possessions, I was very much in the same rush to escape. Wilbur and Orville would be at the house late the next afternoon, and there was much to do to prepare for their return. I wanted them to feel welcomed back to a warm, clean, and inviting home. They had spent weeks living in little better than a shack on the sands of Kitty Hawk, with vermin, insects, and blistering winds. They deserved all the creature comforts that 7 Hawthorn Street had to offer. I very much hoped that Carrie had started on the list of extra chores that I'd left her this morning.

I was happy to find when I arrived home that Carrie had not only completed the list but had also done some extras. She'd even taken advantage of my father being at one of his church meetings to polish his desk until it shone. I was quite pleased with all of it and told her that she could go home early. I would serve Father and myself the vegetable soup she'd made for our evening meal.

She dashed out of the room as soon as I said the words, for fear I might change my mind. I shook my head; I really needed to be a little less stern with that girl.

I didn't expect Father home until late. Many of his church meetings ran well past dinner, and that was especially true now that Father was at the center of a libel case against a reverend in his district. Three years ago Father had discovered that Rev. Millard Keiter had embezzled money from the church's publisher. Father had addressed the issue as he should as the bishop.

Much to our family's dismay, the conference had sided with Keiter, who was very popular among the members. Then, to make matters worse, Keiter had sued Father for libel. Father had countersued. The case had all been going on for months and months. Understandably, the lawsuit upset my father—and all of us—greatly. We tried not to talk of it much. But I knew from his drawn face that it ate away at him little by little.

There was a knock at the front door. I frowned, wondering who it could be at this hour. I went to the door and found Agnes standing on the porch with a scarf wrapped so high over her face that I could see only her eyes.

"Agnes!" I cried. "What are you doing out in this cold? Shouldn't you be at home with your family? It's just about suppertime."

"I just left work and came straight here."

Agnes worked at a small paper store downtown, close to the bookshop where I had bumped into her the day before. She had the very best handwriting and wrote cards for five cents apiece for people to send to friends and relatives. She was most in demand during the Christmas season as everyone wanted a fine card to send to friends and family afar.

I personally thought it was a waste of money, as I could see no reason why a properly educated person could not write out their own card. But I was happy Agnes had the work, since she enjoyed it so much. Even I would admit that her penmanship was particularly beautiful.

"Come in. Come in!" I said. "It's far too cold out there for you."

She stumbled into the house. "I hope I'm not interrupting your dinner." Her voice was muffled behind the scarf.

"Not at all. My father is still at a church meeting. They can go on for hours. I only hope the church committee had the forethought to provide some refreshment. He will be famished."

It took her a good minute to unwrap her scarf. When she was finally free, she asked, "How is everything going with the lawsuit?"

I shook my head. "Not as well as we would like. The conference is being obstinate about the whole thing, but Father has the proof. He will prevail in the end. The greatest disappointment is how long it's taking. As you can imagine, the lawsuit has caused our family great stress."

She removed her coat. "I know it has, and I am so very sorry to hear it. Your father is a good man."

She patted her hair to make sure her pins were still in place. Of all my old friends from Dayton, Agnes was the one most concerned about her appearance and most eager to marry and start a family. As we were twenty-nine now, I knew she was becoming increasingly anxious on the topic of marriage. We didn't talk about it much, because it had reached the point where the subject brought her to tears.

I personally would not cry over such a thing. Although I didn't begrudge my childhood friend for feeling a certain way, I knew marriage and children were out of the question for me. My father would never allow it. My mother had died when I was young, and he had made it very clear that I was to become woman of the house. I had done so with only one small misstep: the engagement, which Father never knew about, during my college days.

"Can you join me for a light dinner?" I asked. "Carrie made vegetable soup. It will warm you right up."

"That does sound nice. I had to work late, and I know Mother didn't hold dinner for me. My father has to eat at six sharp. No exceptions. You would not believe how many Christmas cards I wrote today. It had to be over one hundred. My fingers are cramped. I'm working tomorrow, too, even though it is Saturday, so I can finish all the orders. They all have to be in the mail and arrive before Christmas. There's not much time left."

I nodded. I knew this about her father. There were several times as a child when I had been invited to their home for dinner, and if we were even just a second late to the table, Mr. Osborne would already have said the blessing and be eating. He was a regimented man.

"Vegetable soup it is. Let me just set the table, and we will eat in the dining room."

She hung her coat on the coat-tree by the door. "You don't have to make this a formal visit, Katie. I will help you."

I smiled at her. "All right."

With Agnes's help, the table was set for two in no time at all. I dished soup from the tureen and set it in front of my friend. Then I served myself.

Just as she lifted the spoon to her mouth, I said, "Now, tell me why you are really here."

She set the spoon back into her bowl without taking a mouthful. "Why do you think I would be here for any reason other than to visit my dear friend?"

"Ag, you keep biting your lip, which is a sure sign that you have something to say, but you're nervous about saying it."

She sighed. "Lenora Shaw came into the paper shop today to place her Christmas card order."

I stared at her. "She's just placing her Christmas card order now? It's December eighteenth! How can you even guarantee the cards will make it to all her friends before Christmas Day?"

She nodded. "Many of the wealthier ladies in town wait until the last minute. I believe they hope or think they will do the cards themselves, but when it comes down to it, writing some hundred-plus Christmas cards to all their family and friends is quite daunting."

"Lenora Shaw should have enough in-house staff to handle such a task," I grumbled. "I don't like her putting pressure on you to do it."

Agnes shrugged in her good-natured way. Perhaps this was why she was in the service business. In her position, I would have told Lenora it was just too late, and she was going to have to sit down and write the cards herself.

Agnes sipped her water and then cleared her throat. "While Lenora was at the shop, she mentioned that her son, Benny, came home from school early today."

I frowned and knew exactly where this was going.

"He told her that you kicked him out of your classroom. She said he was quite upset over it. He was close to tears even."

"Oh, I'm sure," I snorted. "I have been a teacher long enough to know boys like Benny Shaw always land on their feet. His ego might be slightly bruised, but he will survive it. And maybe next time, he'll think twice before talking back to a teacher."

Agnes pressed her lips together. "But the Shaws' Christmas party is Saturday night."

I eyed her over my water glass. "And I assume that I am uninvited. That's fine. I can have a grand time at home. Wilbur and Orville should be home tomorrow anyway. I really don't have time for such frivolity. We will have a very nice family celebration of our own. Lenora doesn't have to trouble herself over me. Not in the least. I don't care if I am uninvited to her party. She should have raised a more respectful son."

"Katie, it is not fair to put all the blame on the mother."

"Very well. It's the father's fault too. I don't mind saying that."

Agnes sighed. "Lenora didn't say that you were uninvited. She just said she was disappointed and wanted to speak privately with you about it at the party. She believes that it should have been handled differently because you worked so closely with her on the Christmas tree sale."

"If that is true, why is she talking to you about it?"

"She knows we're old friends and I would relay the message."

"So you are her messenger now, is that it?" I dug into my soup with a scowl on my face.

"She wants only to speak with you. To be honest, she was apologetic about Benny's behavior. She even told me that he could be prideful at times."

"That's one way of putting it," I muttered. "I will talk to Lenora about her son another time. I don't like to mix work with pleasure. It never ends well. If she wants to talk to me about Benny, we can discuss it after one of the committee meetings before the Christmas tree sale. She scheduled several leading up to the event. I'd much rather stay home and catch up with my brothers the night of the party."

"But you have to come to the party. You have to." She sounded desperate.

I set my spoon in my bowl. "Why?" I was truly curious.

"Because Arthur Bacon will be there. I need your help. I'm terrified to speak to him on my own. You will be able to help me start a conversation."

Arthur was the young man whom Agnes had had her eye on for the past year. He was going to medical school and came from a good family. They were a good match, and if Ag married him, her status would rise considerably in Dayton society. Even so, how could I go to a party where I knew I wasn't welcome?

"Please, Katie. My father fears I will become an old maid."

I raised my brow. "And what is wrong with that?"

She held up her hands. "Nothing. Nothing at all. And you're not an old maid at all. You have a career. You're educated and a professional. What am I? A card writer who lives with my parents."

I sighed. "Very well. I will go, but let it be known that I'm going only for you. It's *not* because I want to have a conversation with Lenora Shaw about her son. In fact, I will do everything within my power to avoid it. It's unseemly to discuss such things at such a public gathering."

Agnes jumped out of her seat and threw her arms around my neck. "Thank you! Thank you, Katie! You just made my Christmas."

I would later learn that I'd almost ruined mine.

CHAPTER 6

The next afternoon, my father and I waited anxiously on the platform as Wilbur and Orville's train came in. I twisted my leather gloves in my hands as I watched the passengers disembark one by one. It seemed to me that every citizen of Dayton stepped off the train except for my long-missed brothers.

Finally, I spied them. Orville stepped onto the platform first. His black bowler hat sat perfectly on his head, and his signature mustache was freshly combed.

Father touched my arm. "They are home safe. The Lord is good."

I nodded and waved my gloves at my brother. "Orv! Orv! Over here!"

Orville looked this way and that, but when he finally spotted our father and me standing together, his face broke into a smile.

A moment later, Wilbur exited the train. Wilbur was a bit taller and slimmer than Orville, and I could tell the weeks in Kitty Hawk had both enlivened and drained him. His cheeks were gaunt, but his eyes were bright.

Orville rushed over to us and squeezed me in a great hug

that lifted me from the ground. I couldn't help but laugh. I smacked his arm. "Put me down, you old goose."

He smiled and set me back on my feet. "It is so good to see you both. You're both a sight for sore eyes." He shook our father's hand and patted his arm. "Are you well, Father? We very much enjoyed your letters. We would read them at night, before sleeping. It passed the long hours of darkness that come this time of year on the dunes."

"What about my letters?" I asked, narrowing my eyes in jest.

Orville grinned. "Your letters were good too, Katie. I especially enjoyed your tales of setting mouthy boys straight in your classroom. Oh, to be a fly on the wall there and see it. I'd spend more money on that than a ticket to the pictures."

Wilbur shook his head. "It was nice to hear about the day-to-day of home. I must admit, it made me homesick from time to time, but we were happy to have the distraction. This was especially true on the days when the flying machine wasn't cooperating."

My hands were becoming chilled in the wind, and so I put on my gloves. "Father, Lorin, and I are all so proud of you. To actually fly! What a feather in your cap!"

"How did the papers take it?" Wilbur asked. "Orv wanted us to announce it, but I'm not sure it was the right thing to do. There are many matters that must be perfected before we make too big a fuss of this. We don't want to step on the world stage too early, only to look like fools."

I wrinkled my nose. "I don't think you have to worry about the newspapermen clamoring to interview you. They didn't take it seriously at all. Your achievement was barely mentioned, and the small notations they did make were factually incorrect."

"That's outrageous," Orville said. "I have half a mind to

march down to the newspaper office right now and give them a piece of my mind."

Wilbur shook his head. "No, that's not a good idea. Maybe this is for the best. They will leave us alone." He looked around, as if to make sure no one on the platform would overhear our conversation. "We are the first to understand the need for wing warping and the first to accomplish motorized flight. A motor is essential to stay aloft in the sky in a machine that is heavier than air. I think it is best that we don't attract too much attention until our skills and mechanics are thoroughly mastered."

"We don't need to worry about anyone stealing our discovery of wing warping," Orville complained. "Even if they had the plans for our machine, I doubt fewer than a handful of men would have the understanding to even attempt to make sense of it."

Wilbur shot him a look. "That may be so, but we can't risk it."

Orville shook his head. "You worry too much, brother."

"This is serious," Wilbur said. His face turned red. "You do have the documents, don't you?"

Orville placed a hand on the pocket of his coat. "I have them right here."

Wilbur shot his younger brother a look. "Be careful with those, brother. You know how valuable they are. We don't have any securities until the patent office approves our patent. That could take a considerable amount of time."

Still with his hand on his chest, Orville said, "I will guard them with my very life."

"Sons," Father began, "let us stop the bickering and head home. Carrie has prepared a nice home-cooked meal for you, and she is likely fretting about how to keep it warm while she waits."

The train station wasn't all that far from Hawthorn Street, so despite the cold December day, we walked. My father was a firm believer in walking to strengthen a person's constitution.

I slipped my hand through Orville's arm as we went. I loved both of my brothers dearly, but Orville was my favorite of the two. He was as brilliant as Wilbur, but he didn't take himself as seriously. Orville and I shared many things in common. We loved to read and to debate, and we even had the same birthday. I was born three years after him, on the exact same day. My mother told us when we were young that this was a sign we were always to take care of each other.

Both Wilbur and Orville were shy in public, but Orville was able to warm up to others much sooner than Wilbur, and he was much more willing to have fun. It seemed to me Wilbur's only idea of fun was toiling in the back room of the bicycle shop, where the boys worked on their invention, with his sleeves rolled up and his fingertips covered in machine grease.

"How's business at the bicycle shop?" Wilbur wanted to know.

I wasn't the least bit surprised that Wilbur—who was the more business minded of the two—wanted to get right down to the state of the shop.

"We've received letters from Charlie Taylor, with updates, of course. From the way he tells it, business is good," Orville said.

I wrinkled my nose at the mention of Charlie Taylor. He was my brothers' engine man and worked at the shop year-round. I couldn't deny he was a talented mechanic. There wasn't any engine he couldn't build. He was even able to create engines of his own design.

However, he swore like a sailor and smoked like a chimney. His crude manners rubbed me the wrong way. I had asked my brothers many times to find someone else for the job. There had to be at least one man in Dayton who could do everything that Charlie Taylor could do without swearing every ten minutes. Even the very worst of my students didn't know half of the words he used.

I helped in the bicycle shop, too, and it wasn't easy for me to work alongside the crude Charlie Taylor, but I did my best to ignore him most of the time. I found this to be the best way to cope.

"Charlie was telling the truth," I said. "Business has been good at the shop. It even ticked up a little bit in the past week or so, especially on children's bicycle sales, as so many parents are planning to buy their children their first bicycles for Christmas."

My father clicked his tongue on the roof of his mouth. "It seems to me that buying a child a bicycle in December, when they will be unable to ride it for weeks and weeks, is a poor decision."

"I, for one, am not going to question any parents' decision-making in that regard as long as they keep buying. We need that money to fund our experiments," Wilbur said.

"But you have cracked flight," I said. "What more is there to do?"

"Katie," Wilbur said with a sigh, "there are people all over the world in the race for flight, but now that we've cracked it, as you say, we can't stop. Being aloft for almost a minute isn't enough. We have to solve the issue of practical flight. This will revolutionize the world!"

"Is that possible?" I asked. "Do you even think it can be done? Do you really believe people will fly on a regular basis?"

"Of course it can be done," Orville said. "We just have to build on the principles that all our tests and experiments have taught us. It's no longer a matter of if, but when."

Orville patted his chest, where the documents were concealed. "And it's all right here."

CHAPTER 7

It wasn't until we returned home that I had the chance to tell my brothers about the Shaws' Christmas party, which we were invited to that night. I made sure not to mention my spat with Benny Shaw or the fact that his mother, Lenora, wanted to talk to me about it at the party. A large part of me still wished that I wasn't going, but I had promised Agnes. There was no getting out of it now.

If my brothers went with me, they would cause a stir. Even though the coverage of their first flight wasn't accurate or flattering, their flying machine was still a conversation piece, and I knew many people at the party would want to know what the boys had been up to on the sands of Kitty Hawk.

When he stepped into the house, Wilbur walked right over to the fireplace to warm himself. "Oh, I missed this warm fire while we were away. There is nothing as comforting as a fire in your own home."

Father excused himself and left the room. He was moving a tad slower than normal, and worry filled my heart. I shouldn't have let him walk to and from the train station in this cold. He would deny it had been challenging for him. However, the truth was he wasn't as mobile as he had once been. I would have to remind Carrie to put an extra-warm brick in his bed that night for his feet.

"So are you two going to go to the party with me?" I asked as my two brothers put their feet up.

Wilbur shifted in his seat. "Sterchens, you know that we are not much for parties, and we've had a very long journey."

"It's Christmas. You've been gone so long and working so hard. Don't you deserve a bit of fun, with good food and music?"

He eyed me. "We had plenty of fun in Kitty Hawk, I can assure you. Nothing makes us happier than our discoveries."

"That's true," Orville agreed and then leaned back in his chair. "I'd like to smoke my pipe and relax, but I don't have the energy to fetch it from my suitcase."

I wasn't going to get it for him. I loathed smoking, especially inside the house. It was the main reason that I disliked Charlie Taylor so much. Not that his swearing was much better.

"If you'd like my opinion, you should come along. It will give you a chance to set the record straight about your flight. The newspapers made a mess of it. Randolph Shaw is the owner of Shaw Paper Mill. There will be a lot of newsmen there, as they all use Shaw paper for their publications."

Orville loosened his tie and cleared his throat. "You know, the Shaws have been interested in funding some of our research before," Orville said. "Maybe, considering what we have accomplished, now is the time to talk with them again."

Wilbur stared at his brother as if he couldn't believe the words that were coming out of Orville's mouth. "We don't need investors. We're frugal and make enough money at the bicycle shop to fund our needs. It's when you have investors that the vision is lost and everything goes sideways. Look at what has happened to Samuel Langley. He has all the money in the world offered to him by the Smithsonian, and he still can't crack it the way we have. Money doesn't ensure success. Success comes through trial and error and force of will."

Orville nodded. "I agree with you on this, brother. I prefer to have control over the project, rather than let someone writing the checks pull our strings. Even so, the Shaws are influential people in both Dayton and the state capital. It would not hurt to make friends with them and garner their endorsement, especially after we received such poor coverage in the newspapers. All those newspapers are printed on reams from Shaw Paper Mill. That leads me to believe that if Randolph Shaw took notice of us, the papers would too."

Wilbur pressed his lips together, as if he didn't agree with Orville on the matter but wanted to appear that he was at least giving the conversation some serious thought.

I, for one, thought Orville was onto something. If Randolph Shaw believed in my brothers, the newspapermen would take notice. His opinion was too influential to ignore.

"Even if that were true—and I'm not saying that it is," Wilbur said, "I'm not going to the party. It has been a long and grueling journey home. My only wish is to sleep in my own bed tonight."

"That is fair," Orville said. "You stay home and rest. I'll go to the party with Katie."

"Thanks, little brother," I said.

Even though Wilbur claimed to be exhausted from his travels, he decided to leave shortly after our conversation to walk the two short blocks to the bicycle shop. He said that he wanted to have a chat with Charlie Taylor about how the business was faring. When Orville said that he would go along, too, Wilbur shook his head. "No, little brother. You stay home and catch up with Sterchens. It seems to me that the two of you have much to discuss to prepare for the party tonight."

A strange look crossed Orville's face, and his mustache dipped down into a frown. I tried not to worry about his expression too much, but I couldn't help but take note of it. Unless they were having a dispute over mechanics or engineering, my two brothers were rarely out of sorts with each other. It made me wonder what had happened in Kitty Hawk to cause this kind of tension. True, it was a very subtle tension, but it was still there.

I reminded myself that the brothers had just spent every waking moment for weeks with each other. Even though they lived and worked together here at home, at least they had the chance to be apart for a few hours a day. I didn't believe they'd had that luxury in North Carolina.

"Very well, brother," Orville said and picked up his suitcase to take it up to his room. "I will go unpack and then will see if I have something to wear to the party tonight. I hope that my good suit isn't too loose on me. The dunes were draining, and I lost nearly a stone of weight. I might have to wear two belts to keep my trousers in place."

After Wilbur left, Orville retired to his room, and I went to my own room to prepare for the party. I took time to make sure that my hair was perfectly in place. I didn't do this to impress any of the young men there. There was no one of interest to me in all of Dayton. Certainly no one for whom I would be willing to give up my professional life and my family. Even so, I wanted to look my very best for Agnes's sake. Tonight she had the most at stake. As Arthur Bacon was a very busy medical school student, it would be her one and only chance to catch his eye.

I wanted my friend to be happy, but I didn't like the idea of her moving away if she did marry Arthur. It was impossible to know where he would end up when he finished his schooling. Also, I thought the name Agnes Bacon was ridiculous.

"Katie, the buggy is ready!" Orville called up the stairs.

Before I left my bedroom, I took one last look at myself in my dressing table mirror. My glasses sat perfectly straight on my face. My dark hair was neatly combed and piled on the back of my head, and my blue high-collar dress was neat and without a speck of lint on it. There wasn't anything remarkable about my appearance. I looked exactly like the schoolteacher I was, but I was pleased. I was going to support Agnes, not create a stir myself.

"Katie!" Orville called again.

"I'm coming!" I shouted back and winced. I knew how much Father hated it when we yelled to each other from one corner of the house to the other.

I grabbed my small beaded evening bag, which had been a gift from my friends at Oberlin upon my graduation. It was cream and silver, and I was proud to carry it as I didn't have much opportunity to use it.

Orville wore a long black wool coat over his best suit and was notably quiet as we rode over to the Shaws' estate. My brothers had never been much for making small talk, but they'd always loved to talk to me. There were a million questions I wanted to ask him about the flight and his time in North Carolina, but I decided they could wait until another day. There seemed to be much on his mind.

As we drove through the eight-foot-high iron gate that surrounded the Shaws' estate, he said, "This was a mistake. I should have gone with Will to speak to Charlie, not come here."

Before I could ask him why he thought so, a servant walked up along the side of the buggy and held out his arm to help me out. Not wanting to be rude, I took his arm and stepped out.

I looked over my shoulder as Orville handed the horses' reins to a stable hand.

"Thank you," I said to the servant, who still held my arm. "You don't have to walk me all the way to the door. I will just wait here for my brother."

He released my arm, bowed, and then went to help the next lady out of her carriage. This sort of formality wasn't something I was used to, and it made me feel slightly uncomfortable. From the look on his face, I knew Orville was feeling the same way. We weren't that kind of people.

He smiled at me. "They took the horse and buggy, so there is no turning back now."

"No, I suppose there's not." I cleared my throat. "Can you do me a favor tonight? Well, in actuality, it's two favors."

He raised his brow at me and waited.

"If you see Arthur Bacon, can you please put in a good word for Agnes?"

"Oh? And why should I do that?"

"I can't tell you, but you can probably figure it out."

"All right. Ag is a nice girl, and she has always been a good friend to you. I would be happy to help her." He paused. "And the second thing?"

"Keep me away from Lenora Shaw."

CHAPTER 8

Agnes squeezed my arm, digging her nails through the sleeve of my dress, as she scanned the party.

"Ag, that hurts," I said.

"Oh, I'm so sorry." She dropped her hand and looked at my arm. "I'm just so nervous. Are you hurt?"

I rubbed my arm. "I don't think you broke the skin."

She wrinkled her small nose. "I'm truly sorry, but I have been waiting to see Arthur all night. It's clear he's not here."

"The party began only an hour ago. Guests are coming and going all the time. It's too soon to think Arthur isn't coming. He could have gotten held up at another gathering or party. This is the last Saturday before Christmas. There are going to be many events happening in the city. Surely a handsome young man of his stature would be invited to more than one."

She nodded. "I know you're right, but it's hard not to worry that he changed his mind and no longer plans to attend. You said it yourself—there are so many events going on. I'm sure such a handsome and successful young man has more invitations than he knows what to do with."

She was crestfallen.

"Ag, dear, please cheer up. This is not the one and only opportunity you will have to see him. Didn't you say he is staying through to the New Year? My goodness, it's only the nineteenth."

Her face reddened. "*He* didn't tell me. His sister wrote me."

"Well, if you have an in with his sister, I would say that's a very good thing."

"I wouldn't call it an in. She wrote me and told me that she was coming in order to make sure I stayed away from him. She doesn't believe my social connections are worthy of his potential as a doctor."

I put my hands on my hips. "How dare she! You're just about the sweetest, kindest person in the world. She would be lucky to have you as a member of her family." I narrowed my eyes. "She doesn't deserve to have you in her family. None of them do. What's her name? I want to give her a piece of my mind!"

"Her name is Claudine." She grabbed my arm. "But please don't do or say anything. It will only make the situation that much worse."

"She needs to be set straight, and I'm just the one to do it."

She squeezed my arm a bit tighter.

"Katie, please." Tears gathered in her eyes. "I know you mean well, but I could never survive the embarrassment."

I sighed. When I'd gone off to college, I had asked everyone to call me Katharine, which sounded so much more grown up than my childhood nickname. Nowadays, only my family still called me Katie. I had known Agnes most of my life. She was a dear friend. When she used "Katie," it pulled on my heartstrings and reminded me how far back our friendship went.

I gave a dramatic sigh. "Very well. I won't go looking for Claudine, but if I run into her, I can't promise what I will say, especially if your name comes up in conversation. What kind of friend would I be if I didn't defend you?"

She let go of my arm and squeezed her small reticule in her hands. "I suppose I can't ask for much more than that."

"Would you like some punch, ladies?" A young maid who couldn't be any more than eighteen held out a silver tray laden with crystal glasses that were filled with a bright red liquid.

I eyed it. "What kind of punch is it? We are not ladies to partake of spirits."

"Oh no, miss. It's cranberry-apple punch. It's quite good, and there is no alcohol in it."

With the ingredients in mind, both Agnes and I accepted a glass.

The maid smiled at us as we did. She was very pretty, with bright brown eyes and straw-yellow hair, which was tucked up under her white maid's cap. She wore a long black dress with a stiff white collar and a ruffled white apron. Everything was spotless and freshly pressed.

It was a far cry from the uniform Carrie Kayler wore in our home when she was working, because there was no uniform. She wore a day dress and donned a cap only when she was dusting, to keep her hair clean. I cared much more about her performance than her appearance.

I sipped the punch. "It's very good. Thank you for offering it to us . . ."

"Maggie, miss," she said. "I'm the fourth maid in the house."

I arched my brow. Not because the Shaws had enough money to hire more than one maid, but because they numbered them.

I thanked Maggie again and traded my empty glass for another full one.

"The young people are organizing games in the parlor. You might find that enjoyable," Maggie said before she turned to leave.

I glanced at Agnes. "If Arthur is here, the parlor is the most likely place to find him."

She bit her lip and nodded. "I'm so nervous, I feel as if my skin is crawling."

"I suggest that you take a few deep breaths and let me start a conversation with him."

Agnes gulped down the rest of her punch and set the glass on a table with a thud. "Okay, I'm ready."

As the young people made their way to the parlor for games, the older adults went into the ballroom to enjoy the music of the string quartet. I spotted Lenora Shaw among the older crowd. She wore a peacock-blue gown with cap sleeves and matching elbow-length gloves. I ducked my head so that she wouldn't see me.

As I dipped my head, I bumped into Orville, who was standing in the hallway, reading a sheaf of papers in his hands.

"Where are you going with your head down like that?" He tucked the papers back into his inside suit jacket pocket.

"Staying out of trouble, little brother."

Orville snorted at me. *Little brother* was my nickname for Orville. He was three years older than I, but he was the youngest of the four boys in the family, so I, at least, found the name fitting. Orville tolerated it, but I didn't think he liked it nearly as much as I did.

"It will take a lot more than keeping your head down to keep you out of trouble." He nodded at Agnes. "Nice to see you, Ag."

"You, too, Orville. Katharine has been telling me all about your experiments in North Carolina. It's so exciting. It must be thrilling to fly."

"It is quite a thrill," he said and then looked as if he might say more, but Herman Wheeler popped his head out of the parlor and looked up and down the hallway.

"Anyone else who wants to join in the parlor games, this is your last chance." His face broke into a grin. "Orville, how nice to see you! I didn't know you were back home from your adventures."

Orville's mustache drooped. "We arrived home just today."

"And you came to our little party. We all feel so honored."

I wrinkled my brow when he said, "Our little party." This was the Shaws' Christmas party. I didn't know what that had to do with Herman.

"Yes, little brother, let's play. It will get your mind off other things," I said. "You love games."

Herman's lips curled into a smile, but it was a smile that didn't reach his eyes. Before Orville knew what was happening, Herman had ushered him into the parlor. Agnes and I followed a few steps behind, and as soon as I entered the room and saw the sea of faces in front of us, I knew this was a very bad idea. A very bad idea indeed. The last place Orville wanted to be was at the center of attention, and Herman led him in front of the entire group.

My shy brother blinked, as if he couldn't believe so many people were looking at him at the same time. Now I regretted asking my brother to join in the parlor games. At times, I forgot how entrenched my brothers' shy ways were. The only time they wanted an audience was when deep in an academic discussion about their inventions. Yes, Orville enjoyed games at home with a few close friends, but this was very different.

There had to be at least forty people in the room, and every last one of them was watching Herman and Orville.

To make matters worse, Benny Shaw slouched against the wall in one corner, with his arms folded across his chest. It was a stance I knew well from the classroom and one that he assumed even when I told him time and time again to stand up straight. He spotted me and glared. The phrase "if looks could kill" came to mind. I hoped the Christmas holiday from school would be long enough for him to recover from the apparent humiliation of being kicked out of my classroom. It wasn't as if it was the first time or the last time I would take such action with Benny, or with any other student, for that matter. I would not abide rudeness or disrespect. I didn't care who the student's parents were.

Herman had his arm around my brother's shoulders, and Orville was rigid. I bit the side of my lip.

"We should have the local hero go first. Orville, you are up!" Herman cried. "Did you see the papers mention our local heroes Wilbur and Orville Wright? Brilliant minds both. Orville is sure to master this game, just as they mastered the skies."

Orville tried to step away. "No, thank you. I will just watch."

Herman, the taller of the two men, held him fast. "How can you say that? Is it not true that you and old Wilbur flew through the sky like birds? My heavens, the *Herald* said that you flew three miles. What was it like, Orv? We are dying to know!"

Orville's lips disappeared under his mustache, an expression he most often made when he was especially tense.

"Doesn't such an accomplishment make you a hero?" Herman asked with a slight edge to his voice.

Next to me, Agnes tensed. She had known Orville since we were all children, and being shy herself, she must have known just how he felt in that moment.

"Shall we play?" Herman asked the group.

The people in the parlor cheered.

One called, "Come on, Orv. Show us all how smart you really are."

Orville held up his hand. "No, no. I'm just here to watch and enjoy."

Herman smirked at Orville. "That doesn't sound very brave for a man who supposedly defied gravity."

"We didn't defy gravity," Orville replied. "That shows how much you know about flying."

Herman's eyes went wide, as if he wasn't accustomed to anyone standing up to him like that.

I saw movement out of the corner of my eye as Benny

sulked out of the room. At least that was one less person I had to worry about during the parlor games.

"We're wasting time debating who will go first," I put in. "Aren't we at this party to have fun? I haven't seen an ounce of fun since you started this argument, Herman."

He scowled at me.

I stepped into the middle of the room, where Orville and Herman stood. "I'll go first. I'm excellent at charades and will be able to start the fun in no time flat."

"Leave it up to Katharine Wright to think she excels at everything," someone muttered, but I couldn't see who had spoken.

"No, no. It's all right, Katie. I can do it," Orville said. "If Herman wants to see how well I play this game, I will show him."

"Brother," I whispered in his ear, "I don't think it is a good idea. Herman is trying to get a rise out of you. Don't let him do that."

"Do not worry," he whispered back.

That was easier said than done.

Orville removed his jacket and laid it over the piano bench behind him. The grand piano was massive. Its mahogany top gleamed from the electric lights. It didn't surprise me that the Shaw family had already adopted electricity. They had also been the first family in town to own an automobile. Now they owned several, and it wasn't uncommon to see Benny driving one of the cars to school. All the other students were in awe of the contraption, which built up Benny's ego all the more.

Herman smiled at Orville like the cat that ate the canary, and walked to the center of the room. Reluctantly, I returned to my spot next to Agnes, and she took my hand. I appreciated my friend's support, but I would much rather have been in the middle of the room, making a fool of myself, than watching my brother do so. My feelings were nearly as fragile as his. I taught high school after all.

Herman handed Orville a folded piece of paper. "Here is your word."

Orville opened the paper, read it, and his face creased into a deep frown. He looked at Herman, who grinned back.

"Go on now," Herman said as he stepped back from the center of the room. "The floor is yours, Mr. Wright."

Orville shuddered and seemed to collect himself before he held up two fingers.

The group of people shouted, "Two words. First word!"

My brother nodded. Then he held his arms out and bobbed around the room.

"A bird!"

"An eagle!"

The guesses came fast. Each time Orville shook his head to indicate the guesses were incorrect.

"Flying!"

Orville nodded and held up two fingers.

"Second word!"

Then my brother made motions as if he was turning a crank.

"A well!"

"Machine! Machine!"

"A flying machine!"

Herman pointed at the person with the right guess. "You're right. We could also have called it a delusion of grandeur. Is that not right, Orville? Because man was not meant to fly. Whoever claims otherwise must surely be mad."

The guests burst into mocking laughter.

Orville's face turned red, and he stomped from the room.

My heart sank. Coming to the party might have been the worst decision I'd ever made, as would soon become even more apparent.

CHAPTER 9

Agnes and I left the parlor shortly after Orville. I wanted to stay behind to tell Herman and his band of lemmings what I really thought about them all, but I knew it would only embarrass Orville all the more. For once, my common sense prevailed, and when Agnes gave my hand a light tug in the direction of the door, I followed her.

We entered the ballroom, as I thought it the most likely place Orville would have gone. He wasn't there.

Agnes squeezed my hand again. "He will be all right. Just let him cool off for a bit. That must have been so embarrassing for him."

I nodded. "It is a blessing, at least, that Wilbur isn't here. He would be even more upset than Orville. Let's try to put it out of our minds and have more punch and treats. Those frosted sugar cookies look quite good. I recognize them from the bakery located on the same street as the bicycle shop, and . . ." I trailed off when I realized she wasn't listening to a word I said.

Instead, she was staring across the ballroom at a handsome man who was walking toward us with purpose to his stride.

"Katie, it's him," Agnes breathed.

Arthur Bacon was very good looking. With his blond hair combed back from his face, he strode up to us with perfect posture, and his steel-blue eyes shone with intelligence. I could see why Agnes was so taken with him.

"Miss Osborne, I was wondering if you'd do me the honor of joining me for this waltz. I have been told that the floor is open for dancing."

I glanced at the middle of the ballroom, where only three couples were waltzing to the music. If Agnes joined Arthur on the dance floor, everyone would see it and everyone would be talking about it, including his spiteful sister Claudine, whom I assumed was in attendance as well.

Agnes wouldn't or couldn't speak.

"She would love to." I gave Agnes a little shove in Arthur's direction.

He took her arm and led her to the dance floor.

She looked back at me with shining eyes. I couldn't help but smile. Maybe, despite the horrible sister Claudine, Arthur and Agnes were meant to be together. If I ran into Claudine, I would give her a piece of my mind, with or without Agnes's blessing.

With Agnes otherwise occupied, I went in search of Orville. As I stepped into the hallway, the parlor was emptying out. It seemed the parlor games had not lasted long.

I peered into the parlor, and there were a few people sitting in the corners of the room, chatting. Orville was also in the room, but instead of sitting quietly, sipping punch, he spun frantically around the room like a children's top. Remaining guests watched him out of the corners of their eyes. If my brother didn't want to be seen as an eccentric by the people of Dayton, he should stop acting like one.

"Orville," I asked in a low tone, "whatever is the matter?"

"Katie, have you seen my jacket?"

"Your jacket?" I asked.

"Yes. I took it off to play that ridiculous game of charades." His voice was sharp. "I have to find it." He pointed at the empty piano bench. "I set it right there. I know that's where I put it, but now it's gone."

"Don't worry. We will find it. It has to be in here somewhere."

"It's gone! What am I going to do?"

I put a hand on my brother's arm to steady him.

"Get hold of yourself. I know suit jackets don't grow on trees, but we aren't destitute. You can wear your old one until you have the money to buy another."

"You don't understand." He lowered his voice to a hiss. "The drawings of the flyer with Wilbur's notes about wing warping are in the pocket. If someone took the jacket, they have our plans too."

My eyes went wide. "What? Why on earth did you bring them with you to the party?"

"I thought if things got slow, I could hide away in a corner and work on some calculations for a new version of the flyer." He wrung his hands. "Wilbur is going to kill me. He will never forgive me for this."

He was right. Wilbur would be furious. This mistake could tear our family apart—that was how important the flying machine was to my brothers.

"Wilbur will be upset, of course, but don't be so dramatic. He would never hurt you." I took a breath. "We will find the jacket. Maybe a servant took it away to keep it safe or hang it up. Yes, I'm sure that is what happened. It's most likely in the cloakroom. We'll just find one of the servants and ask."

Orville's shoulders relaxed. "Yes, I'm sure that's it." He let out a breath, and his mustache fluttered above his lip. "It has to be."

I went off in search of a waiter or another servant, and Orville went in the other direction. I had assured my brother the jacket wasn't lost, but I wasn't nearly as confident as I had sounded.

All I could think about was Herman asking me about my brothers' flying machine and how he'd humiliated Orville during charades. After Orville had fled the parlor, Agnes and I had left too. The jacket had been on the piano bench when we left, hadn't it? I tried to remember whether I'd seen it before I left the room. Had Herman or someone else taken it? Why? Did they know that the drawings were in the pocket? If so, how? I hadn't even known that Orville brought them with him. I remembered his removing papers from his pocket and looking at them, but Orville and Wilbur were constantly reading. I'd thought nothing of it.

However, my brother had said that he'd planned to make notes on the papers if he found a quiet moment. Perhaps Herman or someone else had seen the drawings when he was doing that and had decided to steal them at first chance.

A maid rushed past me from the ballroom with a tray of empty crystal goblets.

"Excuse me," I said. "My brother has misplaced his suit jacket. I was just wondering if anyone on the staff would have picked it up and put it somewhere for safekeeping. The last time he saw it was on the piano bench in the parlor."

"I haven't been in the parlor tonight, miss," she said, out of breath.

"Can you ask some of your colleagues to see if any of them picked it up?"

"I can ask, miss." She continued on her way to the kitchens with the empty glasses.

I had a feeling my request wouldn't be fulfilled.

I decided to check the parlor one more time. Perhaps the plans had fallen on the floor and we'd missed the drawings. I knew it wasn't likely, but I had to grasp at something to keep my anxiety at bay. I had almost reached the parlor when Orville came rushing at me. He was very pale. His pallor was made even more obvious by the darkness of his mustache.

"Katharine," Orville said, and his tone sent a shiver down my spine. Whenever he called me by my Christian name, I knew something very bad had happened.

"What is it? Did you find the jacket?"

"I don't even know how to say it. I have to show you." He shook from head to toe. It was almost as if he had seen a ghost.

"Show me," I ordered.

He turned on his heel and headed down the hall, past the family sitting room and the library. Both of these doors were open, and I found myself peering inside as we hurried by. The sitting room was empty, but a couple stood embracing in the library. I didn't recognize them, because they were facing away from the door, but the woman had a white orchid in her hair. I wondered how the flower had stayed fresh through the whole night. It looked as if she had just plucked it.

Orville stopped abruptly in front of a set of heavy mahogany double doors. "In there."

"What is this room?"

Orville shook his head, as if answering my question was too much for him. I studied him. My brother was scared. What on earth could be on the other side of that door?

I placed my fingers on the handle, pushed the door open, and stepped inside. I found myself in a well-furnished billiard room. Like in every room in the Shaws' home, the ceiling was high. From the high ceiling an ornate crystal chandelier hung over the billiard table. The light glittering from the pieces of cut glass was breathtaking.

However, I couldn't spend much time admiring the décor, because Herman lay slumped on his left side over the billiard table, with blood all over his chest and the felt surface.

Orville followed me into the room.

"Is he dead?" I asked just above a whisper.

Herman looked very dead to me, but I had to ask.

"He must be," Orville answered in a thin voice.

"We should check," I said. "If there is any way to save him, we have to try."

Orville walked over to the body and touched his wrist, looking for a pulse. I followed a few steps behind, and up close, there was no question that Herman Wheeler was very dead. He stared at me with unseeing eyes.

It was so shocking to me that this man, whom I had seen walking through my neighborhood just a few days ago and mocking Orville tonight, was dead. Herman was a brusque and frustrating man, but I hadn't wanted him to die, and certainly not like this.

Orville stepped back.

"Katie, that's my screwdriver."

"What screwdriver?"

He pointed at the bloody tool on the billiard table. The blood on it was still wet. I felt queasy.

"Why would you bring one of your tools here?"

"I didn't bring it on purpose. It was in my jacket pocket. I must have absentmindedly picked it up at some point and tucked it into my pocket. You know I'm always picking up odds and ends and putting them in my pockets."

This was true, and especially so when we were children. It was not unusual for Orville to come home after a walk with his pockets full of leaves, rocks, and sticks. All of which my mother would ask him to leave on the front porch before she would let him inside the house.

"Are you sure it's yours?" I forced myself to take a better look at it, which wasn't easy with all the blood darkening the front of Herman's evening vest.

"I'm positive. Do you see my initials carved in the wooden handle?"

I felt ill at the sight of the letters, speckled with tiny pin-pricks of blood. What did this mean? There was no question in my mind that Orville had had nothing to do with Herman's death, but with this kind of evidence, would the police believe that? Also, there was no question that this was no normal death but a murder. It wasn't as if Herman could have accidently been stabbed in the chest. To drive the screwdriver so deep would take a great deal of force, and then it had been yanked out and thrown on the billiard table. There was no doubt in my mind that Herman Wheeler had been murdered.

There was a small whimper to my right. I turned. Benny Shaw cowered in a corner of the room, staring at the dead man with unfocused eyes. Blood soaked the front of Benny's shirt.

CHAPTER 10

"Benny," I gasped. "What has happened?"

His bright green eyes were wild. "I didn't do it! I have nothing to do with this!"

I stared at Benny Shaw. For once, I wasn't seeing the arrogant teenager, but a terrified child. No matter what our disputes in the classroom, I felt for the young man. He was my student. I spent time with him nearly every day. Could he really have killed a man?

My mouth had suddenly grown very dry, and I cleared my throat.

"I didn't kill him!" Benny said again, with even more force this time. "I know you think I'm horrible, but I could never do such a thing. Never."

I held up my hands as if I were surrendering. What I was surrendering to, I didn't know. "No one is saying that you did anything." Even as I spoke, I had to admit that the circumstantial evidence didn't look good for him. After all, his shirt was soaked with what I could only believe was Herman's blood.

He relaxed ever so slightly at my reassurance.

"Why were you in this room with him?" I asked.

"I just came in here to escape. My father decided that the

billiard room—which is his favorite room in the house—was to be closed and locked for the party. I knew if I wanted to get away, this was the best place."

"If the door was locked, how did you get inside?"

He glowered at me, and I was happy to see some of his old spirit back in his eyes, even if it was in the form of anger directed at me.

"I know where all the keys are. I live here, don't I?" His tone was belligerent.

"And was the door locked when you came to it?"

"I—I don't know. I put the key in because I assumed it was, but I must have been wrong. How could he have gotten inside if the door was locked?"

It was a very good question, but one we didn't have the time to delve into at this moment. There was a dead man on the billiard table. The police needed to be notified.

"What happened when you came into the room?"

"Nothing. Nothing happened. He was already dead!"

"Why didn't you go for help? You were standing in the corner when we came in here, and you didn't say a word."

"I—I don't know. I just panicked. It's not like I've ever seen anyone stabbed before." He looked this way and that. "I have to get out of here."

"Benny, you have to stay. We have to talk to the police."

"I'm not talking to the cops! Are you insane? They will take one look at me and arrest me."

He fled the room. The door slammed closed after him.

Orville rushed to one of the leather club chairs in the corner. His jacket was hanging over the arm of the chair, folded as neatly as you please. He picked up the jacket and turned out the pockets. He came up with a handkerchief, coins, a stub of a pencil, but no papers.

"Orville, we have to go tell someone what's happened. The police need to be notified. This man has been murdered."

My brother ignored me and walked back to the body. He began turning the man's pockets inside out, then reached into his jacket, which was no easy task, as Herman was leaning on his left side.

"What are you doing?"

"He had my jacket. He must have the drawings," Wilbur said in a panicked voice. "They weren't in my jacket. They have to be here with him."

"You can't touch the body!" I cried.

"Please, Katharine. I can't lose those drawings. All the work we have done will be for naught if they get into the wrong hands. A man would kill to claim he was the one who made our discoveries."

I stared at the body. Had someone killed for those drawings? I wished the idea sounded more ridiculous to me than it actually did. Unfortunately, what other reason would there be to kill Herman Wheeler?

Orville rifled through Herman's pockets. All the color drained from his face. "They aren't here."

There was a scream outside the door. It could mean one of two things: someone had seen Benny and his bloodstained clothes or another murder had been committed. Either option was dreadful to contemplate.

The doors flew open, and a half dozen people ran into the room.

When one of the women saw Herman slumped over the table, she screamed for all she was worth. It was Lenora Shaw.

"Put your hand in your pocket," I whispered to my brother.

He blinked at me. "What?" Then he looked down at his right sleeve and saw a spot of blood on his cuff. He held his jacket in his other hand, just as if he had been carrying it around that way all night.

"Herman!" Lenora wailed. "What has happened?" She then saw Orville and me standing there. "You killed him?"

Orville was silent, but as I was made of sterner stuff, I did not remain so.

"We didn't kill anyone," I declared. "We just came into this room, and there he was."

A servant ran into the billiard room, and his face turned slightly green at the sight of the body on the billiard table. "Ma'am, we rang the police. They're on their way."

Lenora didn't even acknowledge his words.

"Have you seen your son?" I asked.

She glared at me. "How can you think to speak about my son's school behavior at a time like this? We are in the middle of a crisis!"

So Lenora must not have seen Benny in his bloodstained clothes. I couldn't help feeling a bit relieved. That wasn't an image any mother should have of her child.

"I just wanted to know if he was all right," I said. "My question had nothing to do with the incident at school."

Much as I hated the thought, I knew Orville and I would have to tell the police about finding Benny in the room. It would be irresponsible not to, but the prospect left an ache in my heart. I didn't want to believe one of my students— even the most disrespectful one—could do such a thing. I didn't want to believe one of my students could be capable of murder.

Randolph Shaw stepped into the room, then cleared his throat when he saw the body. "Please, let's all of us step out of the room. The police will want space to work."

No one moved.

"Now, it is best if you all take your leave. We can't carry on with the party after this tragedy." Randolph spoke calmly and clearly.

Slowly, people began to leave the room. Through the door,

I could see the servants running about, gathering up guests' coats, hats, and scarves. Maggie, the maid I'd met earlier, was among them. Just like the rest of the staff, she appeared to be stricken. Her white cap was askew, and she no longer wore her apron.

I stepped forward. "Mr. Shaw, is it really wise to tell all these people to leave? I'm sure the police detective will want to question them about what they may have seen and heard this evening."

"What they saw and heard? It would have been nothing at all," Randolph replied in a clipped voice. "This part of our home was closed off to guests. No one was to come in here."

"That may be true, but Herman was here. Orville and I came into this room as well."

He frowned. "Then maybe you and your brother should stay so the police can talk to you. The rest of my guests followed the rules for tonight's gathering. They did not come into this part of the house and have the right to leave. I will not keep them here indefinitely."

By the time he'd said this, all the other guests had left the billiard room. It was clear to me that none of them wanted to speak to the police. Understandably, they wished to leave before the investigation got underway. In my opinion, Randolph Shaw was probably letting a killer walk right out the front door.

"With all due respect," I said, "I don't think that is wise."

"Miss Wright," Randolph said, "when I want your opinion, I will ask for it. I can see why you are an old maid. No man would put up with the constant second-guessing you seem determined to inflict on everyone around you. If you do ever marry, you would surely send your unfortunate husband to an early grave."

I opened my mouth to make a sharp retort, but he spoke first. "If the officers want a list of my guests' names, they shall have it. However, I don't see any reason to subject my friends to a long night of interrogation when, as far as I can tell, the only people in this house who came into this room uninvited were you, your brother, and the dead man."

That wasn't true. Randolph's son Benny had been in the room as well, and it had been he who'd found the body. What would I say to the police when they asked how we'd stumbled upon Herman dead on the billiard table?

Randolph looked at the billiard table and the bloodstained felt surface. "The whole thing will have to be destroyed. The bloodstains will never come out. How could we play even one round on it? It's a shame, because I ordered the table from a craftsman in Aberdeen, Scotland. It took nine months to arrive. Now it will go into the fire." He shook his head. "How dreadful."

I bit my lip to stop myself from saying that he was clearly more concerned about the state of his billiard table than the state of the lifeless man on top of it.

A wide policeman occupied the doorway of the billiard room. He wore a bowler hat with a sharply pointed silver ornament on the top. If you asked me, the hat appeared as deadly as the pistol at his hip. However, most striking was the shock on his face. "Orv? Katie?"

"Bertie," Orville said in relief. "I'm so glad it's you."

Bertram "Bertie" Fallon was an old school friend of Orville and Wilbur. The three of them used to use whatever they could find in our yard to construct elaborate racing tracks for their marbles. Now Wilbur and Orville were married to their work, while Bertie was married to a sweet woman and was already the father of four children.

A second man—who was in not a police uniform but a tailored suit, with a bowler hat in hand—pushed Bertie aside as he walked in. He was younger than Bertie, with small eyes that didn't fit with his wide nose.

"Looks like we have a murder," were his first words.

It was what I had been most afraid to hear.

CHAPTER 11

"Gaylen," Randolph scoffed. "How can you say such a thing? There could be a myriad of reasons why Herman is dead. It doesn't have to be murder. I must see to my guests." He marched to the double doors and left the room.

The man in the suit watched him go, shaking his head. "Shaw is acting the snob, as usual. Officer Fallon, go make sure he doesn't do too much damage."

Bertie gave Orville and me one more surprised glance, then left the billiard room.

"I'm Detective Patrick Gaylen," the man with the small eyes said. "I will have to ask the two of you to please step out of the way as we assess the scene."

Orville and I shuffled to one side of the room. A doctor and another officer, whom I didn't know, joined Detective Gaylen near the body.

I very much wanted to follow Randolph out of the room and continue walking all the way home to Hawthorn Street. However, since Bertie and the detective were now blocking the doorway, I couldn't see any way to do that.

Detective Gaylen folded his arms. "Has to be murder.

Can't say I have ever seen a person commit suicide by stabbing himself in the chest with a screwdriver. What a horrible way to go." He took a breath. "There is no doubt in my mind this is murder, but it will be up to the coroner to make the official pronouncement. If he knew I was saying anything of the kind, he would smack me upside the head. He can be territorial about these sorts of things."

"I'm not too happy myself that you are making such statements, Gaylen," a tall thin man said as he entered the room.

Detective Gaylen's cheeks flushed. "Captain Grimes, I didn't know you would be here so soon."

Captain Grimes narrowed his eyes. "If you had known, would that have made any difference in your statement about the deceased?"

The detective opened and closed his mouth, as if looking for the right words, but came up empty. Then he said, "I didn't expect you to come to the scene, sir."

"Randolph rang me. We're old friends from the club. Of course, I came when he called. We have to tread lightly in this case. The club has been very generous with financial support for the police department over the years, and Randolph is the club president. Keep that in mind."

Detective Gaylen tried to keep his face neutral, but his jaw twitched. "He let most of the guests go home before we could question them."

"There is nothing wrong with his not wanting to upset his guests."

The detective grimaced.

"Who are these two?" The captain gestured at Orville and me.

"I'm Orville Wright, sir," my brother said. "And this is my sister, Katharine. We are simply guests of the Shaws."

The captain pursed his lips, as if he didn't completely believe what Orville had said.

"I'm going to speak with Randolph," the captain said. "You deal with these two."

With that, he left the room.

The police detective turned to Orville and me. He looked Orville up and down, and his eyes stopped at Orville's mustache. Detective Gaylen placed a self-conscious hand over his own upper lip, as if afraid to be in Orville's presence. I very much hoped that mustache envy would not factor into Detective Gaylen's investigation. I also wondered if there was anyone older who could take on the case. Detective Gaylen had to be fresh from the academy.

Orville and I stood in one corner of the billiard room, near the set of three leather club chairs where Orville had discovered his jacket.

Detective Gaylen pointed at the chairs. "Please have a seat." He glanced at me. "Both of you."

Orville and I sat, but the detective didn't join us. Instead, he came to stand over us, and in the low chair, I felt like a sea urchin looking up to the surface of the water.

He cleared his throat. "I would like to discuss the moment you found Mr. Wheeler in the billiard room."

"We would be happy to answer any questions you might have," I replied calmly. "We're law-abiding citizens and want to do our very best to help you in your investigation. However, I must ask you to have a seat if you wish to talk with us. I'm getting a crick in my neck from looking up at you."

"Oh, I do apologize," he said and settled into the club chair across from my brother. His legs were so long that his knees knocked against the small coffee table between us.

At the very least, it was nice to know he was a polite man. However, I didn't know if that built my confidence concerning his ability as a police detective.

He removed a small spiral notebook from the front pocket of his suit jacket.

"Mr. Wright," he began, directing his questions to my brother.

I wasn't the least bit surprised that he would ask Orville the questions. There were some men in this world who believed women had no observational skills whatsoever. How wrong they were. Women noticed twice as many things as men, because in too many instances, they were expected to remain silent. If one couldn't talk, one might as well look around.

Even so, I was glad he had begun the questions with Orville. Orville and I had had no time to decide how we were going to tell our story. With Orville speaking first, I would be able to follow his lead.

"Can you tell me why you came into this room in the first place?" the detective continued after a moment.

"Katharine and I were just exploring the house. The ballroom and the parlor—where most of the guests were throughout the night—were starting to become too crowded for my liking. I'm not used to being around so many people at one time. I've always loved architecture and wanted to see what the house had to offer."

It wasn't lost on me that he didn't mention the missing jacket. I knew the omission was intentional. Perhaps he didn't want to give the detective a reason to look at him as the killer. Even the thought was startling. I didn't know how anyone could think Orville was capable of such a heinous crime.

"Did you not know that you were not supposed to be in this wing of the house? Mr. Shaw claims he made it very clear to all guests that the festivities were only in the east wing."

"He might have, but I don't remember him saying anything of the kind. It could have been because I wasn't paying much attention to his welcoming speech. As there were so many people around, I felt uncomfortable."

Detective Gaylen seemed to consider this. "Mr. Shaw said that he posted a servant at the entrance to the west wing of the house. Didn't he try to stop you from entering?"

"There was no one there," I said. "It seems to me that Mr. Shaw needs to ask his man where he went."

Detective Gaylen nodded and made a note in his little notebook. "I will do that."

I felt concerned that he had to write down such an obvious task. Did he have trouble with memory? I would have believed having a good memory was a critical part of being a police detective.

All the while Orville spoke to Detective Gaylen, my brother kept his right hand in the pocket of his trousers to hide the speck of blood on his cuff from sight. If Detective Gaylen did see it, he would view Orville in a completely different light. From the way my poor brother was sitting, he appeared very uncomfortable.

"We came into the room and saw Mr. Wheeler lying over the billiard table, just as you and your officers found him when you arrived. Now, I do admit that I touched him when I searched for a pulse. I didn't find any." Orville swallowed. "Judging by the way his eyes were open and unseeing, I knew he was dead." He glanced at me. "We both knew."

I nodded. "That is true."

"It must have been a ghastly discovery," the detective said.

"It certainly was," I said. "Neither of us has ever seen anything like it."

"I should hope not," the detective said. "But I do have a few concerns about you, Mr. Wright."

Orville shifted in his seat. "What are those?"

Detective Gaylen opened his notebook. "I have been told you had a disagreement with Mr. Wheeler not long before he died. Is that true?"

He had his pencil poised, ready to make notes.

Orville shook his head. "We didn't have a disagreement."

"He mocked you in some sort of parlor game," the detective said, looking down at his notes.

"He was poking fun at me, yes, but it wasn't anything to get my tail feathers up about, I can assure you."

"And how was he, as you say, poking fun?" The detective had his pencil poised to write.

"He was teasing me about the work I do with my brother. We like to tinker," Orville said, as if he was a young boy who liked to make things from a pile of sticks. They did a lot more than tinker. My brothers' goal to be the first to fly was an obsession.

"I really don't know," Orville went on to say, "why his teasing has anything at all to do with how the poor man ended up dead."

"I wouldn't think too much about it either," the detective said. "I know young men like to get a rise out of each other." He paused. "However, I have to give it some thought because of this." He held up a brown paper bag. He then reached into the bag and pulled out something wrapped in a bit of cheesecloth. Carefully, as if it was fragile as a butterfly's wing, he unwrapped the object and revealed the bloody screwdriver that had been on the billiard table, next to the body. The shank was encrusted with dried blood all the way to the hilt. "Does this look familiar to you, Mr. Wright?"

I could no longer see my brother's mouth below his mustache.

"It is very likely the murder weapon," Orville said.

"Very true." The detective's demeanor had changed. He was no longer the affable, chatty man he had been when he'd first sat down. He seemed calculating and watched Orville's every mannerism and movement. This must be how he had risen to the position of detective at such a young age. He appeared very good at what he did.

Unfortunately, I didn't know if that was good or bad news for my brother.

"I noticed that your initials are scratched into the handle of the screwdriver. So let me ask you again, do you recognize this item?" the detective went on. As he did, he watched Orville with the same scrutiny with which a cat watched a mouse. Perhaps even with the same deadly intentions.

"Yes, those are my initials," Orville replied. "I won't deny that. I told Katharine when we came into this room that it was my tool." He held up his hand. "Before you ask, I have no idea how it arrived in the billiard room."

"So you didn't bring it onto the premises."

Orville shifted in his seat and seemed to sink into the plush leather as he did so. The club chairs were not the kind of seat that gave one the upper hand with an opponent, mostly because one had to constantly be on guard not to be swallowed up by it.

"I did bring it on the premises, yes."

Detective Gaylen raised his brow.

"It was in my jacket pocket," Orville said. "I am known to tuck odds and ends into my pockets. I must have done so with the screwdriver and forgotten that it was there before I left the house. It's a tool I use often at our bicycle shop."

Detective Gaylen seemed to consider this explanation. I wished I knew what he was thinking. I had to admit that so far he seemed to be focusing on Orville's connection to the case. But who wouldn't? The evidence against my brother appeared damning. The only person who looked more guilty was Benny Shaw. However, as of yet, Detective Gaylen had not mentioned him, and neither had I or Orville. Did I have the nerve to bring the teenager up?

Bertie ran into the room, out of breath. It seemed any movement at all made the officer tired. "Detective, you must come and see this!"

Detective Gaylen looked up from his notes, which were little better than chicken scratch. Penmanship really was a lost art.

"What is it?" Detective Gaylen said.

Bertie wrung his hands. "You need to see for yourself."

"Tell me." This time Detective Gaylen's words came out as an order.

"It's a young man covered in blood," Bertie said, looking as if he might just faint at the memory.

CHAPTER 12

After Bertie made his startling announcement, the detective raced out of the billiard room, and Orville and I were left behind, unsure about our next move.

"What do we do now?" I directed my question to Bertie.

Bertie rocked back and forth in his large shoes, as if he was trying to comfort himself. "I—I think the detective will be occupied for a long while. Did you tell him everything you had to say?"

Before I could answer, Orville said, "Yes, we did."

"What are the two of you doing here?" Bertie asked just above a whisper.

"I was invited and brought Orv as my guest," I answered.

"These aren't our kind of people," Bertie continued in a whisper.

I wrinkled my brow and wondered what he meant by that.

Bertie cleared his throat. "You should go home. All the other guests have already left. We can contact you at a later time if we have more questions. I know where to find you, of course," Bertie said.

"We are glad to see a friendly face here under these circumstances." Orville stood up, still with his hand in his pocket, and hurried toward the double doors. "I trust you will put in a good word for us as your old friends."

"I will, but it's not going to be easy," Bertie said with a great sigh.

Before I could ask him what he meant by that, Orville said, "Come, Katharine. Will and Father will be worried about what has kept us so long."

I followed my brother out of the room. Then we endeavored to gather our coats and scarves from one of the servants. The staff was in a tizzy over the evening's events. Finally, I spotted Maggie the maid.

She was rushing down the hallway with a glass of water in her hand.

"Miss," I called. "Can you find our coats so we can leave?"

When she turned to me, her face was blank, as if she didn't know where she was or how she had got there. I could understand why a man's murder would be shocking, but I wasn't sure why she was so clearly disoriented.

The confusion on her face was short lived. "Yes, of course. Just let me deliver this glass of water." She disappeared down the hallway.

As she was hurrying off, she reminded me of a mouse running away from a cat.

Orville and I waited in the foyer. My brother faced the wall, shifting his weight back and forth from foot to foot. I wouldn't have been the least bit surprised if at any moment he announced we should leave our coats and simply buy new ones. However, the old Wright frugality kept him in place. There was no reason to purchase a new coat if you already had one that you could button up tight.

Unfortunately, Maggie didn't come back in a timely manner or bring us our coats. I didn't know how long she would be, and my patience had grown thin. Another servant walked by, and I asked him to retrieve our coats. He did so right away.

I thanked him and shoved Orville's coat in his direction, and we quickly dressed to face the cold and snow.

Outside, electric lights cast an eerie orange glow on the house's front entrance. They were cast iron, shaped like lanterns, and made strange vulture-shaped shadows on the front steps. I felt as if I was walking over an evil omen. I decided that if my father ever agreed to have our house electrified, I would never allow those particular outdoor lights to be installed on our home.

I stepped on another shadow just as a great wail rose up into the air. I bumped into my brother's back, and if he had not been in front of me, I would have toppled over onto the icy gravel of the driveway.

Had the vulture shadows actually shrieked?

However, I was soon corrected when I saw Lenora Shaw to my right, flailing one arm at Detective Gaylen. Her other hand held Benny in a viselike grip. "You can't take him! You can't take him! He is my son!"

She was still in her peacock-blue gown, but her gloves were missing. The little cap sleeves at the top of her shoulders were fashionable but did nothing to keep her warm.

It wasn't until Benny turned and looked back at his mother that I saw he still wore the bloody shirt. One would have thought the police would at least let him change before taking him to the station.

Lenora Shaw dropped her flailing arm, and her free hand joined the one that gripped Benny. She pulled on her son's arm until one of the police officers attempted to pry her hands off him. Lenora's grip was far too strong. She clung to her son with a mother's love.

"You cannot take him," she said between her sobs. "Randolph? Where is Randolph? Where is my husband? He needs to be here to talk sense into you at once! Benny has done nothing wrong."

The blood on his shirt belied that statement.

"Mrs. Shaw," Detective Gaylen shouted over her protests, "you're only making this worse for your son."

He pushed the officer aside and broke the lady's hold on her son's arm, then held her back as two other officers loaded Benny into the back of the police wagon.

I looked on, stricken for both mother and son. Before the wagon's door closed behind him, Benny made eye contact with me, and the terror I saw on his face shook me to my very core.

"Katie, let's go!" Orville whispered harshly to me.

I nodded dumbly and followed my brother to our buggy. The police wagon passed us as we walked. I glanced over my shoulder as Lenora Shaw fell to the snowy ground in her peacock silk gown.

It would be a long time before the sound of her wailing left my mind.

When Orville and I returned to our home on Hawthorn Street, I discovered that sleep was a fickle friend. Both Wilbur and Father were still up. Wilbur was working on calculations at the kitchen table, and our father was reading the Bible in his favorite chair by the fireplace.

Wilbur looked up from his work. "So tell me, was it worth going?"

"No," Orville said, leaving no room for me to refute him. Not that I was planning to. The evening had been a disaster from beginning to end. The only good thing that had happened was Agnes got her dance with Arthur Bacon, but I didn't know for certain whether that story had ended happily. Orville and I had been in such a rush to leave that I didn't have a chance to look for her. I would check in on her the next day, I promised myself. There was also a very good chance that she'd gone home when Randolph Shaw had encouraged all his guests to leave.

Had we a telephone at home, I would have rung her, but my father believed that the device was a luxury we didn't need, and I was far too tired to walk to the bicycle shop and use the telephone there.

"What happened?" Father asked. "You both look wrung out."

"A man was killed," I said.

Wilbur and Father gasped.

"Was there an accident?" Father asked. "I have been in the Shaws' home only once, and I seem to remember they had an elaborate chandelier in every room. Was that what happened? A chandelier fell and killed him? I always thought such opulence would lead to no good." Father pursed his lips in disapproval.

"It wasn't a chandelier," I said. "He was stabbed in the chest with a screwdriver."

They gasped.

"Tell us from the beginning to the end," Father said. "Leave nothing out."

Father would never admit it even to himself, but he did have an eagerness for gossip.

I excused myself as Orville filled them in on what had happened. That wasn't a normal reaction for me, by any means. Typically, I wanted to be in the thick of it and know every last little detail, but I could not banish Lenora's facial expression or the sound of her wailing from my head. I guessed that a little aspirin powder and a good night's rest were what I needed.

I resolved that I would do something about the situation. I refused to believe that one of my students—even one as disagreeable as Benny Shaw—could take another person's life.

CHAPTER 13

On Monday morning I was never so grateful to have a day free of the classroom. The Christmas holiday had come at the perfect time.

I sat up in bed as I went over the events of Saturday night. Herman Wheeler's body, Orville's screwdriver, Lenora Shaw's wails, and Benny's bloody shirt all came back to me in an avalanche of images.

On Sunday, the day of rest, I had done my very best to put them out of my head. I'd gone to church with my father, read, and wrapped the few Christmas gifts that I already had in hand. My father was staunch about our resting on the Sabbath, and it was a family tradition. I didn't know what the boys had done all day, but I knew they hadn't worked. While they were under our father's roof, they would always follow this rule. I did my very best to do the same, but I would admit that during the school year, I had been known to mark student papers on Sunday afternoons when my father was resting.

On Monday, however, I could no longer push the thoughts of Saturday night from my mind. I worried for Benny, Lenora, and Herman's family. As of yet, I had not even heard if the dead man had any family close by. And maybe selfishly, considering a man had been killed, I was worried about the missing drawings. We had never found them that night. I wondered if little brother had gotten any sleep at all the past two nights. His and Wilbur's life work might have been stolen.

I scrabbled on the small table beside my bed, searching for my spectacles. I finally found them after knocking three books and a pencil to the floor. With the glasses securely on my face, I put the items back in place and then quickly dressed for the day.

There was much to do, and one thing was for certain: this wasn't going to be the quiet, restful school break I'd hoped for.

It was still dark outside when I walked into breakfast. I was not one to sleep late and waste away the day. None of us were. Our parents had instilled in us the need to work hard and make the most of every waking hour.

I expected to find both brothers and Father in the dining room, eating breakfast, but my father was the only one there. He was dressed in a dark suit and a freshly pressed white shirt, which could mean only that he planned to make church calls that morning. His white hair—what was left of it—was combed over the top of his head, and his impressive Dutch beard was stark white.

As if he could read my thoughts, he said, "Both Orville and Wilbur seem to be sleeping late this morning. They are depleted from their travels, and they did not rest for a moment when they arrived home. All that activity catches up with a person in time. I do hope they wake soon. They should have gotten all the rest they needed on the Sabbath. We have yet to reach the shortest day of the year. There are many dark days ahead of us still, but this does not mean that we can sleep away the day."

Not wanting to get in an argument with my father over the boys' sleeping choices, I focused my attention on the paper in my father's hand. "Is there any mention of the Shaws' party?"

He turned the front page in my direction. The headline read in large bold type MURDER AT SHAW MANSION SHATTERS CHRISTMAS PARTY.

I shivered as I went to the sideboard, where Carrie had set out breakfast. It was a simple meal of toast, jam, and oatmeal. I couldn't face the oatmeal, so I made myself a piece of toast with butter and orange marmalade. Oranges always reminded me of Christmas. Our mother would put one orange in each of our stockings every year. It seemed like such a long time ago now; she had been gone for fourteen years.

I poured myself a cup of coffee and pushed my melancholy thoughts to the back of my mind, where I kept them safely locked away. I had enough worries this morning; there was no need to visit old wounds.

"What happened Saturday night was so awful," I murmured as I sat at the table.

My father shook the newspaper. "The newspaper made a tiny, inaccurate mention of your brothers' great accomplishment, and yet this murder is garishly displayed across the front page."

"Well, murder in a prominent Daytonian's home is newsworthy."

"Even so, the papers should pay more mind to the good news in the world. Focusing on all the bad only makes men more despondent and bitter."

I sipped my coffee. I did not bother to tell my father that good news didn't sell papers.

"I'm traveling to Yellow Springs today," Father continued. "To meet with some pastors who are supporting me during this difficult time."

He was, of course, referring to the current lawsuit being waged against him.

"It is a shame there are not more honest men in the church, but sin and evil know no bounds," he went on. "Even with my troubles, I must continue the Lord's work. We are hoping to start a church plant there in Yellow Springs, but I must assess what the community is really like before we do so. A whole study needs to take place. I am going to advise how."

I nodded. "I'm surprised you are doing such work this close to Christmas."

My father's eyes bored into me. "The business of the church cannot wait for a more convenient time. And what better time than Christmas to spread the message of the Word?"

I shifted in my seat. The next question I had for my father was rather uncomfortable. "I passed Orville in the hall when I was going to bed last night. He said he was going back downstairs to talk with you and Will. Did you and the boys discuss the flying machine last night?"

He folded the paper and set it next to his empty bowl on the table. "No. We were just chatting about their life in Kitty Hawk. It was quite fascinating to hear."

"Perhaps Wilbur and Orville discussed it further after you went to bed?"

He shook his head. "I don't believe so. We all retired at the same time." He paused. "Why are you concerned about whether or not they spoke of the flying machine? Would it be a surprise if they had? They speak about it constantly. I, for one, was happy for a respite from all the mechanics."

"Oh, I suppose I just thought you might have discussed it, with their great accomplishment still so fresh," I said. What I didn't say was that if they hadn't discussed the flying machine, it could mean only that Orville hadn't told Wilbur the drawings were missing. I knew my brother Orville well, and I was certain that instead of telling Wilbur straight off, as he should, he planned to set everything right before Wilbur found out. And he was going to ask me to help him do it.

CHAPTER 14

After Father left for his church work, I went in search of my brothers, who still hadn't come down to breakfast. They were so tardy, I began to worry. I knocked on Orville's door first, but there was no answer. I frowned. It wasn't common for anyone in the family to sleep the day away. I opened the door and found the room empty and my brother's bed neatly made. I checked Wilbur's room and found the same.

I put my hands on my hips. "Those boys ran off to work without telling me."

I hurried downstairs, gathered up my coat, hat, and scarf, and then told Carrie I was going out for the day and likely would not be back for luncheon.

The girl was dusting the living room and nodded with wide eyes. "Yes, miss." She was a good worker but always seemed to be a little bit surprised even by the simplest announcement.

The air was brisk outside, and my nose was immediately cold. I pulled my scarf up over my face as I hurried to the bicycle shop. The shop was housed in a two-story flat-faced brick building with two upper windows and windows along the front on the ground level. It wasn't the first location of the shop, but Wilbur in particular liked this new spot because of all the windows. "People can see us working on the bicycles. It makes folks more confident about our products when they can see with their own eyes that we are the ones behind the cycles."

Because I could easily look into the shop, I saw that my brothers weren't in the front room, but their mechanic, Charlie Taylor, was. He was the last person I wanted to see that morning, or any morning, truth be told. With a sigh, I went into the shop.

"Miss Katie, what brings you to the shop this morning?" Charlie asked. "Since you're on school break, I would have thought you'd be out with your little friends, shopping, having tea, or whatever it is unattached young women do these days."

I frowned.

Charlie Taylor was an average-sized man with a thick mustache like Orville's, but his looked more like the bristles of a broom than the refined style my brother nurtured. Charlie's eyes were set deep in his face, and he had a cigar in his mouth. I loathed the nauseatingly sweet smell of the cigar, and I hated that he smoked inside the shop. I had told my brothers time and time again that they should make Charlie take his filthy cigars outside, but they had done nothing.

When the boys were away in Kitty Hawk, Charlie managed the day-to-day running of the shop, selling new bicycles—the Van Cleve, named for our grandmother, still being the most popular model—and fixing bicycles that came in for repair.

I was the one who checked the accounts; made sure we had all the supplies we needed, from tire tubes to pedals; and balanced the books. This meant when my brothers were away, I had to work closely with Charlie, and it was the very worst part of my brothers' absence. Charlie swore, smoked, and was just generally a crude and unrefined man. I had begged my brothers to find another machinist, but they had refused, claiming that Charlie was the best. The best at what cost? I'd wanted to know.

I ignored his question now, because I knew he wasn't actually interested in any answer I might have. "Charlie," I said shortly, "it's not even ten in the morning, and you are already smoking a cigar."

Charlie puffed out a ring of blue smoke. "There's no rules about where and when you can smoke, Miss Katie. Those rules are about drinking." He stood behind the counter. Above his head a Van Cleve bicycle hung from the ceiling. Behind him, small cube shelves lined the wall, filled with bicycle pieces and parts. From where I stood, I could see that we were running low on bicycle bells. I made a mental note to include those in my next supply order.

Next to Charlie, there was a half wall with a window that divided the sales counter from the small bookkeeping office next to it. At the rolltop desk was where I sat when I was crunching numbers for my brothers. Now that they were home, I hoped that meant I wouldn't have to be in the shop nearly as much, with the added benefit of not having to interact with Charlie.

I pressed my lips together. "Well, both are terrible habits."

He shrugged. "That's what you say."

"Are my brothers in the back?"

"Oh yes," he said. "Will and Orv have been back there tinkering away for hours."

I nodded and walked past the office into the next room where a number of bicycles stood in various stages of repair. Bicycle repairs and sales were slower in the winter, and from what I could tell, Charlie had made very little progress on the few cycles he had to fix.

I pressed my lips together. The boys were back, and Charlie was their problem now, at least until they left for Kitty Hawk again.

I had thought many times that Charlie was the product of

not having had the right teacher to set him on the straight and narrow. Had I been his teacher, things would have been different for him. This brought to mind a student who was in dire need of help, Benny Shaw.

Had Benny been arrested? Had they let him go home last night? There was no mention of Benny in the newspaper article, but I had my suspicions as to why that was. Randolph Shaw supplied the newspapers with paper from his paper mill. The last thing a newspaper owner wanted was to lose his paper supply.

Even so, there had been many people at that party. It wouldn't be long before Benny's involvement as a suspect in Herman's murder became a topic of conversation in Dayton.

I found my brothers in the back room of the shop, where they were making adjustments to the wind tunnel they'd built to test their wing-warping theories using the small flying machine models they made.

The wind tunnel was on, and the sound was deafening. The boys were watching their experiment so intently, they didn't even realize I was there. I was about to wave to get their attention when the wind tunnel finally stopped. The model flyer inside the drum fell to the bottom of the contraption.

As I watched them work, I removed my hat, scarf, and coat and set them on a bench by the workroom door.

"I believe all will become clear with these new calculations," Wilbur said. "More control is dependent on the span of the wings. On the train ride, I made a few notes on the drawings before you put them in your coat pocket. Do you have them with you? I'd like to check my hypothesis against what we've learned from the models."

Orville removed the model from the wind tunnel, avoiding Wilbur's gaze. "Oh, I left the drawings back at the house. Would you like me to go retrieve them?"

"No. I will check it later." Wilbur shook his head. "I

shouldn't be fiddling with this now. We had a last-minute printing order come in. I'm going upstairs to finish that, and then I'll return home."

My brothers' printshop was over the bicycle shop, and they still ran a few printing jobs for extra money, even though the bicycle business took up 90 percent of their time. Wilbur and Orville were determined to be self-reliant. Even when benefactors like Randolph Shaw offered to fund their flying machine project, they refused. They wanted to have full control and make all the decisions without needing to please investors. The only way they could do so was to pay for all their inventions themselves, which sometimes meant taking odd printing jobs just a few days before Christmas.

Orville's shoulders sagged in relief; both he and I knew he had no idea where the drawings were. I wasn't sure what he was planning to do that evening, when Wilbur asked for the drawings again. Would Orville then say they were in the cycle shop? It wouldn't be long before Wilbur became suspicious.

"Sterchens!" Wilbur said when he noticed me. "How long have you been standing there?"

"Long enough to have my hearing damaged by that machine," I replied mildly.

Wilbur laughed. "It's not that loud. You should be up in the flyer. Now, that is a noisy experience!"

It sounded like quite an unpleasant experience to me.

"What are you doing here?" Wilbur asked. "I thought you might be off with some of your friends, ice skating or walking in the snow."

I glanced at Orville, who wouldn't meet my gaze. So, he was going to pretend he hadn't lost the drawings? I could play along for a little while.

I frowned at Wilbur. "You make it sound like the only thing I do is amuse myself. While you were gone, I was working two demanding jobs—at school and here. No, it was more than that, since I also had to deal with Charlie Taylor."

Wilbur shook his head. "Charlie is not nearly as bad as you make him out to be."

"No, he's worse. And if you must know, I came here to see if the two of you needed any help. When I couldn't find either of you at home, I figured you came here to catch up on work. I wanted to show you the accounts and our current log of customers. We had a lot of repeat bicycle buyers this fall."

"All business is good, but repeat buyers are extra special." Wilbur removed his work gloves. "I would love to see the accounts. Katharine, I really don't know what we would do without you. You're so organized, and you have a special gift for keeping us both in line."

My gaze slid to Orville. Before the Christmas party Saturday night, I would have said that was true, but then Orville had lost the drawings. I thought Wilbur's claim was no longer always the case. If I had been keeping a better eye on my brother, I would have known he planned to take the drawings with him and could have told him to leave them behind or stay home with Wilbur if he'd rather work. I had been perfectly capable of going to the party on my own. Heaven knew I didn't need a chaperone.

In my heart, I wished none of us had gone to the party. Maybe if we hadn't, the drawings wouldn't have been lost, Benny wouldn't have been taken away by the police, and Herman would still be alive. If, of course, the missing drawings were truly the reason Herman was killed.

"Where did you go just now, Katie?" Wilbur asked. "You had a faraway look on your face. That's not like you."

I blinked. "I'm sorry. I haven't slept well the past two nights. The Christmas party was a tad overwhelming."

"How did you find the party? I read more about the incident you spoke of in the paper this morning. I hope neither of you were caught up in that mess with Herman Wheeler."

"We know little about it," Orville hedged.

"We found his body," I stated plainly.

Orville's eyes went wide. I could not believe he wanted to tell more falsehoods to our brother. The one about the missing drawings was bad enough. We were so close, we were like a set of triplets, and he wanted me to keep the truth from Wilbur? Orville was going to owe me after all this was over. I didn't know how I would ask him to pay up, but I was sure I would soon think of something.

"Did you witness the murder?" Wilbur asked, aghast.

"No, no," I replied. At least that was the truth. "Herman died in the billiard room, which was closed off from the party." I didn't add, of course, that even though it was closed off, Orville and I had gone in there in search of the missing drawings.

Wilbur shook his head. "To kill a man in a crowded house, with dozens and dozens of people there, was taking quite a risk. It makes me think the person who did it had a strong reason to want Herman dead. In his case, it's understandable someone might feel that strongly."

"*Understandable?*" I yelped. "Will, how can you say such a thing?"

"I don't wish anyone dead, but Herman was not a good man. He had engaged in bad business dealings ever since he was a young fellow. He was the type who always wanted a quick fix. He wanted someone else to put the work in, while he took the glory." He pressed his lips together. "I don't have much respect for a person like that. Ingenuity should benefit the individual who uses it. It should not be stolen for someone else's profit. I suppose that's why I'm so anxious about getting our patent approved. The sooner that happens, the sooner we will be able to dispute any claims that we didn't solve the conundrum of human flight."

I suppressed a shiver. Did this mean Herman had stolen the drawings because he'd planned to do exactly that with my brothers' flyer? Had he wanted to take the credit for it as well as any money that might come my brothers' way from their success?

"How did he come to work for the Shaws, then?" I asked. "I would think such a successful paper mill owner would have his choice of applicants. Also, the Shaws are well connected in the community. I can't believe they didn't know Herman Wheeler was problematic if his reputation is widely known."

Wilbur wiped a white handkerchief over the top of his bald head, which had beads of sweat on it. Outside it was close to freezing, but in the shop the woodstove kept everything warm, too warm, in my opinion. "I don't know. It makes no sense that Randolph would hire him, unless Herman had some information that made Randolph Shaw look bad. It's the only reason I can think of for Randolph to hire him."

Or kill him, I thought.

CHAPTER 15

Wilbur and I went over the accounts in the little book-keeping office beside the sales counter, while Orville manned the sales counter. Much to my relief, they sent Charlie home shortly after I arrived. I supposed that it was because I was there, and my brothers were trying to minimize any contact between Charlie and me, but they claimed it was because Charlie had done such a bang-up job managing the shop that he deserved some extra time off.

Wilbur and I had our heads bent over the ledger as the bell over the shop door chimed.

I looked up to see Mrs. Meri Appleton come into the store. "Meri with an *e* and an *i*," as she always said. Mrs. Appleton, who owned a bakery on the corner of West Third Street and Williams Street called West Third Cakes, looked just as a person with her name should. She had round red cheeks, wide hips, and fingers that resembled sausage links.

She made the most delicious and intricate pastries and cakes. People traveled from all over Dayton and beyond to visit her bakery. She was especially popular with the elite of the city, who could afford her delectable treats on a weekly basis.

Even though her bakery was a stone's throw from where we stood, to my knowledge, this was the first time the baker had ever been in the cycle shop. I had invited her to stop by more than once. Cycling was great fun, I'd told her, and she would enjoy owning a bicycle. However, she had always declared she wasn't going to risk breaking a hip on one of my brothers' "two-wheeled death traps."

It made me wonder what she thought of my brothers' attempts to fly. I was certain she knew of their recent accomplishment. Mrs. Appleton was a certified gossip and repeated everything she heard in her shop.

Whatever she had to tell us, it must be big news if she had bothered to travel three doors down to the cycle shop. Mrs. Appleton had told me once she hated walking. She stood all day long while she was baking, and when she wasn't baking, she wanted to sit.

Curious about the purpose of her visit, Wilbur and I rushed out of the little bookkeeping office and joined Orville at the sales counter.

"Have you heard the news?" Mrs. Appleton dug a fist into her back, as if she felt a pain.

My brothers stared at her in dismay, as if she might collapse to the floor. Someone had to take charge here, and as usual, it would be me.

"Take a breath, Mrs. Appleton," I said. "Would you like a glass of water?"

"Yes, please. The cold air sucks the wind right out of you." She coughed.

I hurried into the back room to fetch a glass and the pitcher of water we always kept there. On the sales counter, I filled the glass and handed it to her.

She took a greedy gulp. "Thank you, dear. What I'm about to tell you has shaken me to my very core. To my very core, I tell you."

"Orv, give her your stool," I ordered in my sternest teacher's voice.

Orville jumped out of his seat and moved the stool around

the counter. Mrs. Appleton immediately fell onto the wooden seat, and for a moment, I feared it would topple right over. Thankfully, the stool remained upright. My brothers had made the stool, and it was sturdy enough to withstand even a semi-hysterical baker.

She placed a hand to her chest. "Oh, thank you, Orville. You are such a dear. Your mother raised all of you right. God rest her soul." She then gulped from her glass until it was empty. I refilled it for her.

"What do you have to tell us?" Wilbur finally asked. He wasn't one who enjoyed idle chitchat. He'd much rather be working or researching than chatting with a neighbor over the fence. He cracked his knuckles, making it clear to me that he was anxious to get back to work.

"Lean in and I will tell you," she said in a hushed voice.

My brothers and I leaned in.

But being Mrs. Appleton, she had to draw out her revelation for maximum impact. "It is truly frightful news, and I had to tell someone. My assistant is at the market to buy more butter, so I can't tell her. We're going through it fast with all the Christmas orders. And Lou's Barbershop is closed today. Lou is headed to Maryland for Christmas. Can you imagine traveling at this time of year? You could not pay me to do so. They say the rails are safe, but with snow and ice, how can anyone promise such a thing? No, thank you. I'm perfectly happy right where I am, up to my elbows in éclair dough."

So, Mrs. Appleton was saying we were her third choice of recipient to hear this news. I took no offense. Mrs. Appleton would prefer to share the news with another gossip—Lou the barber was a good choice—but she wasn't going to find any scandal lovers here.

She looked at my brothers in turn. "I hope neither of you want to see a barber before the New Year. Your hair is looking a tad long. Is that the fashion now, to have a man's hair curl over his ears? I can't say I care much for it. In fact, I don't care for it at all—"

"Mrs. Appleton," Wilbur said, finally breaking into her rant, "can you *please* tell us the news? I'm sure whatever it is, we won't have heard it."

"Benny Shaw has been charged with murder."

Her pronouncement came as a shock, even though it wasn't completely unexpected. Orville and I had seen Benny being put into the police wagon in front of the Shaws' mansion Saturday night. However, to hear it from Mrs. Appleton, of all people, was jarring.

And to think before the party, Lenora's biggest worry about her son had been his banishment from my classroom before Christmas break began. Now he had been charged with murder.

"Are you sure?" I asked.

"I'm quite sure. I heard it from a police officer himself." She took a breath. "Officer Fallon comes into my bakery twice a week for a maple cruller. He loves them so much. I used to have them only on my fall menu, because when you think maple, you think of fall."

"Wouldn't you think of spring?" Orville asked, confused. "That's when the maple trees are tapped."

She gave him a look, as if she couldn't believe he'd said such a thing. "That may be true, but it's a fall flavor. I'm a baker. This is my field. I don't question you on how to build a bicycle. Don't question me on which flavor is appropriate for which season."

Orville snapped his mouth closed. He likely feared Mrs. Appleton would cut off his Danish supply.

"I can't believe it. Benny is one of my students," I said. "What a terrible thing to have happened. His poor mother."

My mind went to Lenora as the worried parent rather than to Randolph because he'd been nowhere to be seen as Benny was taken away, while Lenora had shouted in vain for her husband. Was his absence telling? After Wilbur's revelation of Herman's character, it seemed to me Randolph could have been making himself scarce because he was guilty of the crime.

But letting his son take the blame? That was the lowest of the low.

"Oh, can you tell me about Benny? I haven't seen him in a long while, and the last time he came into the bakery, it was with his mother. That was several years ago now. However, I have heard he has become quite assured of himself and planned to go off to college to get his degree before returning to run the paper mill with his father." The stool creaked underneath her as she spoke.

"I don't speak of my students outside of school," I said with a lift of my chin.

Now, that wasn't entirely true. I loved to entertain my brothers and father with stories about my days at school, but I wasn't going to tell this woman anything about Benny—or any of my other students, for that matter. If I did, the whole city would know. Also, as I had nothing flattering to say about Benny's behavior in the classroom, I did not want to add to his troubles.

"Well." Mrs. Appleton stood up, as if offended by my reticence. "I need to return to the bakery. I just wanted to share the news." With that, she walked out of the shop.

"What a distressing story. I could never have imagined a high school student would kill a man," Wilbur said.

My head snapped in his direction. "What about innocent until proven guilty? Just because Benny has been arrested, it doesn't mean he's guilty of this crime."

"But didn't you say yourself that Benny Shaw was one of the most defiant students in your class? He is always speaking to you with disrespect and even malice."

"That doesn't make him a killer."

Wilbur shook his head. "It increases his chances." He turned and walked back into the little office area and sat at the desk. He was back at work, where he felt happiest and most secure.

I cleared my throat. "I think I'll leave now. I am technically on school break and should be enjoying myself while I have the time. Wilbur, if you have any questions about any of the accounts or numbers in the ledger, write your questions down and I will address them at dinner tonight."

Wilbur didn't look up from his work but waved his hand to acknowledge that he had heard me.

I gathered up my coat, hat, and scarf. "Orv, will you walk me out?" I asked quietly as I donned my coat and hat.

He chewed on the edge of his mustache. "Will, I'll be outside for a minute." Orville grabbed the broom by the door. "I need to sweep snow off the walk."

Wilbur raised his hand over his head to acknowledge that he had heard that as well.

I went out the door, and Orville followed with his broom. There was very little snow on the walk, but Orville brushed vigorously at what was there.

"You're going to tell Wilbur, aren't you?" I asked.

"I can't!" Despite the cold, sweat gathered on his brow.

"You have to, and you might have to tell the police as well." I tied my scarf tightly under my chin. "The missing drawings may be tied to Herman Wheeler's murder."

"We can't tell the police, or Wilbur will find out. He'll never forgive me if those drawings fall into the wrong hands."

"Into the wrong hands? What do you mean by that?"

It started to snow, and a snowflake landed on a lens of my glasses. Through the water-speckled lens, I watched my brother and waited.

"The missing papers include our drawings and calculations for wing warping, the breakthrough that led to our successful flight. We are still perfecting the engineering behind our unique way of modifying wing shape, but staying aloft for a few hundred feet is an accomplishment, a huge one that no one else has been able to achieve. Not the Smithsonian, not Lilienthal, not Chanute. No one else has come to our conclusion about wing warping, and it changes everything."

"And you fear the drawings were stolen for this very reason."

"Yes! It takes a skilled pilot to keep a flying machine up in the air. There are tricks we have learned along the way. All those techniques are detailed on those drawings. Our patent is not approved yet. If these drawings have fallen into the wrong hands, someone could falsely claim that he made these discoveries, not us!"

I knew that for my brothers, being recognized as the first to fly was even more important than the potential money that was to be made from their invention. It was a legacy that they were determined to leave behind. If anyone questioned their achievement, they would feel they had failed.

"You can't keep a secret like this from Wilbur," I said. "He has a right to know. It's his life's work too."

"I'm not keeping a secret. I'm waiting to tell him until the time is right. If we could find the drawings before I have to tell him, all the better."

"We?" I asked.

"You, actually. You're better with people, Katie. Everyone knows that. If I go about asking questions, it will appear odd. But you, you are a good conversationalist. You have many friends. Everyone knows you aren't shy. It wouldn't be odd for you to go about striking up conversations with people. It's what you do best."

I stared at my brother. It wasn't the first time one of my brothers or my father had asked me to undertake a difficult task. They always treated me as an equal, as someone who could make up her own mind and come to conclusions just as easily as they could. I appreciated that. It empowered me to be more confident in my life and in the classroom. But Orville was making a very large request. He was essentially asking me to solve a murder.

CHAPTER 16

I left the cycle shop, unsure what to do next. It wasn't often in my life that I didn't know my next move. I prided myself on being a decisive person. That trait served me well in the classroom and in a house full of opinionated men.

Out of habit, I started to walk toward home but stopped in the middle of the sidewalk just a few feet from West Third Cakes. If I was really going to solve this murder, there was only one place I should go right then, back to the scene of the crime.

I wasn't looking forward to it. After spending all of Saturday evening avoiding Lenora Shaw, I was about to seek her out.

I lifted my skirts and ran the rest of the way home. If Mrs. Appleton or any of the other ladies peering out their windows along the street saw me, I knew there would be many whispers about my boldness. I was acting like a young schoolgirl instead of the proper teacher I was. But I wasn't in the classroom at the moment, and truth be told, it was none of their business if I was proper or not.

I burst into the house, making Carrie jump. She was in the midst of polishing the furniture with lemon oil.

We planned to get a Christmas tree this year from my school's Christmas tree sale. The tradition of having a Christmas tree in the home had become increasingly popular in Dayton over the past few years. Carrie was truly a sweet girl and wanted our home to look as pretty as possible for Christmas.

"Miss Katharine, you gave me a terrible start." She held her feather duster to her chest, looking like a woman in a silent movie clutching her pearls.

"I'm sorry, Carrie," I said. "I'm just popping in for a moment to gather a few things, and then I will be out of your way again."

"Do you want something to eat? It's almost luncheon. You said that you would not be home for it, so I just made a simple sandwich for myself. I can make you something if you like."

The thought of food made me slightly nauseous, considering the task I had set out for myself. I was far too eager to start on my plan. "That's very kind, Carrie, but no. I'm just going to run up to my room to gather a few school papers, and I will leave again." I planned to grab the papers to give legitimacy to my claim that I was visiting the Shaw estate to speak with Benny's mother about his behavior in the classroom.

I ran upstairs and found my leather schoolbag on my bedroom floor. It had very few items in it. A pen, a notebook, an extra pair of glasses. My grade book was on the dresser. I put that into the bag, then hurried back to the sitting room, where Carrie had resumed her polishing.

Waving to Carrie, I ran out of the house. Instead of making my way to the street, I went to the carriage house to collect my bicycle.

The Shaws lived too far away to travel to their estate on foot, and I saw no reason to take the buggy. If I had to make a quick escape, it would be much easier to do on my own wheels.

My Van Cleve bicycle was in the very back of the carriage house, where I had stored it that fall. I hadn't expected to ride it again until March, if we were lucky enough to have good weather then.

I wheeled the bicycle out of the carriage house, checked to make sure the tires were in good shape, and hopped on. I realized how much I missed riding as I pedaled out onto the road.

It felt exhilarating to be riding again. Even though there was a light snow falling, the sidewalks were, for the most part, free of snow and ice.

The cold wind bit at my nose, but I didn't care. I made it to the Shaws' in half the time that it would have taken me by buggy because I could weave in and out of the traffic. I slowed my bicycle as I rolled onto the Shaws' property. The driveway was covered by a dusting of snow, and there were a number of wagon and tire marks in it. Apparently, the family had received many visitors that day, but at the moment, I didn't see any carriages or automobiles in the circular driveway. Had all the visitors come and gone?

I tucked my bicycle behind a bush along the driveway and then straightened the hem of my coat and walked to the house. The outdoor staff had been very diligent in keeping the steps clear of snow and ice. I saw nary a snowflake.

I picked up the large lion's head knocker and tapped the door with purpose three times. A moment later, the door opened, and the young maid Maggie stood before me with a tear-streaked face. If she recognized me from the party, she gave no indication. She rubbed her eyes, as if they itched terribly. "May I help you?"

"Hello. I'm Miss Katharine Wright. I'm Benjamin's Latin teacher. I wondered if I could speak to Mrs. Shaw for a moment about her son."

She looked over her shoulder. "I don't know if this is a good time, miss. Mrs. Shaw is not feeling well."

I could imagine why.

"It will take only a minute," I said with the utmost authority. "As his teacher, I care very much about Benny and his success. I'm making this call with the very best of intentions for Mrs. Shaw's son."

She started to close the door. "I'll tell her that you were here, but it really would be better if you came back another day, preferably after Christmas. She's turned all her visitors away."

I stuck my foot over the threshold, which prevented the maid from closing the door. "You are Maggie, aren't you?" She blinked at me, as if she hadn't expected me to ask that.

She swallowed. "Maggie. Maggie Courtier."

"We met Saturday night, before . . . well, before the incident."

She gave no indication whether she remembered or not. I didn't take it personally, as there had been many guests at the Christmas party that night.

"You must know that since I am a teacher, I am here only to help Benny," I said.

"I wouldn't know about that," she replied. "I wasn't any good at school, so I left and went into service."

"Everyone can be good in school with the right teacher. Every child has promise."

She looked dubious.

I wanted to ask her how far she'd gotten in school. I hated to hear that a young person had abandoned her schooling, but I stopped myself before I got too far off track.

In my best schoolteacher voice, I said, "Can you please tell Mrs. Shaw I'm here and would like to speak to her if she is up to it? If she says no, I will leave with no complaint. It is her right to turn me away, and I know you are only trying to protect her. That's what good employees do. They serve and protect their employers. Can you please ask her?" I adjusted my spectacles on my nose. They were ice cold to the touch.

She nodded and closed the door in my face. Normally, I would be offended that I hadn't been asked to wait in the parlor or, at the very least, the foyer, but I knew everyone in the Shaws' home was under tremendous strain just now. Judging by her tears when I arrived, that included Maggie.

I waited a long while outside the door in the cold and began to wonder if I should knock again. Perhaps I would have better luck if a more senior member of the staff answered the door.

Out of the corner of my eye, I saw movement. I turned and spotted a man in a long black wool coat and bowler hat walking around the side of the house. His face was turned away from me, so I couldn't see who it was, but by the ferocity of his steps, I thought that he must be upset or even angry.

He didn't notice me standing there as he marched down the driveway. I watched him until he passed through the entrance gate. Could that be Randolph Shaw?

For some reason, I didn't believe he was the type to leave his property on foot. It was much more likely he would have taken a carriage or one of his new automobiles. I didn't know how reliable an automobile would be in the snow. He was better off with a sure-footed horse and steel-plated wheels on a carriage, in my opinion.

I was about to raise my hand to the lion's head knocker a second time when the door burst open, and Maggie stood in front me.

"She will see you," Maggie announced with obvious surprise in her voice.

"I'm so glad." I was glad because I very much wanted to speak to Lenora, and besides, I was freezing. I couldn't stop shivering.

Maggie stepped back, finally allowing me into the house.

"I will take you to the conservatory. That's where she likes to spend her time when no one else is home."

I nodded.

I removed my hat and scarf and held them in my hand. Maggie did not offer to take them or my coat. That was for the best, I thought. In case I had to make a quick exit, I wouldn't have to find Maggie to fetch them.

We walked by the billiard room. A hand-lettered notice was taped to the door. DO NOT ENTER BY ORDER OF THE DAYTON POLICE DEPARTMENT. I shivered as I remembered what Orville and I had found there.

The conservatory was at the very back of the house, and I marveled at its size when Maggie ushered me inside. Maggie did not enter with me. She turned on her heel and ran in the other direction as fast as her legs could carry her. It made me wonder what I was walking into.

The conservatory's ceiling was twenty feet high, and a crystal chandelier hung down from it. Its electric light illuminated every corner of the room.

There was a wall of windows facing the back of the property. If I'd thought the front lawn of the Shaws' estate was picturesque, it was nothing compared to the back lawn. It was a great white expanse dotted with small outbuildings and trees. Burlap and rope covered and protected what must have been stone sculptures from the winter weather. I saw at least half a dozen of them. There were places where it was clear that gardens grew in the summer, as they were surrounded by fences and gates to keep deer and other wild creatures away. It was beautiful now, but in the height of summer, it would be spectacular.

"Everyone is startled when they come in here. It's so different from the rest of the house, which is so dark and masculine. This is the one room that I requested when we bought the land. I let Randolph do whatever he wished with the rest of the building, but this is my place. I made all the decisions here, from the windows to the throw pillows."

I spun around and found Lenora resting on her side in a chaise lounge that was made for a much larger person. She looked like a small child lying in her mother's bed.

Lenora Shaw wore a floral silk robe, with thick gray socks

on her feet. The socks were so masculine, I wondered if they were her husband's. She held a glass of wine in her hand.

She set the glass on the small table beside her chaise. "You will have to excuse the state I'm in. I don't seem to have the strength to do much of anything today. I take it you heard about what happened to my son. Otherwise, why would you be here? What does it matter how he's doing in Latin if he's been arrested for murder? Now I am more concerned about his freedom than his performance at school."

I could give her a whole host of reasons why Latin was an important language to learn. It helped students master English, for one. I held my tongue. It wasn't the time for one of my lectures on the benefits of foreign languages, even if it was a topic that I could discuss all day.

"Or if you are here about the Christmas tree sale fundraiser, I don't want to discuss that either. Everything is in order. Olive Ann will be able to assist you with any last-minute arrangements."

Olive Ann was another PTA mother who was helping with the Christmas tree sale and carol singing. Even though I wasn't at the Shaws' home for that reason, it was nice to know that the sale was still going on despite the murder.

She sighed and closed her eyes. "I have nothing else to discuss with you."

Her eyes were closed for so long, I thought she might have fallen asleep.

Finally, I said, "I'm so sorry about what happened to Benny and to Herman."

Her eyes opened again. "Thank you. It has been terrible, just terrible." She removed a handkerchief from the sleeve of her robe. "I can't even think of Benny without crying. I've cried so many tears over the past two days, it's a wonder that I have any left at all."

"It must be a nightmare." I pulled up a rattan chair and

sat across from her. She didn't move from the chaise. Even in apparent distress, she was beautiful. She might have been the most beautiful woman I'd ever seen in person. She looked like a stage actress.

"I can hardly think of it. The doctor was just here to help me."

"Oh?" I asked, thinking that must have been the man in the dark coat I spotted leaving the house.

"Randolph asked him to give me some medicine to calm my nerves." She waved her hand and stared at it as if she were noticing it for the very first time. Then she let it fall to her lap, but I had the distinct feeling that she was not in complete control of the movement.

"Did it help?"

She nodded. "I don't feel much of anything at the moment, at least not like before. I have a dull ache in my chest for my son. I just want him to come home. They have kept him at the station for two nights now. What is he eating? Where is he sleeping? He must be so frightened."

"I can understand your concern."

She looked at me, and for the briefest of moments, the focus was back in her eyes. "Can you? You're just a teacher. You don't have children of your own. Unless you are a mother, you cannot possibly understand the anguish I am experiencing. Not having children, you cannot love someone as much as I love Benny."

I bristled slightly at her statement. I loved my family dearly. If Wilbur, Orville, or any of the rest of them were in the same kind of trouble that Benny was, I would certainly feel the same intensity of pain she did. Just because I hadn't borne a child didn't mean that my love for my family was any less than hers.

I cleared my throat but spoke none of the thoughts that came to my mind. She was a grieving mother. This was not the time to argue with her. "I came as a concerned teacher. I heard of Benny's arrest and wanted to check in on your family and offer what assistance I could."

Despite her medically induced stupor, her face softened. "That is kind of you. I . . . We are devastated. Randolph is down at the police station with our attorney to see what can be done. We hope that Benny will be released to our custody until this mess can be resolved." Tears that she no longer thought she had sprang to her eyes. "I can't think of him in a cold jail cell on Christmas. It's all too horrible."

I sat up straight and folded my hands on my lap, just as I requested the students in my classroom to do when the principal stopped by the room to observe me. "Have you seen Benny yourself?"

She forced a laugh. "No. I wanted to go to the station, but my husband told me it was no place for a woman, especially one in as fragile a state as myself. He said he was going with the attorney, and then he sent the doctor in with the shot. I've felt much calmer after that."

I bit the inside of my lip. I had nothing against using medicine to help someone in pain, and it was more than clear to me that Lenora Shaw was in terrible mental anguish. Even so, it didn't sit well with me that her husband had made the decision about medicating her. I would have felt much better if she'd made that choice herself. I hoped the physician had performed a full evaluation before giving her the shot and hadn't just taken Randolph's word on his wife's mental state.

"I can understand why Randolph needs me to remain calm. This is just terrible for him. Just terrible. His right-hand man was murdered in his home, and his son was charged for the crime. And losing Herman was quite a blow to my husband. They've worked together every day for the past five years. Randolph will be at a loss on how to run his business now that Herman is gone."

I wrinkled my brow. It sounded to me that Randolph was

more upset by Herman's death than his son's arrest. I supposed that Benny still had a chance to make things right; all of Herman's chances had been snuffed out. But the fact remained, Benny was Randolph's only son.

"How did Herman come to work for your husband?"

She cocked her head and seemed to consider my question. "I don't really know. One day he was just there, and he slipped into the position so easily. Randolph was very happy with his work. He had more free time with Herman running the day-to-day operation of the paper mill. It allowed him to focus his attention on the club." She paused. "And on his family, of course."

I frowned. The way she had said that made me feel uneasy.

She closed her eyes but continued to speak. "Did you know I worked at the paper mill? That's how I met Randolph. I caught his eye one day while he was making his rounds, checking on all the machines. He felt it was essential that he check all the equipment himself. He still does it to this day." She opened her eyes and stared at the large diamond on her left hand. "It may appear that I have always lived like this, but that's not the case. I was born in a tiny little town in the foothills of the Appalachian Mountains. Life was hard, and work was hard to come by. If I'd stayed, I would be a farmer's wife now, with six children and just enough to eat to keep us all from starving to death. Death would come to us, though, in a slower, more agonizing way."

She took a breath. "I didn't want that life, so I left when I was little more than fourteen years old. I heard there was good work in Dayton because so many factories were opening up. I got a job cleaning machines in the paper mill. I spent most of my days trying not to be crushed by the gears and presses. They usually hired small boys for the job, but there was an uproar starting about children working in factories, so petite women like me were given the chance. That's when Randolph saw me." Her eyes fluttered. "He saw my potential and took me under his wing. I moved up to his office and was an errand girl for a short while. Over time, we fell in love."

I wondered if Lenora would be telling me all this were she not drugged.

I couldn't stop myself from asking, "How old were you when you married?"

"I was seventeen. It's a true rags-to-riches story."

"And how old was Randolph?"

"Thirty-five, the same age I am now."

I tried to keep my face neutral, so my distaste didn't show. At fourteen and even at seventeen, Lenora should have been in school. I reminded myself that not every child had the luxury of education that my students did, and twenty years ago, the free public school system in Ohio was still in its infancy. Even so . . .

"Mrs. Shaw," I began.

"Please call me Lenora. We are acquainted." She gave me a vague smile. "We are on the Christmas tree sale committee together. That should be enough to dismiss any formalities."

I nodded. "Lenora, I know that Benny was found wearing a shirt with Herman's blood on it."

She tried to sit up straight, but when she couldn't keep her balance, she melted back into the chaise lounge. "How did you hear that?"

I bit the inside of my lip. It was very possible that she'd forgotten I was invited to the party, and I wondered if that was something I should remind her about. If I did remind her, would she retain the information in her current state? I thought it was worth the risk.

"I was a guest here Saturday night," I said. "My brother Orville and I both were. I saw Benny when he was being arrested."

She relaxed some. "I was afraid it was in the papers. I

knew with a party as big as we had, it would get out in city gossip, but Randolph promised me he would have that fact kept from the newspapers."

"How would he manage that?"

"He makes the paper they print their stories on, doesn't he? If they want more paper for their stories, they will mind him." She pronounced this last part more forcefully than she had said anything since I'd arrived.

I nodded, completely understanding her meaning, and also her acceptance that word would get out, whether or not the condition of Benny's shirt that evening was recorded by the newspapers.

"So I know why he is a suspect, but what was his motive for the crime?"

She blinked at me. "Motive?"

"Why do the police think that he did it?"

"Because of the blood."

"Yes, but he had to have a reason. People don't kill without a reason."

"I—I don't know. Benny didn't have much to do with Herman." Then her brow furrowed, as if she was remembering something.

"What is it?"

She shook her head. "Nothing." Her eyes were as clear as I had seen them since I'd arrived in the conservatory. She was lying to me. She remembered something, something that might be a motive for her only child to kill another person.

"What did Benny tell you of that night?" I asked.

She blinked at me, as if she was having trouble putting her thoughts together, and for a moment, her eyes cleared. It seemed to me that the medicine was just beginning to take its full effect. I wouldn't be able to ask many more questions before she fell asleep.

"Benny didn't do this. Before the police took him away, he

told me that when he went into the billiard room, Herman had already been stabbed. He tried to help him. That's how he got the blood on his shirt."

I remembered Benny hiding in a corner of the room, with abject terror on his pale face. "How did he try to help him?"

She ignored my question and placed a hand on her pale cheek. "I'm very tired. I think it is best if I rest now."

I was being dismissed, and there wasn't much I could do to prolong my stay. I stood.

"Lenora?"

She looked up at me from the chaise lounge. Lying there, she looked so small and vulnerable. Her eyes were glazed over again from whatever drug the doctor had given her.

"I'm praying for Benny."

Tears filled her eyes. "Prayers are what we need."

Yes, prayers for both her son and for her.

CHAPTER 17

When I left the conservatory, Maggie the maid was nowhere to be seen. As I passed the billiard room to leave through the front door, I hesitated in the hallway. This might be my only chance to see the scene of the crime again.

I stood in front of the heavy mahogany doors, looking this way and that. I half expected a servant or even a police officer to jump out and ask me what I thought I was doing. I wondered what I was doing myself. I was a rule follower . . . for the most part. To follow the rules had been ingrained into my very being by my bishop father. Even so, I ignored the notice on one of the doors, which forbade entry, and turned the doorknob. To my surprise, the doors were unlocked.

The latch gave a light click as I closed the doors after myself.

On the billiard table, a dark stain marred a third of the felt surface. The blood would have soaked down through the felt cover deep into the table. There was nothing that could remove that stain from the billiard table. The stain on the Shaw family wouldn't be removed, either, if Benny was found guilty. Even if he was judged innocent, Dayton's perception of the family would change. For some people, just a hint of suspicion was enough reason to keep their distance.

If I was like that, I wouldn't be a very good teacher. It was part of my calling to help young people who were in trouble, and that included Benny Shaw.

When I could pull my eyes away from the billiard table, I examined the rest of the room with the same steely gaze I ran over my classroom when the students were too talkative. There was no one to shush in this space, but there was much to take in. The fine Oriental carpet on the floor was dusty and marked with muddy footprints. I had to believe they were from the police. The chess pieces on the side table had all been knocked over, save for one pawn. I tried to remember if the game had been set like that the night of the party. Memories of Saturday night came back. I had been preoccupied with Herman's body, Benny, and Orville riffling through Herman's pockets.

I walked over to the corner where Benny had cowered that night. There was a bloody handprint on the side of the bookshelf. Perhaps it wasn't the whole hand, but I could make out at least three fingers, so I surmised that was what it was. Above the handprint a note was posted. *Evidence D*. If this was Evidence D of the crime scene, where were A through C?

I held my hand up to the print. The fingers were thin but much shorter than mine were. Could it be that this print was made by a child . . . or by a very small woman, like Lenora Shaw? If that were true, it would mean Lenora had been in the room at the time of the murder. I shivered. That possibility had not occurred to me before.

Behind me, I heard something hit the floor. The sound made me jump, and I spun around to find a large silver Persian cat standing in the middle of the carpet. She looked me up and down, and I had never felt more judged in my life.

"Where did you come from?" I asked.

The cat didn't answer. She only whipped her long plume of a tail back and forth across the floor. She was a beautiful cat and clearly refined enough to live in the Shaw home. She was nothing like the stray my mother had taken in when we were small children. Wilbur had named our cat Mom. Why he had chosen that name, I never knew, and I had never thought to ask. We hadn't had a pet since. We were all too busy for it, and Father did enjoy a clean house. He believed pets caused mess. I wished he would relent on this small matter. I believed that a cat would add much to our lives.

"Aren't you a beauty," I told the cat.

The silver cat blinked at me, and I took that to mean she was in full agreement.

There was the sound of voices outside the doors. At first, they were muffled, and then I could hear them clearly.

"We just want to take another look at the scene. That's why we blocked it off," a male voice said.

I looked around the room. Should I dive under the billiard or chess table?

"I need to ask Mrs. Shaw if it's all right," a woman replied. I guessed that it was Maggie or another female servant.

"I have just spoken to Mr. Shaw, who is at the police station with his son, and he has given his permission. It is up to him. I do not need Mrs. Shaw's consent."

The cat turned and walked across the room to the window.

Thick velvet drapery covered the entire window, completely blocking the sunlight. If it were not for the electric lights in the room, I would not be able to see my hand in front of my face.

Because I thought it was what she wanted, I followed her. When I stood next to her in front of the drapery, I saw that the bottom third was covered with silver cat fur. The drapery fluttered, and I put a hand to my chest. I felt cold coming from around the side of the drapery.

Behind me I heard the doorknob rattle.

I pulled the drapery back to find the window was open. Why would anyone leave the window open when it was so cold outside?

The doors began to open.

Time was up. I climbed out the window. A group of snow-covered bushes broke my fall. I stifled a yelp as the snow went under the collar of my coat and down my back.

"What's going on in here!" the detective shouted.

I shivered. He surely was going to find me. All he had to do was look out the window, and I would be on full display.

There was a loud meow inside the room.

"A cat! What is a cat doing in this room? This is a crime scene. This is no place for an animal. Who let the cat in here?"

"Nobody *lets* Moonlight do anything," a woman said. I realized that it was Maggie from her voice. "She does what she pleases."

"Well, you will just need to keep her from doing it. This is not acceptable."

"She must have gotten in through the open window," Maggie said.

Soft footsteps made their way to the window. I braced myself against the side of the house.

"Why is the window open?" Captain Grimes asked.

"I don't know. Maybe one of your officers opened it to cool the room. There were many people in here. Even in the winter, it can grow stuffy. Neither the staff nor the family has been in this room since Saturday night, per your orders." Maggie saw me there under the windowsill, and her eyes went wide. But she said nothing and closed the window.

I leaned back against the house for a few minutes, until I worked up the courage to run to my bicycle and ride away.

CHAPTER 18

"Miss Katharine, there is a telegram for you," Carrie said. She held it out to me as I walked into the house a little while later. If Carrie thought it was odd that my hat was askew on the top of my head or that my coat and skirts were soaked from the snow that I had fallen into, she didn't mention it.

"Carrie, how many times do I have to tell you just to call me Katharine? Miss Katharine makes me feel like I'm your primary school teacher, and I've never taught at the primary level."

"Yes, Mis—I mean, yes, Katharine."

I nodded at her use of my preferred form of address, not that I expected her to get it right the next time. It was ingrained in her to speak to a member of the family in a certain way.

I accepted the telegram and unfolded it. I was surprised to receive such a missive. Telegrams came from my brothers now and again when they were in North Carolina, but they primarily corresponded by letter to save on cost. I couldn't remember when I had ever received a telegram just for me.

HEARD ABOUT THE MURDER. FOLLOWING NEWS REPORTS.
YOU MENTIONED THE SHAWS' PARTY IN YOUR LAST LETTER.
CONCERNED FOR YOU. PLEASE WRITE. —HARRY HASKELL

I thanked Carrie. Harry was a good friend, a good *married* friend. He was concerned, as any good friend would be. That was all.

Even so, I carefully folded the telegram and tucked it into my skirt pocket for safekeeping. "I'm going up to my room to rest for a bit and mark papers."

Carrie nodded and went back to her polishing.

I went upstairs to my room and changed out of my wet clothes and into another skirt and blouse. I added a checkered vest to the blouse because of the cold. I was chilled from hiding under the Shaws' window in the snow.

There were so many things that surprised me about my visit there. However, the biggest surprise was Maggie not saying a word when she found me hiding below the window.

The disappointment of the adventure was that I was no closer to finding my brothers' drawings. Based on the people in the room when Herman died, I thought Benny must be the one who had them.

With Christmas a few days away, I would normally be preoccupied with helping Carrie prepare the house for the holiday. My brother Lorin, his wife, and their four children would be having Christmas at our house. With four small children coming over, there was much to get ready in the way of decorations and sweets. I wanted to make Christmas as enchanting for them as my mother had made it for all of us. Even though we hadn't had much money, our mother had always made Christmas special.

I decided the best thing for me to do while I was flummoxed by Herman Wheeler's murder would be to start the Christmas baking. Baking was not my favorite activity in the world. In fact, I wasn't much for cooking at all. I was proficient at it, but I couldn't say that I actually enjoyed it. Even so, my mother had taught me how to make five kinds of Christmas cookies when I was a small girl, and I made them every year. It was one way that I was able to keep her memory alive.

When Carrie saw that I was getting out the flour and sugar, she made herself scarce. I might not enjoy baking, but Carrie disliked watching me do it even more. She was a very talented baker, and it was the one time the urge for her to take over was too much. If Carrie made the cookies, they would be chewy, delicate, and perfectly baked. With me making them, half would be overbaked or even burnt, and there was always the chance I would grab the salt rather than the sugar when making sugar cookies. Even so, it was a family tradition, and I felt it was important for the children to eat cookies made by their loving aunt.

I also knew Carrie would bake her own cookies, so if mine didn't turn out, there was a fallback.

I stirred the dough for the snickerdoodles. They were my favorite cookies, and since it had been such a difficult morning, I thought I would start with the ones I liked the most. I could nibble on them while making the rest of the cookies. Sometimes sugar could help a person think. That wasn't a theory I shared with my students, however.

The door that led into the kitchen opened, and Orville stepped inside just as I was pulling the second tray of snickerdoodles out of the oven. Only a handful of cookies were burned on the bottom, and I blamed that on the unevenness of the oven, not on myself. I could scrape the burned part off, I decided.

"Oh, good. You're here. When did you get home?"

I squinted at him. "Long enough ago to bake four dozen cookies."

"How can you bake at a time like this?" He lowered his voice. "Have you found the drawings yet?"

"No," I said.

"Then what are you doing in here? You're supposed to be helping me." His voice rose in pitch. "Wilbur is asking for them, and I keep putting him off. He thinks that I left the bicycle shop to go fetch them. What am I going to do when I return empty handed?"

I measured vanilla to add to the cookie batter I was in the process of making. These would be banana cookies, which were my father's favorite. Getting just the right amount of banana flavor in them was tricky. I had yet to perfect them the way our mother so expertly had.

I concentrated on the vanilla to suppress my irritation at my brother. Why was it that I was always the one who was assigned to clean up his messes? It wasn't as if I had been the one to take the drawings to the Shaws' home in the first place.

"This is not my fault," I grumbled.

"You talked me into going to the party."

I shook my spoon at him. "Orville, if you keep this up, I will leave you to find the drawings on your own."

"I'm sorry." He smoothed his mustache. "You know I need your help. I always need your help when it comes to this sort of thing."

I arched my brow. "Brother, to my knowledge, this is the first time either of us has ever been included in a murder investigation."

"Not the murder," he said, aghast. "But when I bungle something, the way I have here. You're the one who knows what to say and how to get me out of it."

This was true.

"Losing those drawings could destroy everything." His voice caught.

I studied my brother. I knew his good sense was blinded by the fear of disappointing Wilbur. The two of them were so close, they acted at times like twins. They understood each other in a way I never could. I didn't have the mechanical mind that they'd been blessed with. I was more like our father and understood words and languages. The boys had never had any interest in learning a language.

I returned to mixing my batter. "I believe we have to put this in perspective. A man has been killed, and a young man has been arrested."

"That is because he murdered Herman."

"We don't know that he did," I argued. "That is not what his mother said."

He stared at me. "What mother is ever going to believe her son is a monster?"

"Benny is many things, but a monster is not one of them." I defended my student.

He looked at me as if I had lost every last one of my marbles. "He was covered in blood, in Herman's blood. What choice did the police have but to arrest him?"

"His mother told me that he was trying to save Herman. He went into the billiard room to escape the party and found Herman inside, already stabbed."

He smoothed his mustache with a shaky hand. "And you believe that?"

"You expect me to believe that one of my students could kill another human being? Yes, the truth is that I would much rather believe he was trying to help."

"But he wasn't by the body when we stepped into the room," Orville said.

Of course, this was a thought that had already crossed my mind. "Maybe we scared him," I said, realizing it just might make sense. "He must have jumped away from the body, knowing how it would look."

"I don't know how it looked better for him to be standing in a corner of the room, covered with blood."

He had a point, but I refused to agree with him out of principle.

"What he should have done was find help. What did he really think he could have done?" Orville folded his arms.

"No one knows how he or she is going to react in such a terrible situation," I said. "It's noble that he was trying to save Herman's life."

"If that was what he was doing," Orville muttered.

"I intend to find out." I dropped my spoon into the batter, removed Carrie's apron, tossed it on the kitchen stool, and headed for the door.

"What about the cookies?" he called after me.

"It's about time that you learned to bake!" I shouted back.

CHAPTER 19

After leaving Orville in the kitchen, I went on a long walk through the neighborhood to think about what my next steps should be. As I walked, I remembered that this was where I'd run into Herman a few days before he died. This was the place where he'd asked me about my brothers' flight. How had he known about their success when I had just found out about it from a telegram? Was Orville right that he was the one who'd taken the drawings? But if that was true, where were the drawings now? Had he been killed for them? And if so, were my brothers in danger because they knew that theft was the motive for murder?

My head spun, but I came away from the walk seeing a clear path forward. I had to find out more about Herman and why he had been interested in flying when he worked for a paper mill.

With purpose, I walked back home to find that while I had been gone, someone had baked the rest of the cookies and cleaned the kitchen. Living in a home of men, I knew it could only have been Carrie.

I lifted one of the tea towels. There were two sets of cookies under it. One batch was perfectly baked, uniform in shape and size. The other appeared to be a little haphazard and burned. It wasn't hard to guess which cookies were mine and which were Carrie's. I replaced the tea towel and went to find her.

I found her in the dining room cleaning the windows. "The children are going to love your cookies more than mine. I will be sure to send a plate of yours to Father to take to his next church meeting. They will impress the church officials much more than mine would."

"Your cookies are . . ." She trailed off, as if she couldn't find the right word.

"Please, Carrie, don't trouble yourself searching for a compliment. My cookies are barely edible, but they are made with love and good intentions. Even knowing that, I'm glad you were able to finish up the recipes so that we have some respectable cookies to serve this Christmas."

"Thank you, miss." She draped the rag she was holding over the edge of her bucket.

I smiled. "I am sorry I left such a mess. I had every intention of cleaning it up when I got home from my thinking walk."

"Thinking walk, miss?"

"Don't you ever go on a walk to think?"

"I walk to and fro all day long, but I don't think I've ever walked just to think. I don't have the time for that."

"We will have to grant you time for it in the future. It is good for the soul, because before I went, I was low and didn't know how to move forward. The walk cleared my head."

"Yes, miss," she said in such a way that I knew she was agreeing with me just to agree.

"Has Father returned from his meeting?"

"Yes," Carrie said. "He's in his study."

I frowned. I believed that my father had a hearing Tuesday morning regarding the lawsuit against him. I had written the date down. Could I have made a mistake? I wasn't one to make mistakes when it came to scheduling events on the calendar. I took pride in knowing where everyone in the household should be on any given day.

I thanked Carrie and reminded myself to get her an extra-nice Christmas gift this year before I went in search of my father.

As Carrie had said, he was sitting in his study. He was at his desk, writing in a journal. My father was dedicated to his journal and made a notation in it every day. Sometimes the passages were long and sometimes short. If something particularly interesting happened to him and the rest of us weren't there, he would sometimes read a passage to us in the evening.

Whatever he was writing at the moment wasn't amusing, based on the scowl on his face.

I knocked on the doorframe. He looked up over his glasses at me. "Father, what are you doing here? I thought you had a hearing tomorrow. You should be resting in preparation or going over strategy with Wilbur. Wasn't Wilbur going to go with you? Where is he?"

Wilbur had helped my father with his legal issues from the start. Of my father's five living children, he was the best choice to deal with the issue as he was the most logical and had the most even temperament.

"Wilbur is at the bicycle shop, as you would expect. Tomorrow's hearing is canceled. If the bishops really cared about the issue, they would have wanted the matter put to rest by now. Instead, they drag it on and on. I can only believe they do that just to be spiteful. Even so, we will not back down until we are cleared and found in the right."

"I'm sure that will happen, Father. Good will prevail." I furrowed my brow. "This will just give you more time to gather more evidence and prove your innocence in these ridiculous claims. All you did was try to save the church from a man who was stealing from it."

"I hope you are proven right, daughter."

"I will be," I said with much more confidence than I felt.

He placed a hand on his chest. "I don't know how much more of it I can take."

Alarm filled me. "Is something wrong with your heart?"

"No. It is only the strain of this trial. It can make a man unwell."

I knew this to be true too. When I was particularly upset about something, I felt sick as well. It must have been a trait that I'd inherited from my father.

"How did you learn the meeting was canceled?" I asked.

"Bishop Perch stopped by this afternoon to tell me. Even though we are at odds, I do respect him for having the decency to do at least that."

"Did Bishop Perch tell you why the hearing was canceled?"

"An associate of several of the church committee members died."

"Who was it?"

"Herman Wheeler."

I stared at him. Father didn't know that was the name of the man who was killed at the Shaws' party.

"Was he a member of the church?"

"No, but according to them, he was considering joining. It is my understanding that they are looking for younger members to bring a more youthful perspective to the church. They believe the men of my generation are old-fashioned, narrow minded. Of course, I see things as black or white, right or wrong. They claim there are many unanswerable questions and nuances in life. They think a man can be a member of the church, make a mistake, and it will not reflect badly on the church as a whole. That is just not the case. If they allow a man to steal from the church, what kind of message does that send about right and wrong?"

"Do you know how serious Herman was about joining?" I asked.

"I don't know." He spoke this last part in a whisper. "I have sympathy for his family and friends, but I do wish the hearing could have gone on as planned."

"Father, if he was a close friend of theirs, you can't begrudge the committee members wanting to mourn him."

"But he wasn't a close friend. I heard them speak of him before. When we were all in church together. They hated him back then."

I raised my brow. "Then why ask him to join the church?"

"That is the question they refuse to answer." He stared out the window.

CHAPTER 20

The next morning I got up earlier than I normally would and found Carrie in the kitchen. She was making a hearty pot of oatmeal, which was the perfect breakfast for a cold winter day. Except for the stove, where she was stirring the pot, the kitchen was spotless.

I was on break from school, but that didn't mean I didn't have teacherly responsibilities. The first of those was the Christmas tree sale with the PTA. Lenora Shaw was in charge of the committee, but I couldn't imagine that with her son in jail, she would be at the final committee meeting at school that morning. To be frank, I didn't even know if there was still to be a meeting, but since I hadn't been told it was canceled, I bundled up in my hat, scarf, and wool coat and slung my schoolbag over my arm to make the very familiar walk to school.

Typically, when I walked to school, I reviewed all the lessons I was going to teach that day and which of my students I needed to speak to because they were struggling in class or falling behind. This morning on my walk, my mind was on murder. When I crossed the bridge over the Great Miami River, a gust of wind picked up and nearly blew off my hat. I clapped my hand on the top of my head and knew

I should not have worn the hat with the broad brim. It too easily caught the winter breeze.

I righted the hat on my head and looked upriver at the new factories that seemed to be opening every day. A half mile to the north, on the west bank of the river, Shaw Paper Mill was one of those factories.

As I stepped off the bridge, I had my hat tethered tightly to the top of my head with my wool scarf. It wasn't going to fly away now. Cold bit at my exposed nose and cheeks, and despite my glasses, my eyes watered from the dry, frigid air. I could not have been happier when the school came into view.

The school had been constructed in stone at the turn of the century and was a masterful composition of sharply pointed towers, spires, and countless arched windows. It had been built to show the strength and power of education, and I had thought on more than one occasion that it had been built to intimidate as well.

From one side of the school, there was a clear view of the Great Miami River. My classroom was on that side of the building, and almost every day, I had to rap on my desk to regain the attention of students who were daydreaming while looking out the window.

The school gymnasium was on the opposite side of the school from my classroom, and that was where I was headed now as I approached the building.

The meeting that morning was to be in the gymnasium. As soon as I arrived at the school's back door, I knew that there was a problem. The doors were locked, and as an extra measure, there was a chain tethering the door handles together.

I saw the hand of janitor Langston Fernell in this. In the past year he had been complaining about students breaking into the school to cause mischief after hours. For the most part, they pulled silly pranks, like soaping the windows or stringing toilet paper down the hallways. As of yet, the pranks had been essentially harmless, but they were still a major frustration for Langston, as he was the one who had to clean up the messes. I didn't blame him.

I walked around the school to door after door and found each one locked. We wouldn't be going into the school if I didn't find the janitor to unlock that chain.

I knew I was early for the meeting, but I had wanted to gather my notes and thoughts before the ladies arrived. I was debating walking back home and then coming back at the appointed time when I heard a yelp. The next thing I knew, I was hit in the side by what felt like a streetcar. I braced my hand against the school's stone wall to keep from falling.

"Mae Bear!" a crackling voice called. "You leave Miss Wright be!"

After I gathered myself, I opened my eyes and found Mae Bear, who appeared to be half collie, half bear, staring up at me, with her tongue hanging out of her mouth.

Janitor Langston Fernell stood beside Mae Bear, with his hands on his hips. "Is that any way to treat a teacher?"

Langston was a thin man with round glasses and a great laugh. His daughter, Claire, was one of my best second-year Latin students. I was pushing her to go to college. Personally, I thought Oberlin would be the perfect fit for her.

The janitor shook his head. "She didn't mean anything by it, Miss Wright. She's just beside herself with all the students gone and no one to greet day after day at school. When she saw you standing there, she just lost her head."

I rubbed my side. "I suppose I should take it as a compliment, in that case. No harm done." I scratched Mae Bear behind the ears, and her freshly brushed fur felt like the finest of silks. Maybe I should ask Langston for tips about how to care for my own hair.

Langston was particular about keeping Mae Bear's fur in optimal condition. He brushed her constantly, so she always looked her best. The collie seemed to relish his attention and appeared to take great pride in her appearance.

"What are you doing here today? You should be home, putting your feet up and enjoying the time off."

"I could say the same to you," I replied.

"Oh, Miss Wright, a janitor's work is never done. This time of year, while the students are away, is the best time to wax the floors and polish the woodwork. I can't do that with a bunch of adolescents running about."

"I suppose not," I said. "I'm here for the committee meeting."

"I forgot that you were on that committee with all those uppity mothers."

"Langston, some of them are very nice."

He gave me a look. "If you say so, Miss Wright. All I know is Lenora Shaw orders me about like I'm her hired help." He stood up a little straighter, and Mae Bear looked up at him in admiration. "I am a professional school janitor and should be treated as such."

"I couldn't agree more." I paused. "When was the last time you spoke to Lenora Shaw?"

"Gosh, it must have been Saturday, before school let out. She was here at the school meeting with the principal."

I wrinkled my brow. That was highly unusual. Our school principal wasn't the sort to meet with parents at all, much less on a Saturday. "Do you know why she was meeting with the principal?"

"Well, I did happen to walk by the office while I was collecting the trash and heard her say something to the effect that she wanted him to talk to that know-it-all teacher. I didn't hear the teacher's name and didn't hang around to find out."

My heart sank. He didn't have to find out the teacher's name. I already knew who it was. It was me. Lenora Shaw had been talking about me.

I frowned. But if she'd been so upset about how I had treated her son, why hadn't she revoked my invitation to her annual Christmas party? I certainly wouldn't want a guest in my house whom I was trying to fire.

I had sympathy for Lenora, of course. She was going through a terrible time, but I could feel my anger flaring. How dare she go to the principal like that?

However, as quickly as my anger came, it fell away. Lenora tattling on me to my employer was frustrating, but it could not compare with what she was going through at the moment in regard to her son's arrest.

Langston unlocked the chain and then the door to the gymnasium. Mae Bear ran ahead of us right into the middle of the gym and took in a deep breath, as if she couldn't get enough of the smell.

In the large space there was a smell that was a combination of rubber, boys' sneakers, and floor wax. Mae Bear might have loved it, but to me, it was quite unpleasant. I was happy to find that the tables and chairs for the meeting were in place. I knew I had Langston to thank for that.

I set my heavy schoolbag on one of the tables. "The ladies of the committee should be here within the hour. I wanted to arrive early in order to make sure everything was ready. I know all these mothers have many obligations to their families during the Christmas season."

Langston rocked back on his heels. "That's because we are cut from the same cloth, Miss Wright. We check and double-check that everything is in order."

"It's the only way to be." I paused. "The Christmas trees should be delivered tomorrow morning."

He nodded. "I have a space squared off in the yard where they should go. Is it still seventy-five trees?"

I nodded. "Of various sizes. The tree farmer, who is donating them to the school, has been extremely generous. If they all sell at the asking price, the fundraiser will be a great success and the school will be well on its way to offering more music courses for students."

"That will be wonderful. I do love it when the choir sings," he said. "And the school could use a band."

I nodded. "If we want to stay competitive with the other schools in the city, we do. More and more of them are starting bands, but the instruments are costly."

"It's true. I hated to do it, but I sold my father's old trumpet last year to pay off some debts I had. I'm always wishing that I could come across it again to buy it back."

"I hope you do."

"Thank you, miss." He smiled. "Is there anything else you need me to do before they arrive?"

I shook my head. "No, I don't think so. Before the ladies arrive, I will go down to my classroom and make sure I didn't leave anything out of order when I closed up for break."

He chuckled. "I'm sure you didn't, but again, check and double-check is the way we make our way in the world."

"That is so true."

"If you need us, Mae Bear and I will be working on the ovens in the cafeteria today. One of them is on the blink, and the lunch ladies have been on my back for weeks to fix it. It will be nice for them to return to school after the holidays to a working oven."

I agreed that it would and picked up my schoolbag.

"After the ovens are fixed, I will wax all the classroom floors. There is much to do when the students and staff are away."

It sounded like there was.

When we stepped out of the gym, I turned left, and Langston and Mae Bear turned right. In no time at all, I could no longer hear their footsteps in the hallway.

My classroom was in the language and literature wing of the building.

There was something peaceful and at the same time eerie about walking through the vacant school. My footsteps sounded like staccato taps on a hollow drum, and when I peered through the windows of the classrooms' closed doors, room after room looked as if it had been abandoned. The students' chairs had been flipped onto their seats on the tops of the desks, the blackboards had been wiped clean, and all the windows were closed and locked, with the shades drawn tight.

My own classroom was no different. I was going to use my key to get inside, but when I turned the knob, I found the room unlocked. That wasn't completely surprising. I knew that Langston had to get in and out of the room to collect trash and do the general cleaning. He had also said that he was waxing the floors while all the staff and students were away.

I stepped into the room and was pleased that everything looked tidy, just the way I'd left it on Friday afternoon. But when I turned to grab a notebook from my desk, I saw the wall behind it and froze.

The Latin word *venefica* was sprawled across the blackboard in coarse white chalk lines. In English, the word meant "witch."

CHAPTER 21

My heart sank to the bottom of my shoes as I stared at the blackboard. I dropped my schoolbag on my desk and picked up the eraser from the chalk well and erased the word as quickly as I could. White chalk dust was smeared across the clean black surface, but the word was gone, and that was all I cared about.

Maybe I should have left it, run to find Langston, and written up an incident report, but I had just wanted the word out of my view. I knew Langston would never do such a thing, so my first thought was that one of the students had come in or broken into the school after Christmas break began and had written on the chalkboard.

It wasn't the first time I had gotten an unkind message from a student on my chalkboard, and it wouldn't be the last. High school students tended to be impulsive and reactionary. That could lead to a lot of ill-advised behavior.

However, considering all that had happened in recent days, the message preyed upon my nerves. Was I wrong for immediately suspecting Benny of this insult? If he was the culprit, he must have written on the chalkboard before the Shaws' Christmas party, because he'd been taken into custody by the police immediately after the party was ruined by Herman's death.

I picked up my notebook and schoolbag, left my classroom, and closed and locked the door behind me. I marched down the quiet hallway, in search of Langston. I found him where he'd promised to be: in the cafeteria kitchen, taking apart an oven.

By the looks of it, the oven reconstruction wasn't going well. There were pieces of metal, nuts, bolts, and hand tools covering the gray linoleum floor.

Mae Bear lay on the floor, with her head on her paws, next to her master's feet. Langston lay on his back, with his head and hands in the oven. I could hear him mutter to himself as he tried to fix the problem. However, judging by the state of the oven, I wasn't sure the kitchen ladies were going to return to school to find a repaired oven. It was more likely they would find an oven in pieces, which was even worse than a malfunctioning oven.

It was clear to me that Langston was so focused on the task at hand that he didn't hear me enter the kitchen. Mae Bear did, however, and she lifted her head from her paws for half a second to acknowledge my presence.

"Langston?" I asked quietly.

He continued to mutter to himself about the "blasted" oven.

"Langston," I said a little more loudly.

Still no response.

"Langston!" I shouted.

There was a bang and a curse, and he slid out of the oven as if he'd been shot out of a rifle. "What in blue blazes is going on out here?" He rubbed the top of his head.

"Are you hurt? I didn't mean to scare you!"

He sat up. "No harm done." He rubbed the top of his head again. "It's a good thing that I'm so hardheaded." He looked at my face. "Is something wrong, Miss Wright?"

"When was the last time you were in my classroom?"

He picked up some of the nuts and bolts that were scattered across the floor and collected them into a neat pile. "I peeked in your room just last night. I was looking around the school to see which floors were in the most urgent need of wax. The hallways are a must, but your floor is in good shape. It's lower down the list. I might not be able to get to it until summer," he said apologetically.

"Was there any writing on the blackboard when you went into my room?" I asked.

"On the blackboard? Can't say I even bothered to look. When you leave for the weekend or a school break, your chalkboard is always washed completely clean. I can't say the same for most of the teachers here. If I was given a quarter for every blackboard that I had to clean over the weekends, I wouldn't need this job any longer, let me tell you. However, I always know that I don't have to worry a whit about your room. I much appreciate that."

"Did you lock the door after you left?"

"I did. I always do. You know how I feel about students creeping around the school when no one is here. Troublemakers." He studied my face. "Why do you ask?"

I shook my head. "Nothing. I was just wondering."

He frowned, as if he didn't believe that was the whole story, and he was right.

I cleared my throat. "I should be getting back to the gymnasium. The committee ladies will be here soon, and they will not want to be kept waiting."

"Mothers never do," he said solemnly.

I left Langston to his work on the oven, but I was troubled. Could Langston have missed the giant word *venefica* that had been emblazoned in chalk across my blackboard? Still more worrisome, the culprit must have had a key or some other means of entering the room, because Langston had said that he'd locked the door.

I had to accept that Langston was telling the truth. In all the years I had worked at the school, I'd never known him to lie.

When I stepped into the gym a few minutes later, I was greeted by the entire Christmas tree sale committee except for Lenora Shaw. Lenora's absence was to be expected, but I was still disappointed that she wasn't there. She'd been in such a state yesterday afternoon that I couldn't help but worry about her. I dearly hoped that her husband hadn't convinced her doctor to give her another shot for hysteria, or whatever nervous ailment he'd diagnosed her with.

"Oh good. You're here," Louise Anne Ritcher said. Louise Anne was the mother of four children, who were currently attending Steele High School. She had daughters in ninth and eleventh grades, and sons in tenth and twelfth grades. I currently had her two middle children in my classes. They were sweet, hardworking students who didn't seem to have any aspirations beyond graduating from high school, finding good jobs, and settling down into marriage and parenthood, in that order. There was nothing wrong with that.

Belinda Williams, one of the mothers I was most friendly with, waved at me when I stepped into the room, and patted the empty seat next to her. I gratefully slipped into it.

She patted my arm. "You just made it. Olive Ann has already announced that Lenora Shaw won't be at the meeting today, and she is taking over, as she is the vice-chair." Belinda crossed her legs and leaned back in her chair. "She can have it, as far as I'm concerned. I'd never want to take anything over from Lenora Shaw."

I was about to ask her why she said that when Olive Ann Michaels stepped in front of the group. She was a thin woman with sharp cheekbones and gray eyes, which looked out at the women in the room from behind a thick pair of glasses. "We are a little bit early, but since we are all here now"—she eyed me, as if to remind me that I was the last person to arrive—"I see no reason why we can't start this meeting a little early so that we can all return to our homes and families. I know how busy this season can be, and I am grateful to each and every one of you for attending the meeting today. As I said previously, Lenora won't be here today, as she is feeling under the weather."

"That's one way to say her son killed a man in her house," Belinda whispered in my ear.

As Olive Ann began going over the logistics of the tree sale, detailing where the students would stand when caroling, who had volunteered to provide the food and beverages, the price of trees, and the order of the songs to be sung, I asked out of the side of my mouth, "Is that what people in Dayton think? That Benny is the killer?"

"It's all anyone is talking about," Belinda whispered back. "I heard that he was holding the murder weapon when they found the body."

I wrinkled my nose at this. I knew all too well how rumors could suddenly start spinning out of control. And even if those rumors were proven false, they could still ruin Benny's reputation. I wasn't going to let that happen to him if I could avoid it.

"That's not true," I whispered back.

However, I guessed that I didn't keep my voice as low as I intended to, because Olive Ann glared at me. "What is not true, Miss Wright?" she wanted to know.

A hollow grew in my stomach. I did not like being the reprimanded listener instead of the reprimanding teacher.

"It's nothing," I said as I smoothed my damp hands over my blue skirt.

"It didn't sound like nothing to me," Olive Ann said. "In fact, it seemed that you were engrossed in your conversation."

I wrinkled my nose. I knew that Olive Ann would poke and poke at me until I told her what I'd said, and I saw no reason to draw out the back-and-forth between us. "I said that I know Benny Shaw didn't kill Herman Wheeler."

Olive Ann leveled her gaze at me. "A PTA committee meeting is not the time or place to talk about such unseemly topics. We would do well to let the police sort it out."

"They have, haven't they?" a woman at the back of the room asked. "I heard that Benny was arrested. I can't believe I let him court my daughter. It could have been her!"

Immediately, all the women in the room broke into nervous chatter as they shared their or their children's connection to Benny and the times he could have killed one or all of their offspring.

Olive Ann seethed at the front of the room. "Stop. Stop! Stop! This should not be a topic of conversation among proper women of Dayton. It is not our place to make any determination about Benjamin Shaw's guilt, and must I remind you that his mother is the leader of this committee, and you are speaking recklessly of a child? Let's show his mother and the family some respect."

I had always thought of Olive Ann as a tough, no-nonsense woman; she had to be, as she was the mother of six children, all born within a span of nine years. However, I liked and respected her more for shutting down the chatter about Benny, even if I was at fault for starting it.

I was shocked that everyone had immediately assumed he was guilty. Was he not innocent until proven guilty? And there were other suspects. I frowned. Were the police looking at those suspects?

The murder weapon belonged to my brother Orville. He could just as easily be sitting in jail if Benny hadn't been covered in Herman's blood. Detective Gaylen had been eager to make an arrest. When Benny had presented himself as the perfect suspect, the detective had snapped the young man up.

Olive Ann expertly steered the conversation back to the topic of the Christmas tree sale and settled the final details of the event. After their dismissal, the women disbursed right away. Usually after a meeting like this, they would stay and chat. I could not help but wonder if their haste to leave had more to do with the Christmas holiday or with Benny Shaw's arrest.

Belinda gathered up her papers and handbag. "I have never been in a meeting like that in all my life. For a moment there, everyone was talking at once about the murder. I must say, I was impressed by the way Olive Ann shut it down. She has a real chance of being the next president when Lenora steps down."

My eyes went wide. "Do you think Lenora will step down?"

She set her blue velvet hat on the top of her head and secured it with a hatpin. "She will have to, won't she, if her son is convicted? He will no longer be a student, and without a child in the school, why would she be on the PTA? She was going to have to leave when he graduated, in any case."

She had a point, but it still made me feel slightly queasy to know that Lenora Shaw would be ousted from the PTA. The Steele PTA had been spearheaded from its very beginning two years ago by Lenora. The school would not have the organization without her.

"I hope it doesn't come to that," I said. "However, I have to say that I was pleased with the way Olive Ann handled the meeting."

"I'm glad to hear that you approved, Miss Wright," a voice said behind me.

I turned around, and just as I expected, Olive Ann stood directly behind me.

Before Belinda and I could even greet her, Olive Ann turned to Belinda. "It's nice to see you, Belinda. If you could give Miss Wright and me some privacy, I would appreciate it. We have a matter that we need to discuss."

Belinda's dark eyes went wide. "Yes, of course." She cleared her throat. "I will see you both at the Christmas tree sale on

Christmas Eve afternoon. It should be a very special event."
She quickly backed away.

After Belinda scurried out of the gym, I turned to Olive
Ann. "What can I help you with? You don't have anything to
worry about concerning your children's performance in my
Latin courses. They are both doing very well."

"That is gratifying to hear, but my children aren't the reason that I need to talk to you."

I swallowed. "Oh?"

Her steel-gray eyes bored into me. "Yes. I know who the
killer is, and it's not Benny Shaw."

CHAPTER 22

Istared at her, gape-mouthed, for a moment, but then I snapped my mouth closed, remembering the hundreds of times that I had reprimanded my students for putting on a dumbfounded expression. I told my students not to overdo their surprise, and here I was, overdoing it. However, who could blame me? The very last statement I had expected to come from Olive Ann Michaels's mouth was that she knew who Herman's killer was.

"Who is it?" I asked.

"It's not just one person. It's a conspiracy," she revealed in a hushed tone.

"A conspiracy?" I asked.

"Yes, it is a group of men."

"Who are they?"

"The club. They are the ones who orchestrated Herman's murder. I'm sure of it."

I gaped at her. I was going to have to stop reprimanding my students for gaping, because I realized that there were times when it just couldn't be helped. "The club?"

"Yes," she said with the utmost confidence. "They are a group of men who are all members of the Gem City Club. They sit around and think of ways they can gather more power and control over Dayton society. They are both scholars and powerful men of industry. Every last one of them is in it for his own gain. They will stab each other in the back if given half a chance."

I winced at her statement because Herman had been stabbed to death. Her turn of phrase was a little too close to the truth for comfort.

I stared at her. "You believe the members of this club got together and killed Herman?"

"Yes, and I'm comfortable telling you this because I know how your father feels about such clubs and how they distract from church work. Men should spend their free time away from their jobs and families doing good works for the church, if you ask me."

It was true that my father was not a proponent of private clubs or societies. He'd actually started a new denomination of the Church of the United Brethren and taken his congregation with him because the younger generation of the church had wanted to have the ability to join men's societies, such as the Freemasons and others like it. My father had been dead set against the change. To this day, my father would not speak of the Freemasons, and my brothers and I knew not to bring them up.

But it was still hard for me to believe that members of a social club would conspire to kill a man, and so I studied Olive Ann with uncertainty. What were her motives for telling me this, and how much of it could I believe?

I cleared my throat. "Yes, it's true that my father doesn't care for such organizations, but I have never heard of them murdering someone."

"Maybe that is the case for the majority of the members, but I know for certain that the most powerful men in this club have their hands in all the corruption in Dayton."

"How would you know that? I believe Gem City is a men's

only club. They wouldn't even allow a woman inside the building."

She pressed her lips together. "My brother told me. He's a member, or he was a member until they kicked him out on his ear because he was raising the alarm about their exploits. As soon as he did that, they ousted him."

I adjusted my schoolbag on my shoulder. It sounded to me as if Olive Ann was bitter that her brother had been kicked out of the club; her attitude made me wary of the information she'd shared with me. How much was true, and how much was shared out of resentment?

As a high school teacher, I knew that when a student tattled on another student, there was usually more to the story than what that student reported, so I had doubts about everything Olive Ann had told me.

"What's your brother's name?"

She straightened her shoulders. "I don't believe you need to know. He is no longer a member of the club, so there would be no reason for you to speak to him."

I frowned. "There is all the reason in the world for me to speak to him. I have to verify that everything you are telling me is true. Your accusations of murder and conspiracy are not claims that I can simply accept at face value. I have known you through school, but other than your being on this committee and having your children in my classroom, I know nothing about you, and I certainly know nothing of your brother. How can I trust you, with so little knowledge of who you are?"

She opened and closed her mouth. "I have never been so offended in all my life. You should never speak to a parent of one of your students in such a way."

"Right now, I'm not speaking to you as the teacher of your children. I am speaking to you as someone who is trying not to jump to any conclusions. I am trying to be fair to all involved in this tragedy. I do want to know what happened to Herman, because I, too, believe that Benny was unjustly arrested, but that doesn't mean I am going to march into a members-only club and accuse someone of murder." I took a breath when I finished my speech.

Olive Ann wrung her hands, as if she was in the midst of some personal struggle over what to do.

When she still didn't tell me her brother's name, I asked, "And what reason did the club give for removing your brother?"

She pressed her lips together. "They said that he didn't meet their standards of success. He has a delivery company, which has been floundering these past few months. He refused to switch over from horse and carriage to trucks, as many delivery companies have." She paused. "They say he is stuck in the past." She licked her lips. "Since his ousting from the club, his business has taken even deeper losses. He begged to be reinstated, but they refused."

It sounded to me as if both she and her brother were bitter that he'd been booted from the club and were telling stories about its members as payback. However, their claims were still something that I had to look into if I wanted to free Benny from jail.

"I know you are thinking that my brother is just trying to get back at the club, but that's not true. He's had misgivings about them for years."

"Then why didn't he leave earlier of his own accord?"

"It's not that simple," she snapped.

I took a step away from her and glanced around the gymnasium. We were the only ones left in the large room.

She took a breath. "Being a member of the Gem City Club was good for my brother's business. He knew that if he ended his membership for any reason at all, they would ruin his business, and that has been proven to be true. He's worked too hard and too long to give it all up now."

"Ruin it how?"

"Many of the club members used his delivery service. When he left the club, they hired another company, one with automobiles and trucks."

"If your brother believes that these men were involved with the murder, why hasn't he gone to the police?"

She didn't meet my eyes. "He doesn't care for the police."

The way she said that made me wonder if her brother had had some run-ins with the law.

"Did he say who was behind his dismissal?" I asked.

She nodded. "Herman. He said Herman Wheeler was behind it."

My heart dropped to the soles of my boots. "But Herman is dead."

Did she even realize that she was pegging her very own brother as a suspect? I had to know his name.

I frowned. "I'm not speaking to you any further until you tell me your brother's name."

"I can't tell you. He would be furious with me for speaking to you at all about this."

"Then I believe this conversation is over." I turned to go.

I was halfway across the gymnasium floor when she called out, "Gil. Gilbert Penney."

And I had a new suspect.

CHAPTER 23

Langston and Mae Bear came into the gym shortly after Olive Ann shouted her brother's name, putting an end to any further discussion on the matter.

"My land," Langston said. "I didn't know that anyone was still here. I have to lock up the building. Ladies, I'm sorry, but I have to ask you to leave."

"We understand, Langston," I said. "I hope you will be able to go home and put your feet up."

"For a little while I just might, but the missus has a long list of chores for me to do. She thinks that since the school is closed, I should be at her disposal. She doesn't understand that I still have responsibilities here," Langston said.

Olive Ann hurried out the exit without so much as a goodbye, leaving me to wonder what I should do with the information she'd shared and how I was going to find her brother, Gilbert Penney. It was clear to me that she wasn't going to tell me where he was.

"Well, she seemed in a rush to get away from you, Miss Wright. What did you say to her?" the janitor chuckled.

"It's what she said to me."

His thick eyebrows touched each other in concern. "What do you mean by that?"

I shook my head. "Never mind. I do thank you for all the extra work you are doing for this fundraiser, Langston."

"I'm happy to do whatever it takes for the students." He scratched Mae Bear behind the ears. "Mae Bear feels the exact same way. She has a hankering for music too. She wags her tail when I get my harmonica out to play a little tune."

I smiled at the image. "And our students are the better for it."

I said goodbye to Langston and Mae Bear and left the school. My mind spun as I made the mile-and-a-half walk home. On the way to the school, I had been bothered by the cold, but on the return trip, I didn't even feel the bite of the wind off the river. I was far too preoccupied with what I'd learned from Olive Ann and the memory of the cruel message on my chalkboard.

What I didn't know was how the person who'd left that message could have known that I would be the one to see it. It was the Christmas holiday. As far as the students knew, I would be away from school for the entire two weeks. It was more likely that Langston would discover the word on the chalkboard, but I was certain that it hadn't been written there for him, and I knew he didn't know Latin. Furthermore, *venefica* was the feminine form of "witch." It could also be translated to "hag." I knew in my heart that the word had been left for me to find and me alone.

And how was the hateful epithet connected to the Gem City Club? I had heard of the Gem City Club before, of course. It was the most exclusive gentlemen's club in the city. As a woman and a member of a bishop's family, I had never been there. However, I had walked by it many times. I had no plans for the rest of the day. What harm could it do if I rode my bicycle by it?

I hurried the rest of the way home, so I could collect my bicycle and put into action the next step in my investigation. I didn't even go inside the house when I arrived home. Instead,

I went straight to the carriage house for the bicycle and was riding away before anyone even knew that I was home.

The club was in the opposite direction from the school, and so I followed the Great Miami River to the south. It was a pretty ride along the river, and I would have enjoyed it more if it had been a bit warmer and there had been far less ice on the path.

Nearly two miles from my home, the large Tudor-style hall came into view. It was constructed of red brick and huge dark beams. Nearly a dozen chimneys poked out of its slate roof.

There was one automobile in the large circular driveway. I parked my bicycle near the middle of the driveway, by an old hitching post, and walked through the snow up to the front of the building.

My feet were frozen by the time I reached the front door. I tried to open it. It was locked. I knocked, but no one came.

I frowned, went back down the steps, and walked around the building.

Near the back of the building, a window was cracked open. I found that odd in the middle of winter, so I went over for a closer look.

I peeked in the window and saw that the interior space was some sort of empty boardroom. There was a long, heavy table in the middle, with at least a dozen chairs running the length of it. In the middle of the table was an envelope. I could be wrong, but it looked like it had Herman Wheeler's name on it.

I shivered. Was that envelope a clue to the identity of his killer?

Before I could change my mind, I pushed the window up, but it went up one foot before getting stuck. I squinted at it. The opening was tight, but I thought I could get through it if I removed my hat.

I untied the scarf that held my hat in place, then put the hat and scarf on the bush next to me.

I put my arms and head inside the window and, with the tips of my boots, climbed the jagged bricks on the side of the house to push my torso through.

I thought I had almost made it when my hips got stuck in the window.

With my body half hanging out the window, I began re-thinking my plan to climb into the hall. What was I going to do if I actually made it inside? Was I really going to take that envelope?

"Hey, what are you doing?" an angry male voice de-manded from behind me.

I was caught, and there was nothing I could do but lie there, with half of my body inside the window and the other half outside.

A second later, a pair of rough hands grabbed me by my legs and pulled me out of the window.

"What in God's green earth do you think you're doing?" the man asked. He wore a servant's uniform. It consisted of a short buttoned jacket, a white shirt, and pleated trousers. He blinked at me. "Miss Wright?"

I felt a blush creep up my neck, and then I took time to compose myself by straightening my coat. How embarrass-ing to be caught breaking and entering by one of my former students. "Samuel Burrels. I have not seen you since you graduated from Steele last spring. I see that you landed on your feet. Are you working for the club?"

He blinked at me. "Yes, I am a footman for the club."

I picked my hat and scarf up off the bush as if it made per-fect sense for them to be there and dusted them free of snow. "Very good. This is a great start for you."

He blinked at me. "What are you doing here? And why were you in the window?"

I thought fast. "If you must know, I was out on a long ride and had an urgent need to use the water closet. I knocked on the door, but no one answered. I am in such a desperate state that I walked around the building, looking for a bit of privacy, and then saw the open window."

The blush started at Samuel's neck and went all the way up to the very tips of his ears. "Oh my." He cleared his throat. "I can let you in to use the privy." Without another word, he started around the building, and I followed him to the back entrance. I knew this had to be where the servants came and went from the club.

He pointed at a closed door. "The water closet is right through there. You can let yourself out when you're done."

"Thank you," I said as primly as possible and went into the water closet.

CHAPTER 24

As I expected, the club had electric lights and indoor plumbing. Only the best for the elite of Dayton. After what I thought was an appropriate amount of time, I opened the water closet door. Samuel was nowhere to be seen.

Something I had learned in my years of being a schoolteacher was that the easiest way to rid yourself of a young man was to say something he would find embarrassing. He would make himself scarce after that.

I left the small room and decided to risk taking a look around the hall. I didn't know if I would be able to find the boardroom, because the building was massive. I knew I mustn't tarry—I certainly didn't want to be caught by poor Samuel again. I wasn't sure the poor boy's heart could take it if I asked him to show me to the privy a second time.

The hall was quiet. There was a very good chance that there were more servants in the building other than Samuel, so I had to keep my wits about me.

I walked through the servants' quarters to the empty kitchen. The kitchen itself was huge, bigger than the whole house I shared with Father and the boys. Everything was clean and put away, leaving me to conclude that there were no festivities at the hall that evening.

Beyond the kitchen was a set of double doors. I went through them and found myself in a grand ballroom, a space far larger and grander than the one in the Shaws' home. Above my head were four giant chandeliers with thousands of crystals hanging from them. They were electrified, but at the moment, the lights were off. However, I could easily find my way because of the giant arched windows on three sides of the room.

The floor was marble, and a marble fireplace that could practically hold a horse and carriage was located at one end of the ballroom.

As the space was essentially empty, I moved through it quickly to the next set of double doors. This exit led me into a hallway. To my delight, the doors on either side of the hall were open, allowing me to quickly peek inside each of them. The very last door opened into the boardroom. In the middle of the table was the envelope, and I was right. Herman's name was on it.

I stared at it for a long moment. I had been so focused on the idea of finding the envelope, I had not thought of what I would do when I found it. It would be wrong to open a letter meant for someone else, but then again, the man was dead. If the envelope held some kind of clue as to why Herman had been killed, Bertie, Detective Gaylen, and the rest of the police force would want that. I was doing a public service by opening it.

Before I could change my mind, I picked up the envelope, opened it, unfolded the note inside, and read it. *I need more time. It should all be settled by the New Year.*

I stared at the words.

And it was signed *Yours.*

"Yours?" I asked aloud. "Yours who? Who is yours?"

There was a loud bang somewhere deep in the building, and I jumped. I shoved the note back into the envelope and left it where I'd found it. I hurried out of the room. It was time for me to leave; I had dithered here in the club long enough.

I went out another set of double doors to a hallway that was lined with photographs. On a golden plaque above the framed pictures were the words *The Members*.

I stopped in front of the wall of faces, then looked at each one in turn. Olive Ann was right. The members of the club were the high society of Dayton. Many of them were moguls of industry, bankers, and heirs to fortunes. I stopped in front of one of the photographs, and Randolph Shaw's face stared back at me. Hadn't Lenora said that Randolph had met Herman at his club? This could be the very club.

At the end of the hallway, there were other, smaller photographs with a much smaller plaque. The plaque read *The Junior Members*.

The men on this part of the wall were younger. They looked less jaded than the older members and had a clear hunger for wealth and success in each of their expressions. Herman Wheeler's photo was among them. His smug demeanor came through in the photo, and I remembered how little I had cared for him in life. Odd that now I was spending a great deal of my free time trying to solve his murder.

The photograph next to Herman's took my breath away. It was none other than Arthur Bacon, the man my sweet Agnes was in love with.

I stared at Arthur's photograph. Did Agnes know that he was a member of this club? Did it even matter whether she knew or didn't know? I didn't have the answers to those questions, but I was surprised that Arthur and Herman had known each other. That seemed to me to be an important piece of information. Arthur could give me more insight into the man who'd been killed, and maybe that insight would lead me to his killer.

I heard footsteps on the other side of a door to my right. Before I could find a place to hide or flee, the door opened, and Samuel walked out. He gaped at me. I couldn't say I could blame him; this was the second time he'd caught me where I wasn't supposed to be.

"Miss Wright?"

I cleared my throat. "Hello, Samuel. I was just letting myself out when I got all turned around. This building is so large. Can you point me in the right direction?"

"How did you get lost?" he sputtered. "The servants' exit is right beside the loo."

I put on an equally shocked face. "I can't believe I missed it."

"I'll show you out," he said.

He started down the hallway, clearly thinking that I would fall into step behind him.

"Samuel, before I leave, can I ask you something?"

He turned, with a pained expression on his face. "Yes?"

I pointed at Herman's photograph. "Is that the man who died at the Shaws' home?"

He rocked back and forth on his feet, and I could almost hear his mind turning while he tried to decide how he should answer my question.

When he didn't say anything, I spoke again. "I'm sure it is. His name is Herman Wheeler, isn't it?"

"Yes, that is Mr. Wheeler, and he was a member of the club. We have all been very shaken up by his passing."

"Because he was well liked at the club?"

He pursed his lips. "No, that isn't the reason."

I see, I thought.

"It is a shame that he passed in such a terrible way."

"It's worse for the Shaw family. They are the ones who have to deal with the aftermath of it all," he said in a clipped voice.

"Because their son was arrested?" I asked.

He didn't say anything when I asked that.

"Did you know Benny Shaw when you were at Steele?"

"Everyone at Steele knows Benny Shaw," Samuel replied.

"But if you are asking if we were friends, no, we were not. I didn't have enough money to move in Benny's circle."

I nodded, as I was well aware of the divisions in the school between the haves and have-nots. Public education was supposed to even the playing field for all students, but in reality, that wasn't happening. The students still knew who among their classmates came from money and who didn't.

"What was your impression of Herman?" I asked.

He sighed. "He was ambitious. I heard him say once that he planned to be the president of the club within a year, and when he was, he was making changes."

"What changes?" I asked.

"I don't know. I was passing by him and a group of other gentlemen when he said it. I don't stand and listen to members talk."

I had my doubts about that. I thought that anyone who happened to be in the Gem City Club would have his ear to the ground to hear what all the members were up to. I knew I would. These were some of the most powerful men in Dayton. Their decisions could have a great impact on everyday Daytonians, like Samuel and me.

"Who is the president now, and is he planning to leave office?"

He brushed imaginary dust from the sleeve of his jacket. "Randolph Shaw. And no, I doubt he will ever be willing to leave his position."

Randolph Shaw's motives for murder grew by the hour.

I pointed at one more photograph. "And Arthur Bacon?" I asked. "We share a mutual friend." There was no way I was going to tell him Agnes's name.

"Arthur Bacon is fake," Samuel said. "Herman was unkind and greedy, but at least he showed his true colors. Arthur hides the worst parts of himself, which makes him far more dangerous."

CHAPTER 25

I decided that speaking to Agnes was a top priority now that I had learned Arthur Bacon was a member of the club, and I would be lying to myself if I didn't admit I was concerned to hear Samuel claim that Arthur was "dangerous."

The cold wind brushed my cheeks as I rode my bicycle along the river to the paper store downtown where Agnes worked. Just as I parked my bicycle by the front of the shop, Agnes came out the front door, carrying two very heavy-looking wicker baskets. She smiled at me. "Katie! It's so good to see you. You came at the perfect time. I just finished my last batch of cards." She held up the two baskets as proof.

I hurried over to her and took one of the baskets. It was like picking up four jugs of milk at one time. I had to use two hands to hold it. "How are you able to carry both of these?"

"Practice, I suppose, and determination. Besides, I don't want to make another trip. These are my last ones to mail, and after this, I can go home and enjoy my own Christmas."

I looked down at the basket full of letters. There had to be over one hundred. "How did you finish all of these? You must have been up all night."

"That's exactly how I did it. If you compare the handwriting from the cards I did in the middle of the day and those I did late last night, you will be able to tell. However, I still believe I did my very best." She set her basket on the cold sidewalk and fished in it for two envelopes. She held them side by side.

I couldn't tell the difference at all. Both were beautifully written. Agnes had the best penmanship I had ever seen. I could see now why so many society ladies wanted her to be the one to write their Christmas cards.

I blinked when I saw the envelope that she said she'd written in the middle of the night. It was made out to Herman Wheeler, and the return address was the Shaw family.

I set the container I was holding inside my bicycle basket and was relieved to find that it just fit, but I had to concentrate to keep the bicycle upright due to the weight of the cards. I patted my stack of cards. "You can drop those in here. They will lighten your load a bit."

She laughed. "Katie, you are ridiculous. Two cards aren't going to make much of a difference."

"You would be surprised," I said with a seemingly carefree smile as she dropped them in.

I fell into step behind Agnes and removed the envelope addressed to Herman from the basket, then tucked it into my coat pocket. Since Herman was dead, I thought it would do no harm if that one card went undelivered. My guess was Lenora had ordered it for him before Herman died, and Agnes had been so exhausted while addressing the cards last night that she didn't put two and two together and realize he was the murder victim.

She looked over her shoulder. "What are you doing back there? Aren't you going to walk beside me?"

"Yes, of course. It's just a little precarious with my bike." I rolled the bicycle up next to her. "With everything that happened at the Shaws' the night of the Christmas party, I never got to ask you how your time with Arthur was."

She closed her eyes and smiled, as if recalling a sweet memory. "Oh, Katie, I have never felt this way before. Arthur is a dream come true. He's so handsome, sophisticated, and successful. I'm lucky that he is paying any attention to me at all."

I adjusted the bicycle's weight. "You are a dream come true for him. He's the one who is lucky that you are paying any attention to him."

She waved her hand. "Oh, Katie. Don't be silly." She beamed. "And I have even better news."

"Oh?"

"He asked me to go with him to the holiday formal at his club! Can you believe it? I keep pinching myself to prove I'm not dreaming."

"Wow! He's a member of a club?" I asked, as if I didn't know.

"Yes. The Gem City Club, the premier gentlemen's club in the city. Can you believe a girl like me would be escorted to such a place by a man like Arthur?"

"Yes, of course. You're a prize, Agnes. I wish you'd believe me when I say that. When is the formal?"

"Christmas Eve night. I'm so thrilled to go."

"I didn't know the club allowed women into the building. I thought it was for men only."

"It is, except for this one event each year, when guests and spouses are allowed inside for the Christmas party. Isn't that grand! And I am so glad that you showed up today, because I have a favor to ask of you."

I made a face. The last time she'd asked for a favor, I'd found a dead body, so I didn't believe that anyone would blame me for my hesitation. "What is it?"

"Arthur has a friend in the club who doesn't have a date. The young men are expected to show up with a date. If they don't have a date, they are relentlessly teased by the other men."

I wrinkled my nose. "That doesn't sound like a very supportive group."

She shook her head. "You know how men are."

I did. I lived with them, but my father and brothers wouldn't tease each other in such a way.

"Arthur asked me if I had any single girlfriends who might be willing to be his friend's guest, and you immediately came to mind."

I shook my head so hard, my glasses slipped down my nose and I almost lost control of the bicycle. "No, no, no. We have plenty of other friends that you can ask. Besides, the Christmas tree sale at school is on Christmas Eve. I can't possibly do anything else that day. I will be exhausted."

"The Christmas tree sale is during the day. This is at night. It doesn't even begin until seven. Your school event will be long over before you have to get ready for the formal. I know for a fact there are ladies on the committee who will be at the Christmas tree sale and then accompanying their husbands to the dance."

"Still. I will be tired, and it's right before Christmas. I don't feel I have had much of a holiday break from school at all this year."

"Please, do it for me. It will impress Arthur that I was able to find a date for his friend. I promised him I would try." She looked at me with her big blue eyes.

I groaned. "What is the friend's name?"

She thought for a moment. "I can't remember, but if he is a friend of Arthur's, you can trust that he is a kind and respectful gentleman, just like Arthur."

I knitted my brow. Her description of Arthur was in stark contrast to the one Samuel had given me at the club. I knew Agnes far better than I knew Samuel. In fact, I had not seen Samuel since he'd graduated from Steele. But which assessment could I trust more: that of a young man whom I had known only as a student or that of a friend who was clearly infatuated with the person in question?

In any case, what I did know for certain was that going to the formal would give me the opportunity to learn more about Arthur and make my own determination of his character.

"Very well. I will go with you."

"Oh, Katie! You are the best friend a girl could have."

CHAPTER 26

After we left the post office, where Agnes had sent off all her clients' cards except for the one addressed to Herman, which was sitting in my coat pocket, I said to her, "I am glad I can help Arthur's friend out by going to the party, but not everything I have heard about the Gem City Club has been good."

Her eyes were wide. "Oh?"

"There is a member of the Christmas tree sale committee who told me her brother had a bad experience and was asked to leave the club."

"I know club members put a lot of pressure on each other to be successful. Perhaps her brother wasn't up to snuff."

"Maybe," I said. "The committee member believed there was more to it than that."

Agnes pulled at her cuffs as we made our way down the sidewalk. "It's only natural for a sister to take her brother's side. You know that better than anyone."

This was true.

"Who is her brother?"

"Gilbert Penney." Now that I said his name, I realized that I hadn't seen Gilbert's photo on the club's wall of junior members.

"Oh my. I do know that name. Arthur told me that he was asked to leave the club because of some poor behavior."

"What poor behavior?" I asked.

"He didn't say, and I don't pry into such things with Arthur. I know my place."

I wrinkled my nose. It was clear to me that I would not know my place if I was the woman involved with Arthur. I would want to know all the goings-on at the club in great detail.

Agnes shook her head. "I can tell you wish that I'd asked him more about it. I suppose you can ask him at the dance."

"I will."

As Agnes and I parted ways, she promised me that she would find me the perfect dress from her closet. That was a good thing, as I didn't have the money to buy a new dress for the dance on my teacher's salary.

I rode my bicycle home, wondering whether I should have warned Agnes about Arthur Bacon as I'd planned. In the end, I had decided not to say anything because I had thought I could get a better take on Arthur if I spoke with him in person. I was still cautious, though, and didn't want Agnes to get too far into her romance with Arthur until I could judge his character for myself.

At the very least, I would be able to enter the club when members were there and find out if it was as awful as Olive Ann claimed. Maybe I could even find out what had caused Gilbert Penney to be kicked out the door.

A block from home, I pulled my bicycle over to the side of the road and leaned it against a tree. I couldn't wait any longer; I had to see what the Christmas card the Shaws were sending to Herman said.

I felt the slightest twinge of guilt as I opened the envelope. There was something wrong with looking at a dead man's Christmas card, I thought. I shook the feeling away.

The illustration on the card was of a stand of fir trees in

the snow. There was a lamppost in the middle of the trees with a red bow tied around it. *Season's Greetings* was written in gold lettering.

I opened the card and recognized Agnes's perfect handwriting immediately.

> *We wish you a happy Christmas and the very best into the New Year! Many congratulations on your upcoming installation as president of the Gem City Club.*
> *The Shaw Family*

I stared at the card. Randolph Shaw was the president of the Gem City Club now. That was set to change after the New Year? I thought back to the photographs I had seen on the wall of the club. Herman Wheeler's photograph had been among those of the junior members. How could he jump from being a junior member to club president?

I put the card back in the envelope and tucked it into my bicycle basket. I felt I had learned something very crucial indeed to my investigation. The only problem was I didn't know what made it crucial.

Back at 7 Hawthorn Street, I found Orville in a state.

"Katie, you're home. Where have you been all this time?"

I frowned at him. "I had a meeting at school for the Christmas tree sale. Father knew where I was." I thought it best not to include my other excursions in my answer.

"Father isn't here. He went to the church offices to prepare for his next hearing. Why, I don't know. It is unlikely that a hearing will be held before the first of the year. And it's well into the afternoon."

I wasn't surprised that Father had gone to the office. It was impossible to get him to sit still. The only time he came to a full stop was on Sunday, and that was because the Bible decreed it. Were it not in the Ten Commandments, I doubted he'd ever take a day of rest.

"We have to find those drawings." Orville wrung his hands.

"I have been looking," I said. "However, with the murder, things are more complicated." I would not be surprised if the theft of the papers and the murder were connected. However, I wasn't ready to tell my brother that. He was already on edge. I thought this new information would only make him more nervous.

"Did you learn anything at all?" he asked. "Wilbur is getting impatient to check his notes on the drawings. I am running out of ways to put him off."

"Maybe it's just time to tell him the truth," I said. "He's your brother. He will be upset, of course, but he will forgive you."

"I can't, Katie. You don't know how important the flying machine is to us. For Wilbur—for us both—it is about being the first to fly. If I've lost those notes and they fall into the wrong hands, I might have undone years of work. I could never live with myself if something like that happened."

The last thing I wanted was for the special bond between my brothers to be broken over Orville's carelessness. He had not lost the drawings on purpose, but I knew that Orville was right about how upset Wilbur would be.

"I do have some leads, but I'm not even sure they have anything to do with the drawings. I have learned some interesting things about Herman, though."

"Oh?" Orville asked. "I'm still convinced that Herman was the one who stole the drawings. He used that ridiculous game to distract me and then ran off with the jacket when I wasn't looking."

"What does the Gem City Club mean to you?"

"It's a men's social club," he said. "Some of the most powerful men in Dayton are members. Wilbur and I have been asked to join."

"You have? What did you say when asked?"

"I met with members of the club not long before we left

for Kitty Hawk this past season. Wilbur wouldn't go to the meeting, but I thought it was only polite that I hear what they have to offer. There are many very powerful men in the club, and it's a place where we could make connections that would benefit the business."

"Which business?" I asked. "Bicycles or flight?"

"Frankly, both."

"But Father dislikes groups like that." I removed my hat and coat and hung them on the coat-tree by the door.

Orville frowned. "It's not the Freemasons. It's just a social club. It is not the same thing. There are no ritual overtones to the Gem City Club. That is what Father doesn't like, when such gatherings step into the realm of religion."

"Even so . . ."

"Yes, even so, our father would not like it. He believes a person's life should be devoted to the church, family, and occupation, in that order. If you can combine church and occupation, as he has, all the better." He paused. "In the end, I decided not to join. The membership fee was far too steep, and I knew Wilbur and Father would never approve of paying that kind of money merely for status. And if I participated in all the events the club requires of its members, it would take away from my work. That would never do."

"Did they have interest in your flying experiments?" I asked.

"As a matter of fact, they did. I thought they'd invited us because we have had so much success at the bicycle shop and the popularity of cycling. However, when I got there, all they wanted to speak about was the flying machine."

"Was Herman there?" I asked.

"Yes, I saw Herman there. He was seated with Randolph Shaw," Orville said. "From what I could tell, they were the ones most engaged in the conversation about flying."

CHAPTER 27

The next day, I was busy with final preparations for the Christmas tree sale, but the murder of Herman Wheeler and my brothers' missing drawings were always in the back of my mind.

I was spinning my wheels when it came to the missing drawings and the murder, and I didn't know where to turn next. I couldn't get access to the club until the dance. I certainly wasn't going to try to break in for a second time. I had been lucky that Samuel was one of my former students. Had I been discovered by anyone else, I would have been in a whole mess of trouble.

When I arrived at school that day, Langston was expecting me, and he had the gymnasium door unlocked and the tables and chairs already set out. I could always count on Langston to be ready for anything.

However, when I went into the hallway, there was no sign of Langston or his collie, Mae Bear. They could be anywhere in the school, waxing floors or washing windows. What I knew from working with him for so many years was that he just never stopped. It was a quality I respected, because I was the same way.

I returned to the gymnasium and got to work. The first order of business was to gather together the tablecloths I needed. I knew they were stored in the secretary's office.

I left the gymnasium a second time in search of the tablecloths and found them just where I thought they'd be. The school secretary was one of the most organized women I'd ever met, and I admired that about her. She had to be organized, working with our principal, who had great ideas but was never able to execute them without Lucy's help.

I returned to the gym, holding a stack of white linen tablecloths, and pulled up short when I saw Bufford Lyons flipping through one of the songbooks I had left on one of the tables. "What are you doing here?"

"Miss Wright," Bufford said. "I'm pleased to find you volunteering with the PTA. The experience will serve you well when you have children of your own and participate as a mother someday. You won't be teaching then, of course."

I had been working on this project for weeks, and as the chair of the Foreign Language Department, he knew that because I had to tell him when I left the building early for the day to attend to PTA business. He'd delivered his little speech just to be condescending. He was much better at belittling people than teaching Greek. I was certain of that.

"I'm helping with the Christmas tree sale, as you well know, because I believe the school should expand its music programs. It is a great way to broaden student horizons. The more we expose them to now, the better and more thoughtful adults they will be."

He pulled at the collar of his jacket. "Yes, well, I hope when the time comes, you will work as hard for the Foreign Language Department."

I didn't bother to respond. I worked far harder for the Foreign Language Department than he did. I knew he had said it only to get a rise out of me. To cover my anger, I walked over to one of the tables and set the tablecloths on a chair. After selecting the tablecloth on top, I shook it out and spread it over the table.

Bufford cleared his throat.

I glanced over my shoulder. "Was there something else?"

He frowned at me. "Yes. I have been told that you were at the party where that unfortunate death occurred."

"You mean the Shaws' Christmas party." I went to the next table with another tablecloth and smoothed it over the top.

"Must you move about when we are speaking? It's very distracting."

I went to a third table. "Yes, I must. I don't have much time to set up today. Everything must be in place for the program."

He clenched his jaw but said nothing more about it. "Randolph Shaw has told me that you called on his wife and upset her. He asked me to remind you that a certain distance should be maintained in the parent-teacher relationship. Unless you are going to a parents' house about a school matter, you shouldn't be there."

I studied him. "I *was* there about a school matter. Benjamin Shaw is one of my students, and I was concerned about him."

"But his arrest was not related to school, so you should not have been involved. In fact, it was inappropriate for you to even be in attendance at the party."

"Lenora is—or was—the chair of this committee. She invited me to the party."

"Out of generosity. You didn't have to accept the invitation. The right thing to do would have been to politely decline."

"Is that why you are here today? Just so you can tell me what I did was wrong? You could have waited to do it when school started up again and you had a full audience at a faculty meeting."

He glowered at me.

"Why did Randolph Shaw ask you to deliver this message? You're not on the PTA, nor do you have anything to do with it."

He pulled on the collar of his shirt, as if it was a little too tight around his neck. "He came up to me in our club and asked me to speak to you."

I arched my brow. "The Gem City Club."

He narrowed his eyes. "How do you know that?"

"It's the club where Randolph Shaw is a member. That is common knowledge."

He looked dubious.

"How can you afford to be a member of the club on a teacher's salary?" My question was blunt, but I didn't care. Bufford had gotten on my last nerve when he'd stolen advanced Greek from me at the faculty meeting, and today's conversation was only making it worse.

He glared at me. "My father was a man of industry and a member of the club. As his son, I can join no matter my occupation."

I frowned. Was this how Herman Wheeler had gotten in, or even Agnes's young man, Arthur Bacon?

In any case, Bufford's chumminess with Randolph Shaw was not good news for me.

He cleared his throat. "I will let you get back to your task. It is a good use of your time as you have no family to care for."

I glared at him. Who did he think took care of my brothers and my father? Santa Claus? It was true that I had Carrie to help me, but the majority of the decision-making for the household fell on my shoulders. Also, just because I wasn't married with children, that didn't mean I had no family to care for.

"I just stopped by to collect my textbooks so that I will be able to teach advanced Greek in January," he said smugly.

I knew he'd said that just to get a reaction out of me. He wasn't going to get it. I smiled. "If you need any help with that, don't hesitate to ask."

He pressed his lips together for half a second. "Don't worry. I won't." He stomped out of the gymnasium.

After Bufford left, it took me no time at all to finish setting up for the fundraiser. The tablecloths were on all the tables, the chairs where students would sit before going outside to sing were perfectly lined up, and the stacks of sheet music were organized by song.

I didn't know where Langston was, so I left him a note on one of the tables, thanking him for all he had done. Then I bundled up in scarf, coat, and hat and went out through the gymnasium doors.

While I had been inside the school, it had begun to snow again, and the sky was the color of faded newsprint. I skirted around the side of the building until I came to the front of the large redbrick school. It was a formidable and impressive building.

I was about to step on the sidewalk when a shaky voice asked, "Miss Wright?"

I turned and saw Benny Shaw sitting on the school steps.

CHAPTER 28

Benny and I stared at each other for a long moment. It was as if both of us had been trapped in the presence of a ghost.

I snapped out of it first. "Benny! What are you doing here?"

He stood up. "I need to talk to you."

"I thought you were . . ."

"You thought I was in jail."

I nodded.

"My father got me out," he said with a bitter tone.

The sound of his voice surprised me. Shouldn't he be happy for his father's influence and help?

"Does this mean you are no longer accused?" I pulled my scarf more snugly around my neck.

"No, I'm out on bail." He looked down at the sidewalk. "My father paid it."

My heart sank. "I am sorry for what has happened. I know we have had our differences in the past, but I don't believe that you killed Herman."

He looked at me with tears in his eyes. "Thank you. That means a lot to me coming from you. My father isn't even able to say that. He doesn't care if I committed murder or not. He just cares about how it looks to the city."

"And the members of his club?" I asked.

His eyes went wide. "How did you know that?"

I adjusted my spectacles on my nose. "It's well known that your father is the president of the Gem City Club."

"I guess." He shivered. He wasn't wearing a hat or gloves, but I believed he shivered less from the cold than from fear of his father.

"But if your father was willing to post bail, he must believe you are innocent."

He shook his head. "Having a son in jail looks bad at the club, so he had to do something about it." He swallowed. "My mother told me that you wanted to help prove I didn't do this."

"I do. That's what I have been trying to do."

He nodded. "If that's the case, I need to tell you the whole story." A shiver racked his whole body.

"You're cold. Why aren't you wearing a hat or scarf?" I asked.

Once a teacher, always a teacher. I couldn't help being bossy.

"I'm not cold," he said with some of the petulance back in his voice. I was relieved to hear it. If Benny had any chance of staying a free young man, he had to have his confidence about him, even if it came off as arrogance. This was not the time to show weakness.

"Well, in any case, I don't want to stand out in the cold and speak to you, so let's go back into the school."

"I don't want to go back into the school. I can never go back there."

"What are you talking about? You're a senior. You have to finish out your final year. You're so close to graduating."

"I can't. Do you have any idea what a pariah I will be to my classmates now? No one will respect me."

"Your true friends will stand by you."

"I don't have true friends," he said. "I only have people who want to benefit from my status or who fear me. Did any of them call on my family while I was in jail? Did any one of them telephone my house to see how my mother was doing?"

"My guess is no," I said.

"You were the only one." He wiped the tears from his eyes. "Of all the people in this school, you were the only one."

I had sympathy for Benny, but I also knew how he'd behaved in school over the past four years. He'd kept the other students around him in line because they knew he could ruin their reputation or status among their classmates with a single word. If they stepped out of line, they would no longer be invited to the fancy parties at his home. To have a true friend, one had to be a true friend. I couldn't remember ever seeing evidence that Benny had that deep kind of friendship with another student.

"If you don't want to go back into the school, let's walk. I have to keep moving to avoid frostbite." I started walking and wasn't surprised when Benny fell into step next to me.

I glanced at him. "I want you to promise me something, no matter what happens."

He scowled. "What?"

"No matter what happens, you finish your education. You don't finish only high school, but you graduate from college."

"What would be the point of that if I am found guilty?"

"You can't assume you will be."

"They will find me guilty," he said. "In their place, I would think I was guilty too."

"Tell me about that night. Maybe if you explain your side of the story, we will have a better idea of what really happened."

We walked in silence for a few minutes, but after a deep breath, he spoke. "That night, I was upset and didn't even want to come down for the party. It was my parents' event, and because of my poor grades, my father would not let me invite anyone."

"But I saw you in the parlor before . . ." I trailed off. I had been about to say, "Before I saw you with the dead body."

"Yes, my father insisted that I make an appearance. I walked from room to room for a while. I was in the parlor when Herman was making a fool of the man you were with."

"That was my brother Orville," I said.

He shrugged, as if that didn't make any difference to him. It made me wonder then whether Benny knew or cared who my brother was. If that was true, why would he steal the jacket with the drawings in it? Orville had assumed that it was Herman who'd taken the jacket, but Benny had been in the billiard room with Herman's body and Orville's jacket. He could have just as easily picked it up in the parlor and dropped it when he entered the billiard room and saw Herman's body.

I shook my head. The jacket had been lying perfectly folded over the arm of the chair. It hadn't been dropped or tossed aside. Whoever put it there had done it with care. That didn't fit with anything I knew about Benny, or Herman either, for that matter.

"How long were you in the parlor?"

"Not long."

"Can you be more specific?"

"I don't know. Less than ten minutes. I wasn't interested in the silly games. You would think adults would have better things to do than play charades."

He had a point, but I didn't comment, because I didn't want to get off track.

"Where did you go after that?"

"Outside."

"In the cold?"

He made a face.

"Benny, if you want me to help you, I need to know all your movements."

"If you have to know, I went out to smoke. My mother despises the habit, so I never do it in the house. She can smell cigarette smoke even if she's in the conservatory and I'm on the third floor."

That was something Lenora and I had in common. I hated the sickeningly sweet smell of tobacco myself. I always wished that Charlie Taylor wouldn't smoke in the bicycle shop. It was almost unbearable at times.

"How long were you outside?" I asked.

He shrugged. "A while. It was cold, so I came back in. I didn't want to rejoin the party, but if I went to my room, my father would send a servant looking for me. He was making me attend the party as punishment. He was furious with me for being booted from school." He took a deep breath. "So I went to the billiard room. I knew no one was supposed to be in there, and it was my father's space. Because of that, the servants rarely went in that room, unless they were cleaning it. But I did see what I thought was a shadow of someone as I came down the hall. I assumed it was a servant, because who else would be there? But I don't know for sure it was."

I nodded and encouraged him to continue. "Was it a man or a woman?"

"I couldn't tell. All I saw was a shadow. It could have been my mother's cat, for all I know."

"What did you find when you went into the room?"

He closed his eyes for a moment. I wasn't sure if he was trying to conjure up the memory or forget it. "Herman. He was slumped over the billiard table. He was trying to stand up."

I shivered. So Herman was still alive when Benny saw him lying across the billiard table. "Did you go for help?"

"I was going to, but I thought he was going to fall over, so

I went to help him. He—he was trying to pull the screwdriver from his chest. I—I didn't know it was a screwdriver at the time."

"What did you think it was?"

"I don't know. A knife maybe. He kept trying over and over again while I was holding him, so finally, I—I just pulled it out." He stopped in the middle of the sidewalk and covered his eyes, as if by doing so, he could block out the memory. "Blood spurted out all over the table, all over him, and all over me."

I shivered at the image. It was too horrible for words.

"There I was, holding the screwdriver in my hand, and I heard someone outside the door. I knew how it would look. I dropped the screwdriver and looked for a place to hide. There wasn't anywhere, so . . . ."

"So you went to stand in the corner."

He nodded and began walking again, more quickly this time. As I was shorter than he was, I had to double my pace to keep up with him.

When I came alongside him, I asked, "Did you tell the police all of this?"

"No, not exactly. I didn't tell them I removed it from his chest, just that I was trying to help him, and that's how I was covered with blood."

I did not tell Benny that removing the screwdriver had cost Herman his life. The presence of the tool had temporarily kept him from bleeding out. With it gone, there was nothing to stanch the flow of blood. This was something that Benny didn't need to know.

"Before Orville and I came into the room, did you see anyone? Maybe even before you went into the billiard room? Was there anyone in the hallway? Did you hear any strange noises?"

He frowned and was quiet for a few paces. Finally, he spoke. "I heard someone crying."

"Crying?"

"Maybe. It could have been crying. At the time, I thought it was just my mother's cat whining. When there are parties, my mother puts her in the conservatory, so that she doesn't bother the guests. The cat hates that and wails and moans the entire time. I thought it was Moonlight, but it could have been a person crying."

I remembered the large silver Persian I'd met in the billiard room the day I went back to visit with Lenora. "Does the cat sound like a person crying?"

"She can. My father says it's because my mother spoils her and treats her like a human baby. Father hates that cat."

He had just given me another reason not to like Randolph Shaw. The reasons were piling up. He medicated his wife. He was unkind to his son, and he hated cats. None of these were admirable traits.

"All right. Let's assume that it was a person crying and not the cat. Who could it have been?"

He shook his head. "I don't know."

I tucked that bit of information into the back of my mind and asked another question. "Did you see any papers around Herman's body?"

"Papers?"

"Yes, any papers. They might have been folded up in quarters, as if they'd been kept in a man's suit jacket pocket."

"There was nothing there." He paused. "If there was, it would have been covered with blood too."

CHAPTER 29

We passed the bakery, and Benny stopped at the front window. "I know this place. It's my mother's favorite bakery. She sends our maid here all the time to pick up cakes and pastries." He removed his wallet from his pants pocket. "I'll take her a cake. Maybe it will cheer her up."

There was a sadness in his voice, and I wondered what was truly wrong with his mother, other than her controlling husband.

Benny went into the shop, and the bell over the door rang. I hesitated before I followed him into the bakery. As soon as I stepped inside, my glasses fogged up, and I had to remove them to clean the lenses on the edge of my scarf.

"Is that you, Benny Shaw?" Mrs. Appleton asked. "I haven't seen you since you were knee high. Your mother used to come in here all the time with you when you were just a little sprite."

"I remember," Benny said. "It was one of our favorite outings."

Mrs. Appleton glanced at me. "Katharine, I'm surprised to see you here with Benny. I saw the two of you walking down the street, in deep conversation. I hope everything is all right."

I put my glasses back on my nose. I wasn't surprised in the least that Mrs. Appleton was waiting and watching by her window to see who passed by. Sticking her nose into other people's business was one of her favorite pastimes.

"Benny is one of my Latin students," I said. "I had a meeting at the school today, and he was nice enough to escort me back to the neighborhood, which gave us time to discuss his grades and so on."

Mrs. Appleton squinted her apple-green eyes at me, as if she wasn't so sure that I was being truthful. I certainly wasn't going to tell her what we had really been discussing.

"It seems that a teacher is always on call these days, doesn't it?" Mrs. Appleton asked. "I remember when I was in school, our teachers wouldn't even look at us after class was over, and if we had a question, we just had to wait until the next time we were in class." She looked from Benny to me and back again. "What can I help you with today?"

Benny shifted back and forth in his brown leather boots. "My mother isn't feeling well, and I thought one of your Christmas cakes would cheer her up."

Mrs. Appleton rested a hand on her cheek. "I am so sorry to hear it. Lenora is one of my very best customers. She always puts in the largest orders for her parties. Believe me when I say I am grateful for the work." She winced. "Unfortunately, a few days before Christmas, all my cakes are spoken for. We have been so very busy with custom orders. My girls have been working around the clock. I just don't think I can ask them to make one more without their walking out completely."

"Oh," Benny said.

Mrs. Appleton's face brightened. "But I have a Yule log that I can sell you. I promise you that it tastes just as good as your mother's favorite layer cake."

"Yes, I will take that."

Mrs. Appleton clapped her hands. "Very good." She opened the kitchen door. "Mary, can you bring out one of the Yule logs for the Shaw family?"

A high-pitched reply of agreement came back.

Mrs. Appleton smiled at us and folded her hands over her apron. "It is so good to see you, Benny, but if you needed a cake, why not send the maid, the way you usually do?"

"As Miss Wright said, I was walking her home and came into the shop on a whim. I remember the many times my mother brought me here when I was small."

"I'm sure you do. You always had a special bond with your mother, but that doesn't surprise me in the least. Boys love their mothers best of all until they marry, and then things become more strained," she said, as if she spoke from some sort of experience, and a painful one at that. "I do hope that you'll tell sweet Maggie hello. I'm used to seeing her every few days, and she has not been here yet this week."

Benny shifted uncomfortably from one foot to the other. "My mother hasn't wanted much to eat lately, not even sweets. I'm sure that's the reason why she hasn't sent Maggie here. I'm hoping this Yule log will change her mind."

"I hope so too. Lenora is far too thin. I tell her so every time I see her." She patted her ample hip. "She needs some meat on her bones. Maybe not as much as I have." She laughed. "But she needs her strength. The only way she is going to get that is with a good meal."

One of Mrs. Appleton's young assistants came into the front room, holding a long bakery box. Benny paid for the cake and thanked the baker. "I'll be sure to give it to my mother right away. It will put a smile on her face. That's what she really needs right now. It's what we both need."

Mrs. Appleton nodded. "Yes, I can see that. Always care for your mother, Benny. It's the most important thing you can do."

He nodded and went out the door. I thanked Mrs. Appleton and followed him back into the cold.

Outside the bakery, I pulled on my gloves.

"I should go back home," Benny said. "My parents don't know I left, and my father promised the police that he would keep an eye on me. I don't know how he's going to do that when he's always at the mill or the club, but I don't want to be caught out wandering the city by the police either."

"Do you think your father is at work or the club now?"

"The club. He's most definitely at the club, trying to control the damage my arrest has done to his reputation. He says he's disgraced at the club because of me. Some of the members won't even speak to him."

"I would think being snubbed by some uppity men wouldn't be as bad as your son being falsely accused of murder."

"You don't know my father. The only reason he posted bail was because of how it looked to have a son in jail. He's more worried about his reputation than what will happen to me."

"How do you know that?" I asked.

"He told me." With that, he walked away with the Yule log in his hands as a fresh snow began to fall.

CHAPTER 30

As soon as I stepped into my family home, Orville jumped out of his chair by the fire. "Katie! What have you learned?"

I put a hand to my chest. "Orv, for goodness' sake, don't jump out at me like that."

"I'm sorry." He nervously smoothed his mustache. "I just have to know if you had any luck finding the papers."

"Not yet, but does the name Gilbert Penney mean anything to you?"

"Gil? Yes, we went to school together. He runs Penney's Ponies downtown."

I nodded. That was why the name had sounded so familiar. "If you want to find those drawings, I suggest we go talk to him."

On the buggy ride to Penney's Ponies, I filled Orville in on what I had learned from Gil's sister Olive Ann about his being kicked out of the Gem City Club by Herman.

"So you think Gilbert had something to do with stealing the papers?"

"He could have, but I certainly think he is a good suspect for Herman's murder. If we solve the murder, I believe the drawings will also be found."

He gave me a dubious glance, as if he wasn't in full agreement with me.

Penney's Ponies was on the northeast side of the city, along the Mad River.

Gravel crunched under the horse's hooves and the buggy wheels as Orville brought the buggy to a stop next to a large stable. A sign was posted on the side of the building: CARRIAGES AND WAGONS FOR SALE. MAKE AN OFFER ON A HORSE TOO!

We got out of the buggy, and I caught a whiff of the stable. I covered my nose.

A man dressed in overalls and a thick jacket came out, leading a horse and carriage. A train engineer's hat sat on the top of his head, and his ears were bright red from the cold. "Orville Wright! My goodness, you haven't aged a day since school. But I see you have added a mighty impressive mustache."

Orville stepped forward and shook the man's hand. "It's nice to see you, Gil. How have you been?"

"Life's full of hard knocks, my friend, and I've gotten my share." He removed his hat and slapped it on his left thigh before setting it back on the top of his head. "I'm selling what I can and making this a small operation. People don't want to ride in wagons and carriages as much anymore, and my business is hurting. I have to get rid of some of the extra expense." He glanced at our family buggy. "I see you travel the old way. I have a new-model carriage right there I can take an offer on. I'll give you an old friend discount."

Orville shook his head. "I think we will buy an automobile next."

"You and everyone else," Gil said bitterly. "I know next to nothing about autos and have no interest in them at all. If automobiles are the way the world is going, you can count me out."

"But if you don't change, your business will be ruined," Orville said, aghast. He couldn't imagine not wanting to learn something new.

Wilbur and Orville had been inventors and innovators from a very young age, and they could not understand why everyone else didn't think the same way they did.

Gil didn't seem concerned by Orville's response. "Folks get killed every day in those death-trap cans of metal. I'm not traveling around with my children in one of those, no sir." He looked at me.

Orville cleared his throat. "This is my sister, Katharine."

"Nice to meet you," I said.

"Likewise," Gil said and then studied us. "I see you have your own carriage there, so you don't need a ride, and you're not interested in buying anything from me. Why are you here?"

"We have some questions about the Gem City Club," I said.

He bristled. "I do not want to talk about that place. They did me wrong."

"That's what I heard," I said quickly. "I am on the PTA with your sister Olive Ann, and she told me about how you were asked to leave the club."

He folded his arms. "I was. They said my business wasn't successful enough for the club. I expect they don't want anyone less than Henry Ford himself as a member."

"I'm sure you've heard that Herman Wheeler was killed at Randolph Shaw's home Saturday night."

"I did. It seems fitting that he would die there, since all he ever wanted was to be Randolph. My guess is Randolph didn't know it until it was too late."

"What do you mean by that?" Orville asked.

Gil just shook his head. "Not my place to speak ill of the dead."

"What was Herman interested in?" Orville asked.

"Anything that could make him money or give him more prestige."

Orville and I looked at each other, and I knew that we were both thinking the same thing. A flying machine, or the knowledge of how to make one, could bring money and prestige aplenty if you were the one to patent it.

Gil went on, "I have never seen a man so hungry for success in my life. He wasn't a good sort of person to be around. You start to think the same way after a while. It's not the sort of person I want to be. Really, he did me a favor by asking me to leave the club."

"Where were you Saturday night, when Herman was killed?" I asked.

He eyed me, and for a second, I thought he wasn't going to answer the question.

"I was at home with my wife and children, trying to figure out where we can cut costs. It's not going to be much of a Christmas at my house this year, I can tell you that."

He had an alibi. I mentally scratched Gil from my list.

"One last question," I said. "What do you think of the other men at the Gem City Club? How did they feel about Herman Wheeler?"

"If you ask me, every last person in that club both feared Herman and wanted to be him." With that, he walked his horse back into the stable.

CHAPTER 31

When I went to bed that night, my head was spinning with all the new information I had learned, but none of it compared to Benny Shaw's release. Benny's story about how he had got the blood on his shirt made sense. It was plausible, but the police must not believe it, since he was still their primary suspect.

I wondered what the police thought Benny's motive could be. He knew Herman because the victim had worked for his father and been a member of his father's club, but what reason could he possibly have to want the other man dead? I wished that I had thought to ask him.

Even if I saw Benny the following day, I didn't know if I would have enough time to question him further. It was the day of the Christmas tree sale. It was also the day of the dance at the club that I'd agreed to go to with Agnes. I hoped I would learn more at the club that night.

The next morning, the sky had barely lightened when I dashed out of bed. With much to do, I quickly washed and dressed.

Even though I was awake early that morning, I knew Father would already be up, reading the papers or writing letters. He believed that the best thinking happened in the morning light. "Poor decisions always come late in the day, Katie. I want you to remember that. As the day goes on, thoughts become muddled, because so many choices have to be made. A man's willpower lags, and he makes mistakes, some of which may be the most costly of his life."

The memory of what my father always said brought to mind Herman Wheeler's murder. The murder had happened at night, so perhaps my father was correct that the poorest decisions were made after dark.

"Yes, yes, I understand. There has to be something we can do." Carrie's voice floated to me through the kitchen door as I stood in the hallway.

I couldn't hear the response of whomever she was speaking to.

I adjusted my glasses on the bridge of my nose and marched into the kitchen. "Carrie, who's with you?"

"Thank you!" she shouted out the door and closed it before I could see who was on the other side.

She spun around to face me. "Miss Katharine. Good morning! Would you like coffee?"

I narrowed my eyes at her. "I asked you a question."

"Oh, yes." She hurried to the stove and removed the pot of coffee. "It was the milkman, making his deliveries. He does that quite early, you know."

"Where is the milk?" I asked.

"I—I guess we got to chatting, and he forgot to leave it. He's a good man. I'm sure he'll be back."

I stepped around her and opened the back door into the alley. There was no one there, but there were fresh boot prints in the snow. I put my foot beside one of those prints. The boot print was roughly the same size as my shoe. That certainly didn't look like our milkman's foot, as he was built like an ox.

I went back into the kitchen and closed the door. "The milkman was here?" I asked again. "Those boot prints don't look like they belong to him."

She licked her lips. "One of his sons. The boy is no more than twelve. I'm sure that's why he forgot to leave the milk. I can't believe I didn't ask him. I suppose with all the extra duties that the Christmas season requires, I simply lost my head."

I didn't believe her.

I pressed my lips together. Carrie was seventeen, and I knew she must be getting to an age where she was thinking about marriage. She wasn't destined to be an old maid like me. A happy old maid, I might add. Even so, I hated the idea of losing her help around the house. I couldn't possibly take care of everything and teach as well. Even though I lived with my father and brothers, it was very important to me to have my independence. I couldn't bring myself to ask them for money when I wanted to go somewhere or buy something.

"I hope you're telling me the truth, Carrie," I said in my sternest teacher voice.

She went on with the task of making my father's breakfast. "Yes, ma'am."

I was about to leave the kitchen when there was a knock on the back door. Carrie made a move to answer it, but I stepped in front of her. "Let me get that."

I opened the door to see William the milkman standing on the other side. Even though it was cold out, he wasn't wearing a coat, and his head was bare. He was wearing thick leather gloves, and his impressive beard must have kept his face warm enough.

"Miss Wright," William said. "I didn't expect you to be the one to open the door. It's nice to see you this fine Christmas Eve." He held out the four jugs of milk that we ordered each week. "Do you have any empty jugs for me to take back?"

"I'm sure we do." I turned. "Carrie?"

But when I looked behind me, Carrie was gone. I frowned and turned back to William. "I'm so sorry. Carrie must have taken breakfast upstairs. I don't know where she stores the empty jugs. I can go find her to ask."

"Oh, that's quite all right. I have plenty, and I can get them next time." He turned to leave.

"William, did you send your son here earlier to deliver milk?" I called after him.

He turned around, with a confused expression on his face. "Son? No, ma'am," he said. "I don't have a boy. Five daughters, and my wife said that was enough." He laughed. "They all are strong as any man, and a daughter is the one who takes care of you when you get old. I'm lucky to have five of them."

"Oh, my mistake, then." My chest tightened. Carrie had lied to me. I didn't believe that had ever happened before.

"You have a Merry Christmas, Miss Wright," William said. "And tell your brothers congratulations on their flying machine. I saw it in the papers. The human mind never ceases to amaze."

I thanked him and shut the door. It seemed that I needed to have a conversation with Carrie sooner rather than later. I set the milk in the icebox and shook my head. Today wasn't a day that I had time to deal with Carrie's romantic entanglements. Until I could talk with her, I had to trust that she wouldn't make any rash decisions.

I went in to breakfast and found not only my father there but Orville and Wilbur as well.

Wilbur was buttering his toast. "Today is the last day we can get in a full day of work before Christmas. I need those drawings, Orville, and I need them today. I believe I have been as patient with this delay as I can be."

Orville took care not to look at me as I sat at the table across from our father. "Yes, yes, today, of course."

Wilbur set his knife on the table and scowled at his younger brother. "You have been telling me that for days."

"I'm sorry, brother. Like you, I get caught up in our work and forget minor tasks."

"It's not a minor task," Wilbur snapped. "There are notes on those pages that are necessary for our success."

"Katharine, when did you last see the papers?" Orville asked.

I narrowed my eyes at my brother. He wasn't going to put the blame for this on me. "I don't know that I have ever seen the papers. You patted where you kept them in your pocket at the train station, but I didn't see them. And I certainly didn't see any writing on them. Even if I had, I would not expect to understand it. I don't have the engineering mind the two of you have."

Father folded his newspaper and set it to the side. "I must say, I tire of hearing you argue about these drawings. Orville, go fetch them now and give them to your brother. If the three of you are going to act like children, I will treat you as such."

Orville pulled at his mustache, and sweat gathered on his brow. "I can't do that."

"Why not?" our father wanted to know.

I waited to see if Orville was going to make up yet another excuse. There had been so many by this point, I didn't know how he kept any of them straight in his head.

Instead, he surprised me by saying, "I can't, because I don't know where they are. I misplaced them, brother. This is why I haven't had them for you to review."

Wilbur stood up so quickly that he knocked his chair over. "You what? Orville, how could you be so careless? You know that we need the notes to continue developing the project."

"Maybe you can re-create them," Orville suggested. "If you thought of those ideas once, you can again. In fact, I know how ingenious you are. You will likely come up with something that is even better."

"Don't try to flatter me so that you can worm your way out of blame for this." Wilbur glared at Orville.

"I'm not," Orville said. "I take the blame. All of it."

Wilbur turned to me. "I expect you knew about this."

I lifted my chin. "I have been helping him look for the drawings, yes."

"Why haven't you found them? It shouldn't take long to search every possible location in the house."

I looked at Orville.

Orville's shoulders sagged. "They're not in the house. I took the drawings with me to the Shaws' Christmas party, and they were lost there. We haven't found them yet."

"You took them to the party! You are a fool!" Wilbur shook with anger. It wasn't often I had seen my brother so upset.

"Now, please. Let's all calm down," Father said. "Orville made a mistake, but he is your brother. It was not intentional."

"Those drawings could have been picked up by anyone at the party. How are we to know that someone won't use them for his own gain?"

"We don't know that," Father said. "But I doubt that many people could make heads or tails out of what you drew."

"It takes only one person to find those drawings and steal our ideas. They don't even have to understand the designs to sell them to the highest bidder."

"Orville has been trying to find them for you," I said.

"Why have you been lying to me all this time? That is worse than the lost drawings. As my brother and partner, I have to be able to trust you, and now I feel I cannot. How can we build a flying machine and operate it if we can't trust each other?"

"I trust you," Orville said.

"Yes, but I don't trust you. And I don't know if I will be able to in the future." Wilbur stormed out of the room.

Orville folded his cloth napkin and set it carefully next to his plate. "If you will both excuse me, I believe it's time for me to leave for the shop." He stood and left the room.

"I hope this doesn't mean Christmas is ruined," Father said.

I couldn't agree more. I had to find those drawings.

CHAPTER 32

When I left the house later that morning, Orville and Wilbur weren't speaking. They had both left for the bicycle shop in silence. As always when it came to my brothers, I felt it was my job to bring them back together. Unfortunately, this time I didn't know how I was going to do that. Wilbur was just as mad at me as he was at Orville over the lost drawings. I had kept the secret as well. In my mind, the only way I felt I could resolve the situation was by finding the missing drawings. It seemed to me that I needed to go back to the scene of the crime again.

I rode my bicycle to the Shaws' estate for a second time. The snow had stopped, and a deep freeze had fallen over the Dayton plains and rivers. The wind whipped over the flat road ahead of me and bit into my skin, and I was chilled to the bone when I arrived.

Shivering, I tucked my bicycle into the same spot where I'd stowed it the last time I was on the estate. This time, I wasn't planning on jumping into any bushes, but one never knew if it would be required.

After straightening my hat, I knocked on the door.

A moment later the young maid Maggie stood in front of

me. Her welcoming smile faded as soon as she saw my face. "You again?"

I arched my brow at her. "Is that any way to greet someone at the door?"

Her face turned bright red. "You're right. I'm so sorry. The past few days have been so difficult. Mrs. Shaw has taken to her sickbed. She won't even eat sweets."

The Yule cake Lenora's son had bought her came to mind. Apparently, it hadn't worked to lift his mother's spirits.

My glasses fogged up as soon as I stepped into the house. "Thank you for allowing me inside."

"It's cold," she said, as if that was reason enough.

I cleared my throat. "I would like to speak with Mrs. Shaw again. Is she in the conservatory? I know the way. There is no need for you to trouble yourself." I took a step in the direction of the hallway.

Maggie jumped into my path. "I don't think Mrs. Shaw will see you. As I have told you, she is unwell."

"That's what you said last time, and she agreed to see me right away."

"Yes, that was before . . . She hasn't been well. Recent events have been a strain on her nerves. Mr. Shaw had to call the doctor twice."

I took that to mean that Lenora had been given even more sedatives. No wonder the poor woman was confined to her bed.

"I very much want to see her. I can help."

"I can assure you that she doesn't need any more help. She has her servants, and she is under a doctor's care. We are doing all we can for her."

"I don't doubt that you are, but she might also need a friend. Companionship is just as important as medication when a person is ill. In fact, I believe it does even more than drugs to improve a patient's prognosis."

Maggie's shoulders sagged. "You may be right. She has been

lonely. It has broken my heart to see it. On a normal Christmas, she received call after call from friends, but there has been nothing since the party. I know people don't want to be associated with the family at this difficult time, but where is their compassion for their friend? You can go to her, but please don't tell anyone you pass that I let you in."

I promised her I would not. "Maggie, before you go, I have one more question."

She stared at me, as if she couldn't believe that I would dare make another request when she had granted my first one.

"The night of the party."

"Yes?" she said slowly.

"My brother Orville left his jacket in the parlor during the game of charades. When we went back for the jacket after the game, it was gone."

"People misplace items all the time when they come to parties. There's a little too much fun and a little too much to drink. Things are forgotten."

"Yes," I said. "Orville was distracted by the game. However, we found the jacket eventually."

She wrinkled her brow. "If you have the jacket, your problem is solved. Why are you telling me all this?"

"My brother had a sheaf of papers in his jacket pocket. It would have said 'Wright brothers' in the corner. Two of my brothers, Wilbur and Orville, are working on a project together, and those papers are essential to their work."

She eyed me. "I know they are making a flying machine. I read the newspapers."

"The papers weren't inside his pocket when we found the jacket."

"Perhaps they fell out. Guests misplace all sorts of things when they are here. I have worked in this house for two years, and I can promise you common sense goes out the window at these parties." She turned and walked away.

As she left, her back was straight as a board, but as she disappeared around the corner, her shoulders sagged and her head bowed, as if she were a deflated hot-air balloon.

My footsteps echoed on the parquet floor as I made my way down the hall to see Lenora. Each step sounded like a gunshot that reverberated off the high ceilings. Maggie seemed to think I shouldn't be there, so I increased my pace on the way to the conservatory. Maggie might have let me inside, but another servant or even a member of the family could easily show me the door.

Just like the last time I'd come, Lenora was lying on her chaise lounge in a silk robe in the conservatory. If my memory was correct, she was wearing the very same robe. I couldn't help but wonder if she had left the room since the last time I was there. The scent of the orchids covered the worst of it, but there was a sickening tobacco smell lingering in the air. I wondered if the smell came from her. Hadn't Benny said he had to hide his smoking habit from his mother because she hated it so much?

Moonlight, her large silver Persian cat, lay beside her with a protective paw on her side and stared at me with her amber eyes, as if she was daring me to make one false move.

Lenora's eyes remained closed, but she spoke. "Maggie, can you please thank Benny again for the cake and apologize to him that I didn't eat any of it. I'm just not hungry. He was a sweet boy to walk all the way to West Third Cakes for me. I know he was trying to cheer me up, but the only thing that will relieve my pain is knowing that my son is safe."

"Lenora, it's not Maggie," I said. "It's Katharine Wright from school."

She opened her eyes. They were bloodshot, which was very apparent because of their unusual green color. Dark circles hovered beneath her eyes. "Miss Wright, what are you doing here?"

I was relieved that she recognized who I was. I hadn't been

sure she would. "I came to check on you. The Christmas tree sale is later this afternoon, and I know you must be disappointed that you can't attend."

"I haven't decided yet if I will attend or not. I know Olive Ann has done a fabulous job of taking over the last few details, but I would like very much to be there. Shaws don't show weakness, and I believe not going is a sign of weakness. I wish my husband and son would accompany me so we could present a united front." She pressed a hand to her forehead as if gauging her own temperature. "Randolph would like me to stay home," she added bitterly.

"Will you be going to the dance at the club this evening?"

Lenora dropped her hand to her side. "No, I don't go to events at the club. I haven't for years. That's Randolph's place, and I want nothing to do with it. He's more married to the club than he has ever been to me. He loves that place much more than he ever loved his bride." She studied me. "How do you know about the dance tonight?"

"My girlfriend Agnes asked me to go with her. There is a young man there whom she likes very much."

"It is a good place to find a husband, if that's something you want."

"I'm not interested in husband hunting," I said. "Marriage is something that my friend wants, though. I am going to support her."

"You are a better friend than I would be. You couldn't pay me to set foot in that place. It's too stuffy, but then again, as I have told you, I came from much more humble beginnings than Randolph did. Being around all those pretentious men makes me uncomfortable."

If that was the case, I would have thought all the fancy parties she hosted at her house would make her uncomfortable too. Perhaps she felt those were different because she was the hostess?

She studied me. Her pupils were dilated, and she just missed making eye contact with me. I had to wonder how many shots the doctor had given her that day.

"Why are you here?" she asked.

"I told you that I wanted to check on you before the Christmas tree sale."

"That isn't the real reason. You have never checked on me about anything before this week. We're not friends." Her words were slightly slurred. "We don't travel in the same social circles. You have to have a better reason than that to come not once but twice to speak to me privately."

Despite the slowness of her speech and her tired eyes, Lenora was far more lucid today than the last time I had been there, and I was happy to see it.

"If you have something to say to me, say it. We don't have much time to speak. The doctor will be here soon with my second shot of the day."

"What kind of shot is he giving you?" I didn't even bother to keep the concern out of my voice.

"I don't know exactly, but it numbs the pain." She looked at me. "It all feels like one long day. There doesn't seem to be any beginning or end. It's just the same over and over again. And Benny is still in trouble."

"He's home now," I said.

"Yes, but for how long? Until I know that this is truly over and he is safe, I will worry."

I supposed that any mother in her position would feel the same way. It must be unbearable to know that your only child could spend the rest of his life in prison or, worse, face the death penalty, a possibility in Ohio.

"Are you sure you need the medicine the doctor gives you?" I asked tentatively. "In the time we've spent together, you have seemed all right. Upset, of course, but to help Benny, you must have your wits about you. I'm afraid the shots you are given rob you of your will."

"The doctor says it's what I need. Who am I to question

him? I am merely a wife and mother." She placed a hand on her cheek.

Moonlight looked up at her and shifted his silky body closer against her, as if he knew she needed protection. I was very much in agreement with Moonlight on that.

"I don't believe there is a 'merely' in that statement. Those are the most important roles in our society," I argued. "My mother had *only* those roles, and you could not have met a more ingenious and formidable woman. My brothers and I would not be where we are today without her, even if our time with her was shorter than it should have been."

"I thought once before that I failed at both." She stared at a bright pink orchid perched on the plant stand next to her chaise lounge.

I wanted to ask her what she meant by that, but I needed to get on with the real reason I was there. I certainly didn't want to be caught in the conservatory with Lenora when the doctor or, worse still, her husband arrived.

"I saw Benny yesterday."

She looked at me. "Where?"

"He came to the school while I was setting up for the Christmas tree sale. I think he wanted me to hear his side of the story."

"You are his teacher. He respects you and doesn't want you to think ill of him. I told the principal that when I met with him on Saturday. I thought it was important to clear the air about Benny's behavior before the Christmas holiday. Considering what we are dealing with now, it seems so trivial that I worried about his being kicked out of class. That night at the party, I wanted to speak to you in person to extend my apologies about Benny's behavior."

I remembered Langston saying that Lenora had been at Steele High School on Saturday to speak with the principal. It wasn't often that parents of high school students would ask for such a meeting, and as far as I knew, such meetings never happened on the weekend during a holiday break. I had supposed the urgency was to get me fired as quickly as possible. But Lenora had wanted to apologize for Benny's behavior? I couldn't have been more shocked.

I bit my lip. I should be apologizing to her for misjudging her, even though she had no idea that I had. I cleared my throat. "Benny told me what happened the night of the party, when he found Herman."

"Yes, he was just trying to help. He thought he was helping by removing the screwdriver. Anyone would have thought that."

Maybe not a doctor, I thought.

"I understand why the police are suspicious of him because of the compromising position he was in, but I still don't know why he would kill Herman," I said. "I have not been able to discover what his motive could possibly be."

She sat up, disturbing the cat in the process. Moonlight opened one eye and hissed softly to himself before curling up and going back to sleep.

"He didn't kill anyone. My son would not do that."

I held up a hand. "I know that. What I meant to ask is, What reason do the police have for thinking he murdered Herman? There has to be a motive. I suppose it's possible, but people don't just stab others for no reason at all."

"The police don't have a good reason." She twisted her handkerchief in her hand over and over again.

"The police accused him of murder with no motive to explain the action. They believe he killed Herman in cold blood because the opportunity arose. I don't believe that for one second."

She looked at her hands, and a single tear slid down her face. "He was trying to protect me. That is what the police say. Benny is always trying to protect me. He is the very best son, and I failed because I have not been able to protect him."

"Protect you from Herman?" I asked.

"From Herman revealing my secret," she said.

"What secret?"

To my surprise, she said, "There is no point in hiding it now. The police know. The men at the club know. The very worst is that Randolph knows. I am waiting for him to ask for a divorce."

My eyes went wide. "What could you have done to warrant that?"

"Benny is not Randolph's son."

I stared at her. Her tone was so matter of fact that I wondered if somehow I'd misheard her. "How?" I blushed. I knew how, yes. I wasn't that prudish that I didn't understand how children came into the world, but she was married. "You had an affair?" I guessed.

She shook her head. "No, no, I was always faithful to my wedding vows. I was pregnant with Benny before I married Randolph. He wanted to marry me. He made no secret of that when I met him at the factory, but he was fifteen years older than I, and I was in love with a boy my own age from back home. We loved each other and planned to get married just as soon as he could save up the money." She looked away from me. "He died in an accident before that could happen."

"What happened to him?"

"He drowned in the river." Tears came to her eyes. "A few weeks later, I realized I was expecting. I wanted to keep Benjamin's child. The baby would be all I had left of him. Marrying Randolph seemed like the only way out. I would marry him, and he would believe Benny was his. That is what happened."

"His name was Benjamin? That's your son's name."

She wouldn't look at me. "It was my way of honoring the man I really loved. In hindsight, I know it was a mistake to be so obvious about it. It must have been Herman's first clue that my marriage to Randolph wasn't all it seemed to be."

"How did Herman guess?"

"I think Randolph always suspected that he might not be the father because of the timing of Benny's birth and when we married. Over and over again, I repeated the story that Benny came early and what a blessing it was to have a baby so soon, especially considering the age difference between Randolph and me. I got married and had Benny. That was the end of the story until Herman showed up."

"He showed up how?"

"He started working for Randolph at the paper mill five or so years ago."

"What did he do?"

"Everything. He had his hand in everything concerning the business and Randolph's life. He even ate dinner with us twice a week. He was always around." She closed her eyes. "I did not like it, but who was I to argue with my husband on such a matter?"

I frowned. Something about that arrangement sounded off to me. "If he was so close to Randolph, why would he want to expose this secret about your family?"

She shook her head. "There was something calculating about him. To know Herman was to know he was always looking for an angle. He wanted to figure out how people ticked. At first, I thought it was because he was truly interested in people, but I soon learned it was just a way to manipulate them."

"Why did he want to manipulate you?"

"It wasn't me he was after. He was trying to hurt my husband. He wanted to embarrass him."

"Why?"

"I don't know, but he must have had a reason."

I didn't know if Lenora realized it or not, but she was making her husband look more and more like a suspect with everything she said. I'd had a bad feeling about Randolph from the start. I thought back to the night of the murder, when Benny was being arrested and Lenora was screaming to her husband for help. He had been nowhere to be found. Wouldn't a loving husband and father want to be there for his wife and child when they were in such distress?

She covered her eyes. "Before long, everyone will know the truth about Benny. My family is destroyed. Randolph told me today that he doesn't have a son. Soon he will ask for the divorce. I came from nothing and will return to nothing. All I have is Benny now, and the police will rip him away from me as well."

"Benny is Randolph's son," I argued. "He raised him like a son. He is the one who has been a father to him."

"That doesn't mean much to Randolph. He is furious with me. He said that I tricked him and made a fool of him."

"When did he say this to you?"

"The day before Herman died."

"How'd he find out?" I asked.

"Herman told Randolph and said that he was going to expose my secret to the club. That would destroy Randolph. His biggest point of pride is how well respected he is at the club. If his reputation were tarnished, he would never recover."

"But you said that everyone at the club knows."

"They do now because the police leaked the information. The police captain is a member of the club as well and told one of the other members. From there, one after another heard the news. It spread fast. It was the most scandalous thing anyone ever had to say about Randolph, and they were all enjoying his fall from grace. They enjoyed the fact that he was tricked into believing Benny was his."

It sounded to me as if the men in this club gossiped more than a roomful of teenagers, and from working at the high school, I knew how quickly rumors could pass through the building.

"Can I bring up a more difficult topic?"

She looked at me. "More difficult than my son possibly going to prison?"

"Perhaps not. But do you think the medicine your doctor is giving you actually helps?"

Tears gathered in the corners of her eyes. "It takes the pain away. It always has."

"Have you taken these injections before?"

"Many times. Randolph says that I need it for my nerves."

I balled my hands at my sides and for a moment was unable to speak. "Have you ever wanted to tell him no?"

"I can't do that. He's my husband. It is his job to know what is best for me."

The conservatory door opened, and a man in a dark suit, with a medical bag, walked into the room. "Mrs. Shaw, it is time for your shot." He looked at me over his reading glasses. "Would you like me to come back when your guest has left?"

"No, Doctor," she said. "I know you're a very busy man, and I know you don't have time to travel back and forth. I will take the shot now."

"What's the medicine?" I asked.

The doctor frowned at me. "It's just something to help calm her nerves."

"What is in it? What is the medicine called?"

"I'm not in the habit of sharing my patient's private information with anyone." He set his medical bag on a white wicker table and removed a metal box. He opened the box, and inside were half a dozen syringes and twice as many vials of cloudy-looking liquid. He picked up one of the syringes and removed the rubber cap on the needle. The needle glistened in the sunlight coming through the conservatory windows.

He filled the needle from one of the cloudy vials.

"Why does she need this?" I asked. "I think she is fine as she is."

The doctor scowled at me. "I don't believe this is your place, Miss . . ."

"Wright," I said. "Katharine Wright."

He stepped between Lenora and me. "It's not your place, Miss Wright."

Lenora pushed the sleeve up on her silk robe, and he plunged the needle into her arm. She winced, and when he removed the needle, she lay back on the chaise lounge and closed her eyes.

"You should rest well the remainder of the day," the doctor said.

I cleared the lump from my throat. "Lenora, I should be going to the Christmas tree sale. I'll look in on you again."

She didn't even notice when I left.

CHAPTER 33

I had just enough time to ride my bicycle home and change before the fundraiser. When I arrived at the event, snow was beginning to fall, and students and PTA members were already gathering in the gymnasium. Laughter and voices filled the air. Everyone was so excited, you could feel the Christmas spirit. I felt it, too, but my holiday cheer was dampened by my conversation with Lenora Shaw, and I was even more worried about Benny than I had been the day before.

Langston walked over to me, with Mae Bear in tow. Langston smacked the side of his leg every few feet to keep Mae Bear's attention. It was clear the collie was fascinated with the proceedings. She stopped often to sniff the air and stare at the crowd. I was happy with the turnout. It would be a good fundraiser for the school, and I was even happier that so many students were taking part on their Christmas holiday.

"You did a mighty fine job putting this together, Miss Wright," Langston said. "When I heard what you planned to do, I thought you'd never be able to pull it off. I said, 'The young folks aren't going to want to come back to school and volunteer when they are enjoying their Christmas break,' but here they are. Many more of them than I expected."

I smiled. "Thank you, Langston. I can't take all the credit. The ladies of the PTA spearheaded the sale, but I have to admit that I'm quite proud of the turnout, even if my father would say that pride is a personal failing."

"Oh no, you should be proud, and I overheard the principal and superintendent say they were impressed too." He lowered his voice. "I wouldn't hold your breath on their telling you that, though. You know how stingy they can be with compliments."

"I'm very well aware."

"Students! Students!" Olive Ann called. "It's time to go outside. Remember, sing clear and with a smile on your face. This is for the future of music at Steele!"

The excited chatter died down as the students took their places in line. Another PTA member handed out the sheet music to each student. The inside of the gymnasium was abuzz. It was moments like this when I loved being a teacher. I knew this event would be a forever memory for many of these students. They would look back at it happily and have fond memories of their time at Steele High School and of this particular day. In the end, the good memories were all the other teachers and I wanted them to take away from their time here.

Olive Ann led the students out of the building as they sang "The First Noel." It was only in that moment that my heart sank just a bit. It should have been Lenora at the front of the line. If only things had gone differently. I knew in my heart that even though she had wanted to, Lenora would not be at the school fundraiser that afternoon, not after the shot she had received from her doctor. I could not help but wonder how much had been stolen from her in the name of calming her nerves.

Benny was one of the students who had signed up to sing that afternoon, but I didn't expect to see him either. I couldn't say that I blamed him for deciding to stay away. His presence would take away from the event, as his arrest would be the main topic of conversation, and if the members of his father's club knew the truth about who his biological father was, it would not be long before that information reached the students. Perhaps this was the real reason Benny had said he could never show his face at the school again. He wasn't the son of a paper mill mogul but of two poor kids from Appalachia.

I followed the line of students outside and was happy to see that Langston had made a firepit in the middle of the schoolyard to keep folks warm.

The flames flickered on the faces of onlookers gathered around it for warmth. The students were leading the singing, just as I'd hoped they would, but a good number of guests were joining in. For five cents, someone could request a song, and I saw girls walk around the crowd with notepads and coin purses as they asked for requests and gathered the money. Others were collecting money for hot chocolate and coffee.

Everything was going perfectly. However, I didn't feel much Christmas cheer in my heart. Herman's murder still remained unsolved, Benny's life was in shambles, and I didn't have the faintest idea where my brothers' drawings were. To make matters worse, Wilbur and Orville weren't speaking to each other. It did not promise to be a very happy Christmas on Hawthorn Street, or on the Shaw estate, for that matter.

At this moment, there wasn't much more I could do about Herman's death, Benny's predicament, or my brothers' drawings. As for my brothers' fight, I wasn't touching that with a ten-foot pole.

Mae Bear stood proudly next to the students as they sang. She wore a big red bow around her neck and appeared to be quite pleased with herself. Behind the students, the Great

Miami River glistened in the late afternoon sun. It was three o'clock, and by five the sun would be completely gone until the next morning.

Olive Ann joined me at the edge of the schoolyard. "I'm so pleased with how everything is going. I only wish Lenora was here to see it too. She put so much work into this event."

"She did. She truly has a talent for planning."

"She would have to with all the parties she has to plan for her husband and his company. It surprises me that she has time for anything else. Those parties are incredibly elaborate."

"Have you been to one of the company parties?"

She nodded. "Many times. My husband's law firm used to represent the mill and the club, so the partners are invited to all the parties." She paused. "After what happened with my brother, my husband's law firm no longer represents either. Family loyalty always comes first."

"I can understand that," I said. I was doggedly loyal to my own brothers.

She wrinkled her nose. "There was a time before Gil was asked to leave the club that my husband, Cramer, was also asked to be a member. He couldn't, because he represented the club as their attorney. It was a conflict of interest, you understand. I was relieved he didn't join. Between his work and family, he had very little time for other interests. The club made it very clear that members had to spend a certain amount of time there to remain in good standing. Cramer also said the bylaws were always changing, and he wasn't happy with that."

"Who changed the rules at the club?"

She was quiet for a moment and then said, "Herman Wheeler. As far as I'm concerned, Herman Wheeler changed everything about that place, and Randolph Shaw just stood by and let him. Perhaps Randolph was tired of trying to please everyone. If Randolph had still been in charge, Gil would not have lost his place at the club."

"But Randolph was still the president when Herman was alive, wasn't he?"

"In name only." She waved at someone across the yard. "Oh, there is Mary Lee's mother. I must talk to her about the graduation celebration we are planning for our children. It's never too early to plan a party."

After Olive Ann walked away, I wondered if Herman's involvement in the club had led to his death. However, I had to admit at this point that it was Benny who had the best motive for wanting Herman dead; wanting to protect his mother from shame was a very strong motive.

As people began purchasing the trees we'd brought in, I shook these thoughts from my mind and walked around the schoolyard, chatting with onlookers about what the PTA planned to do with the money from the fundraiser. There would have to be many more events to raise the money for the music department, but I was gratified to see the community's support for the cause and the students who'd worked tirelessly to learn all the songs.

Across the parking lot, a young woman hurried down the sidewalk. She had her head bent, and her scarf was covering most of her face. Even with most of her face covered, I recognized Carrie Kayler immediately. I had told her about the event, but she hadn't expressed interest in coming. I would have brought her with me if I'd known she wanted to be here. Carrie was always a great help, and the extra set of hands would have been welcome.

I frowned. Was Carrie here to enjoy the caroling? Was her family buying a tree for their home? I didn't think so. Money was always tight in the Kayler home, and a tree would probably be too much of an extravagance. Finances had been so much of a concern for the Kaylers that Carrie had come to work for our family when she was just fourteen to help her parents with the bills. There had been times I felt guilty that I had hired a girl who was the same age as many of my students. She should have been in school, too, not working cleaning my home. However, her family needed the money.

I left the schoolyard and walked after Carrie. She looked visibly upset. I wondered what could be wrong. She was always such a cheerful girl.

I immediately thought of my brothers. They weren't getting along. Were they arguing? If that was the case, Carrie might be looking for me to put an end to it. Yes, that had to be the reason she had come. She must have gone around the back of the school because she thought I was still inside the building.

Next to the school was an empty lot with a few trees. It was school property and might be used in the future if the school were to expand, though I doubted it ever would. The building was too close to the river as it was, and flooding during the rainy springs in Dayton had been an issue from the day the school opened. Certainly, the school board would not want to move closer to the Great Miami River.

I spotted Carrie standing on the edge of the lot with another young woman.

Carrie was facing me, but I couldn't see the other girl's face. As I drew closer, I heard Carrie say, "I think you need to leave. Dayton isn't safe for you anymore."

"I will. Just a few more days. I want to know that she will be all right."

"What about you?" Carrie asked. "You have to think about yourself. You did nothing wrong."

I increased my pace. "Carrie?" I called.

Carrie looked at me, and the other girl turned.

I pulled up short. "Maggie?"

Maggie's face turned as white as the snow at her feet.

Neither of them spoke.

"What are the two of you doing here? Are you here for the caroling?" I asked.

Maggie recovered first. "Yes, that's why we are here. Isn't that right, Carrie?"

"Y-yes," Carrie stammered.

I frowned as I realized that this was the second time Carrie had lied to me. The first had been about the milkman. I hadn't even addressed that lie, and already she was lying again.

"The singing is at the front of the school," I said. "You two are in the wrong place."

"Oh," Maggie said. "That's good to know."

"I didn't realize you knew each other."

"We are old friends," Carrie said.

"Yes," Maggie replied. "Carrie has always been a good friend to me and has been here when I needed her." The way she said this suggested to me that she was sending some sort of message to Carrie. What the message was, I didn't know.

"How's Lenora?" I asked Maggie. "She wasn't well when I left the house."

"She's sleeping." Maggie looked over her shoulder. "I should return to the mansion and check on her. She's there alone. Mr. Shaw would not want her to be alone for long."

"But you didn't hear any of the singing," I said.

"It's quite all right. I mostly came to wish Carrie a Merry Christmas." She forced a smile. "We don't get to see each other much, as we both work long hours."

"You're welcome to visit Carrie at our home whenever you like," I said.

She looked at me, and I thought that there might be tears in her eyes. "Thank you. I appreciate how kind you have been. Carrie speaks very highly of you and your family. Not every girl can say that about her employers." She gave Carrie a tight hug. "Your friendship means everything to me. I could not have survived without you." Then she turned and ran down the sidewalk in the direction of the Shaws' home.

I turned to Carrie. "Carrie, what is going on?"

Her cheeks were bright red, but I didn't believe it was from the cold.

"Nothing is wrong, Miss Katharine," she said.

I didn't believe her. "Are you in any kind of trouble?"

She looked me in the eye. "No, but my friend might be."

CHAPTER 34

"Katharine!" Agnes called as soon as I walked through my front door an hour later. "I have your dress."

"Agnes, how did you get into the house?"

"Your father let me in. I love chatting with the bishop. He has the best stories of his travels. We had a nice chat over tea."

I smiled. My father wasn't much for the parties that I held for friends at our house, but he did like talking to them one-on-one. He approved of anyone who liked to hear about his travels. It also saved my brothers and me from hearing the same stories over and over again, so we also approved.

"Are the boys here?" I asked.

"I haven't seen them. I've been up in your room, getting everything ready, after my tea with the bishop."

I squinted at her. "What's everything? I thought you were only bringing me a dress."

"We have to do your hair too. You can't possibly wear it up in that schoolteacher bun."

"I am a schoolteacher."

"Not tonight you aren't. You're a young woman going to the Gem City Club Christmas Eve formal!"

I wasn't sure I liked the sound of that.

She waved me to the stairs. "We haven't much time."

Agnes raced up the stairs in her excitement, and I followed at a much slower pace. What I really wanted to do was go to the kitchen to see if Carrie was there. However, if my father was the one who'd let Agnes into the house, it was unlikely Carrie had returned from the Christmas tree sale.

I didn't believe for a moment that she and Maggie had been there for the caroling. They were up to something, and with Carrie's last ominous words, I feared Maggie was in some kind of trouble.

"Have you thought about going without your glasses? You have the prettiest, most intelligent eyes, and it's a shame that they are hidden behind those lenses."

"If you want me to be able to see, I will need my spectacles."

She sighed. "All right. Your hair will be so beautifully set that no one will notice your glasses."

"What is wrong with wearing glasses? I'm sure no one says to a man, 'You should take your glasses off to improve your looks.' It's ridiculous. Is female appearance more important than sight?"

She waved away my questions. "Don't ruffle your tail feathers over it!"

I sighed and followed Agnes into my bedroom. The dress she'd picked out for me lay across the bed. It was navy blue, with an embroidered high collar and oversized long sleeves.

"It has a black lace train that can be added to it."

"Don't push it, Ag. I'm not wearing a train," I grumbled.

She smiled. "I thought you'd say that. I will put it on my dress."

Her dress was similar to mine in cut but had cap sleeves and was cranberry red.

"These had to be expensive. Where did you find the money to pay for them?"

"I've saved my money from the paper store. The blue dress I wore last season, when I went to visit my cousin in Louisville. I can't wear it again."

"Why not?"

She blushed. "Because Arthur was there. He's already seen me in that dress."

I shook my head at the impracticality of it all. I wore the same two or three dresses every week. Everyone I'd ever met had seen me in the dress I had on today.

"You have a corset, don't you?"

I frowned. "Yes, but don't tie it too tight. Breathing is very important to me."

She smiled. "We have to find a way to make the dress fit. You're a touch thicker around the middle than I am."

I didn't like the sound of that one bit.

"Sit, sit, so I can do your hair first, and then we will worry about getting you into the dress."

The worrying part was the reason I was so concerned.

"What about your hair?" I asked. "I'm not going to the party to impress a man as you are. It's much more important that your hair be perfect, not mine. Your time would be much better spent on that."

"Oh, my hair won't take me but a few minutes. I put it up all the time. I could do it in my sleep. Your hair is going to be the greater challenge, as it has been tied back in a knot all day. It must be full of knots and snarls."

If she was trying to flatter me, she was doing a bang-up job of it.

I sat on my dressing table chair, and Agnes began removing the pins from my hair. Before too long, my brown hair fell down my back.

"Oh, Katie, when was the last time you brushed your hair?"

"I brush it every night before bed," I said defensively.

"How many strokes?"

"You expect me to count strokes?"

"Yes, everyone does."

"Not me," I said defiantly.

"You should brush it one hundred strokes, and you need to brush it in the morning, too, since it's so thick and long." She placed her brush at the back of my head and pulled.

"Ouch!" I cried.

"Don't be such a baby, Katie. Beauty is pain."

I muttered under my breath what I thought about that sentiment. "Whoever came up with that saying should be the one sitting here right now being tortured."

She didn't even bother to respond to my comment. "I'm beyond excited about the party tonight. Thank you again for agreeing to go. The thought of going by myself is terrifying. I've never been to such a fancy place before. It's so kind of you to go as Arthur's friend's guest. He was so happy when I told him. And you never know, you might like him very much, and then we could have a double wedding."

I much preferred her yanking at my hair to suggesting the idea of a double wedding.

"I very much doubt that will be the case," I said. "But I'm happy to go. Maybe it will take my mind off things."

"You mean Benny Shaw, poor dear."

"Among other problems," I said vaguely and then changed the subject. "You're certain that Arthur will be there?"

"Yes, he promised he would be," she said. "He was the one who asked me to come. I had a good conversation with Arthur yesterday."

In the mirror, I saw her face flush.

"Oh, and what was that conversation about?" I asked and then winced as she ran her brush through my tangled locks. Maybe the double wedding conversation wasn't that bad after all.

"I think he might propose this Christmas. He said that he's making great plans for the future."

"What?" I jerked back, and the bristles of her brush raked the back of my head.

"Hold still, or you are going to get hurt."

"I'm already hurt," I complained. "What do you mean, he's going to propose? That seems awfully quick. When we went to the Shaws' party, you were just hoping to catch his eye, and now he wants to marry you!"

"We were close during the season I spent in Louisville with my cousin. At the time, I thought he might even propose then, but he said he wasn't ready to settle down. I was heartbroken, but he said he wanted to be sure he could support a wife and family. He says now that he's confident about his future. He's even having a house built in the Oakwood neighborhood."

"That's practical," I said, thinking of my brothers Reuchlin and Lorin and how they married young and had struggled to make ends meet for their families ever since. Many times, I thought if they had waited to start their families, they would be farther ahead in life now.

Not that I begrudged them their marriages. I loved my nieces and nephews dearly.

"He must be doing very well if he's building a house," I said.

"He is. He's moved up in society very quickly. It's startling. You know that he came from nothing."

"I didn't. I can't say that I know much about him at all."

"He's self-made. He's putting himself through medical school on his own. That is very hard, you know."

"When will he be done with school?"

"I don't know."

I frowned. If I was about to marry a man, I would want to know everything about him, but I knew Agnes was different. She was in love with the idea of love. I prayed the stars in her eyes wouldn't get her in trouble farther down the road.

She stepped back. "Done!"

I put my glasses back on and gazed into the mirror. Agnes had arranged my hair in a pile of curls on the top of my head, held in place with countless hairpins. The style was set off by my mother's jeweled combs. "I look like my mother," I said.

"And she was a very pretty woman indeed." Agnes clapped her hands. "I will quickly do my hair, and we can put on our dresses!"

Agnes's excitement was contagious, and I found myself smiling.

After Agnes finished her own hair, which was done in the same pile of curls as mine but was adorned with feathers and ribbon, she undressed. "We need to tighten your corset if you want to fit into that dress."

I frowned. "Fine." I wasn't one for a tight corset, especially when I was teaching and moving around the classroom. Breathing was an important part of life to me. However, this was just one night, and Agnes was so excited that I agreed to the tightening.

She turned me around and yanked on the strings at my back.

I held my breath. "Be careful. I don't want a broken rib!"

"You can't actually get a broken rib from a corset. That's just a rumor. I have never met anyone who experienced such a thing." She pulled even harder.

"That's because the women are too embarrassed to tell the truth about how they fit into their impossibly small dresses."

"Oh, Katie—"

There was a knock on the door. "Girls, is everything all right in there?" my father asked. "I keep hearing shouting."

"We are fine," I grunted. "Ag is just torturing me."

"All right. Carry on." His footsteps receded down the corridor.

"I'm not tightening it more than I absolutely have to in

order to button the dress." She yanked one more time and tied the corset strings off. "There! Now, put the dress on and we will see if we have to tighten it any more."

"Good heavens, I hope we don't. I feel like a sausage in its casing."

I stepped into the dress, and she helped me pull it up. It took some doing, but she was able to button the back.

"It's still a little snug around the middle," Agnes said. "And I'm not saying you're a big person at all, Katie. You are very thin. Our shapes are just different."

That was one way of putting it.

She started to unbutton the dress. "Two more pulls and we should have it."

"Oh no." I hopped away from her. "We will have none of that. It's fine the way it is. I'm not going to this dance to impress anyone. You are. I am simply going as your friend. My only request is that I not be in pain. I don't believe that's too much to ask."

She dropped her hands and sighed. "Very well." She smiled. "It is going to be a night to remember, Katie. This night will change my life."

What we didn't know at the time was it was a night that would change all our lives, and not for the better.

CHAPTER 35

Before we left for the dance, I stopped in the kitchen to see if Carrie was there. I didn't expect to find her, as it was after dinnertime, but I was disappointed all the same. I was worried about her. I was also curious as to why she had never told me that she was friends with Maggie Courtier when she knew I had been to the Shaws' estate so many times recently. She also knew I was looking into Herman Wheeler's death.

It made me wonder if Maggie had seen something the night Herman died. If so, had she told the police? Had the police even spoken to her about the murder?

So often, servants were overlooked. That was even more likely to happen in a large home like the Shaws', where there were so many servants.

I found Agnes in the living room, peeking out the window. "Oh good. You're here. The hansom cab is out front waiting for us." She pulled up short. "Is everything all right? You look troubled."

"I'm fine. I'm just worried about Carrie. I saw her earlier today, and she wasn't herself."

Agnes relaxed. "I'm sure it's only the Christmas season. For some, this time of year can be difficult. Is everything well with her family?"

"She hasn't mentioned any problems at home, but I haven't asked either."

Agnes opened the front door. "Talk to her after the holiday. With all the excitement of your brothers' return, it must be a lot to care for four people when she was just used to you and your father for so many weeks. Perhaps she needs a few days off."

I nodded. Giving Carrie time off wasn't a bad idea.

After thanking the driver, we climbed into the cab and set off for the club.

I was quiet during the ride and looked out the window as we traveled along the river. The flames from gas lampposts reflected off the parts of the inky water that were frozen in place.

Our arrival at the club this time was much different from my first visit. I was much relieved to see a different footman at the entrance. I had been bracing myself to run into Samuel again.

Agnes anxiously pulled at the hem of her silk gloves as the footman looked over her invitation.

He then handed the card back to her and stepped back to let us in. "We hope you have a good evening."

Agnes smiled politely and went inside.

There was no entry hall leading into the club from the front doorway. We were in the ballroom the moment we stepped inside.

The space was like the grand ballroom of a castle. I knew there were other rooms in the building, but the ballroom, with its high dark-beamed ceiling and polished marble checkerboard floor, had to take up the majority of the building.

"It looks like it's set up for a wedding," I said.

Round tables surrounded the dance floor, and each one of them had an elaborate red and gold floral centerpiece in the middle. A giant Christmas tree stood against one wall. I guessed it was at least eighteen feet high. Lit candles glowed on its branches. None of this had been here the day I broke inside. It was amazing what the staff had been able to do in such a short amount of time.

A band played in one corner of the room, but at the moment, no one was dancing. The space was only half full as more and more guests arrived. The giant fireplace I'd noted before was lit tonight. I had only ever seen one that big in pictures of medieval castles. Three men could have stood inside it without hitting their heads.

Agnes looked around, searching every face for Arthur's.

I couldn't say how I felt about the possibility of Agnes getting married to Arthur Bacon. I wanted her to be happy, yes, but Arthur was ambitious. I feared if he ever thought Agnes might hold him back socially or in any other way, he would leave her. I hoped that was a groundless fear.

A footman appeared at our sides. "Can I take your coats?" He gasped. "Miss Wright."

I removed my coat. "Hello, Samuel. It's so nice to see you again." I smiled.

Agnes and I handed Samuel our coats, and I said to Agnes, "Samuel is one of my former Latin students from Steele. He graduated last year." I looked at him. "Isn't that right, Samuel?"

He swallowed. "Yes, ma'am."

"How nice to see one of your old students, Katie," Agnes said. "I told you coming to the formal would be worthwhile for you."

Samuel took the coats and hurried away.

I hoped that he would try to avoid me the rest of the night. It would be best for both of us.

"Everything is so fancy," Agnes whispered as she looked around the room. "Did you ever imagine that we would be in a place like this?"

I hadn't. When I was a student at Oberlin, there were many fancy parties and galas I attended, but I never thought I would enter a gentlemen's club. The crowd was certainly older than the students at those college parties. I guessed that Agnes and I were some of the youngest people in the room. Most of the men appeared to be in their forties and fifties. The women were far younger, although there were a few wives who were of a more appropriate age for the men present.

Agnes gripped my arm. "There he is!"

I turned in the direction she was staring and spotted Arthur Bacon standing across the room, with his hands in his suit pockets, leaning against the wall. When he saw Agnes, his face broke into a smile, and he began to walk toward us.

She spun me around to look at her. "How do I look? How's my hair?"

"Agnes, we just got here. There hasn't been enough time for your hair to fall out of place."

She patted her curls self-consciously all the same.

"Agnes, you are lovely this evening. When I saw you, my breath caught," Arthur said.

She blinked up at him as if she were unable to speak.

"It's nice to see you again, Arthur," I said.

He turned to me. "You too, Katelyn."

"Katharine," I corrected.

"Yes, I'm glad that you were able to come with Agnes. I would have picked her up at her home myself, but you know how people talk."

Agnes looked around his shoulder. "Where is your friend? Katie is eager to meet him."

Not that eager, I thought.

"Oh, I'm sorry. I forgot to tell you. He has a touch of the flu and wasn't able to come." He gave me a lopsided smile. "I am sorry about that, Katharine. Maybe we can double-date another time."

I shook my head. "That's not necessary. Really." I paused. I was far more concerned about something else he'd said.

"Did you want Agnes to arrive separately because you were afraid club members would pair you together as a couple?" I arched my brow.

"Katie," Agnes gasped.

"No, of course not." He smiled at Agnes. "I would just like to keep our relationship private for as long as we can. It's more special that way. Don't you agree, my sweet?"

"Oh, yes." Agnes beamed.

"I don't agree," I said. "It looks like you might be up to something."

"Katie!" Agnes glared at me.

Arthur laughed. "Please don't be vexed at her, Agnes. She's just defending her friend. I admire that."

"If you do admire it, I believe you should be a little more forthcoming about your intentions toward Agnes."

"When the time is right, certainly. For now, the dancing is beginning." He held out his arm. "Agnes, will you do me the honor of this waltz?"

"Yes," she said and then shot an angry glance in my direction.

It seemed to me that it would be a long ride home in the hansom cab.

Arthur and Agnes joined the other guests on the dance floor, and I sighed. I hadn't meant to upset Agnes, but at the same time, I wanted Arthur to know that he had to take her feelings into account. I still wasn't certain whether he really cared about her or was just taking advantage of her obvious adoration of him. I was concerned he didn't really intend to propose and was only stringing Agnes along.

I walked over to the food table and made some selections of the desserts.

"Did you come here with Agnes Osborne?"

I had a cream puff in my mouth and chewed it as quickly as I could before responding. "Yes," I croaked.

The woman, who was older than I, pressed her lips together. "I would appreciate if you would tell her to stay away from my little brother."

I set the cream puff that was in my hand back on the plate. "Excuse me?"

"Agnes—she needs to stay away from Arthur. As her friend, you ought to tell her that."

I stared at her. "I will do no such thing."

"You will." She shook her finger at me. "My husband's family are longtime members of this club, and he had to pull countless strings to get my brother inducted. Arthur and I don't come from high society. My husband helped us both get where we are today. I can't have Agnes pulling him back into the working class."

She said "working class" as if it was the ultimate insult.

"Who are you?"

"Claudine Kezler. Don't you forget what I told you," she said and stomped away.

Agnes was right: Arthur's sister really was awful.

CHAPTER 36

With a glass of punch in hand, I walked around the hall, looking for anything that would give me a clue as to who in this club might have wanted Herman dead. It was no secret that Herman had made a meteoric rise in the club and Dayton society. How he'd accomplished that was the burning question. I thought of the note that I'd discovered in the boardroom. It had said, *I need more time. It should all be settled by the New Year.* The note had had no date on it. I wished it had, but I believed that it was written before Herman was killed, or at least before the writer knew Herman was dead. Who would write a note to a dead man?

As I made my second lap around the hall, I spotted Randolph Shaw standing in a corner of the room with a balding man. Randolph was wearing a black coat with tails, and his trousers were freshly pressed. I realized Randolph was still my number one suspect. Perhaps I was biased because of the way he treated his wife and son; that wasn't completely fair. But my suspicion remained.

I stepped behind the large Christmas tree a few feet from the two men. It was the perfect place to eavesdrop without being seen.

"The club will recover," the balding man said to him. "We hate to lose one of our members, especially one so young and with so much promise. We expect the old fellows to die off one by one, but he was only forty if he was a day."

"It's a tragedy, of course, but I believe that everyone in the club is breathing easier now that Herman is no longer in the picture." Randolph held up his glass of bourbon and said, "I personally had been wanting to let him go from the mill for months but had had no way to do it."

"Yes, yes, I could see how that would have been a problem." The other man paused. "Am I right to assume that things at home are better with him gone?"

"I'm breathing easier."

I wrinkled my brow. He was breathing easier because Herman was dead? And life had been more stressful when Herman was alive than now, when his only child might be going to prison for the rest of his life? Was that what I was hearing?

Of course, considering what Lenora had admitted to me about Benny's real father, perhaps Randolph didn't consider Benny his true son. If that was the truth, it was a terrible shame as Randolph was the only father Benny had ever known.

"The club will need firm leadership after this tumultuous time. I know Herman was poised to lead by the New Year."

By the New Year. There was that phrase again, the one written in the note I'd found.

"The club," the balding man went on, "will want you to take the reins again. You have the most experience."

A smile curled on Randolph's lips. "I'm happy to be of service any way I can."

My brow shot up. Had Randolph killed Herman in order to secure his presidency of the club?

"The young members will need to be convinced, of course."

Randolph sipped his drink, and when he lowered his glass, he said, "The young are clamoring for change, but when they see how much effort it requires, they give up. The one compliment I can give Herman is that he was dogged in his pursuit of success, whatever the cost."

"Good. Good," the other man said. "This news comes as a relief. I didn't have the money—"

I leaned forward, and one of the branches I was hiding behind broke. I lost my balance, and the tree toppled over, scattering glass ornaments across the marble floor. Several men jumped into action, snuffing out the candles with their boots before anything could catch fire. One stamped on a tiny flame on the hem of my skirt. I would always be thankful to him for his quick action.

I lay on top of the fallen tree, with the pine needles digging into my skin.

"Miss Wright, what on earth have you done?" Randolph asked.

Two men helped me to my feet. I brushed soot and pine needles from my skirt. "I'm so sorry. I—I was walking around the tree, admiring all the ornaments. In my clumsiness, I tripped and fell into it, causing it to fall."

While I spoke, a team of servants were cleaning up the mess, and the tree itself was whisked away. I was sorry to see it go. It really was a beautiful Christmas tree.

"I just feel horrible," I said. "It was such a gorgeous tree."

"Katie," Agnes gasped as she and a number of other guests ran over to see what all the commotion was about.

"I'm fine." I looked down at the dress I was wearing. "I'm so sorry about your dress."

"Don't you worry at all about that. When I heard that someone had tripped over the Christmas tree, I knew it had to be you. You could have caught on fire."

Looking at the burned hem of my skirt, I said, "I almost did."

She put a hand to her chest. "Oh, Katie! How frightening."

"I'm glad you are unharmed, Miss Wright," Randolph said, but his tone told me that he was thinking the exact opposite. "We would not want you injured." He looked me up and down. "I must say I'm surprised to see you here. Your brothers are not members of the club." He said it in such a way as to imply that my family had no chance of becoming members of the club. I could assure him my father and brothers had no interest in joining, but I didn't want to waste my breath.

I lifted my chin. "I'm here as a guest."

"Of whom?"

"Arthur Bacon," I said.

"Yes," Agnes said, coming to my defense, even though her voice did shake a bit. "Arthur invited me and said I could bring a friend. He knew he might be occupied for much of the night with speaking with members."

"I imagine he would. He was Herman Wheeler's protégé of sorts, and Herman knew how to work the room better than anyone."

I wrinkled my brow. "What do you mean by that?" I asked.

He ignored my question and asked one of his own. "Why isn't Arthur with you, making sure you don't destroy the hall? Where is he?"

"He is with another guest at the moment," Agnes said.

"Wily young man to invite two young women," a portly fellow said. "That's not how they did things in my day."

"I should say not," another agreed.

Part of me wanted to tell them I was there as the guest of Arthur's friend, who had gotten sick at the last moment, but I thought it was best to save my breath.

Samuel hurried over to the tree with a broom and a dustpan. He pulled up short. "Miss Wright?"

"Samuel," I said. "We have to stop meeting this way."

Randolph scowled at Samuel. "Stop chatting and clean this up."

Samuel ducked his head. "Yes, sir."

"Please excuse me," I said. "Agnes and I must do some-

thing about this dress if we are to have any hope of saving it."
I wrapped my arm around Agnes's shoulders and steered her
away.

We went out of the ballroom, and found ourselves in a
narrow hallway that led to the kitchen. Pots, pans, dishes,
and spoons clanged together inside. Waiters hurried back
and forth as they made their way in and out of the ballroom.

"Agnes!" I grabbed my friend's arm. "Money. It's about
money. I should have known that all along."

She squinted at me. "What are you talking about? What
money?"

"The money that got Herman killed. Money has to be the
reason he's dead. It's the oldest motive in the book. I should
have thought of that right away."

"Can't I enjoy one night without your speaking about this
murder?" she asked.

"Agnes, this is a major revelation. If the motive is money,
Benny is innocent." I glanced back at the doorway from
where we'd come. Concerned we might be able to be overheard, I pulled her into the kitchen where the noise of the
staff would drown out our words.

She frowned. "I just want to spend time with Arthur. He's
told me that I shouldn't get involved in all of this. He heard
that you were asking questions. It could upset members of
the club and ultimately reflect badly on him."

I stared at her. "It will reflect badly on him if I ask questions?"

She wrung her hands. "You are his guest here."

"But, Ag, I have to find out what happened."

She looked me in the eye. "Why? What does it have to do
with you really?"

I couldn't tell her about my brothers' lost drawings. I didn't
want to tie them to the crime in any way. Instead, I gave my
other reason for being involved. "Benny is one of my students."

Her face softened. "I know that you care about your students, and I admire that. I really do." She took a breath. "But for Arthur's sake, please leave me out of it." She left the kitchen.

I stood on the edge of the room and watched the staff run this way and that with hot plates and empty glasses. I hoped this murder didn't cost me my friendship with Agnes.

CHAPTER 37

Because I had been in the club before, I knew where the back servants' entrance was off the kitchen. I needed fresh air after that close call with the lit Christmas tree, so I left the kitchen and went out the back door. As soon as I was outside, I regretted my decision, as I didn't have my coat or scarf to shield me from the cold. I wished I knew where Samuel had put our coats. I turned back to the door, only to find it locked. I knocked. No one came. I knocked even louder. Still no one came. I could hear laughter and the clatter of pots and pans on the other side of the door. No one could hear me.

I'd certainly placed myself in a pickle.

After one more futile attempt at pounding on the door, I realized that the only way I was ever getting back inside the club was through the front door.

The building was massive, and it took me several minutes to trudge around it through the snow. I was halfway there when I came upon the window where I had been stuck. My toes were numb from the snow, and my arms and fingers ached from the cold. Even so, I could not stop myself from going up to the window to see if the note that had been addressed to Herman was still on the table.

A soft yellow light glowed from the boardroom window. I walked over to it and peeked around the corner of the window-sill. The envelope with Herman's name on it was no longer on the table, but there were three men in the room. I recognized only one of them, Randolph Shaw.

He sat at the head of the table, while the other two men remained standing. They were speaking, but I couldn't hear what they were saying.

I knew it was a risk, but I had to know what they were saying. I pushed up on the window, and to my surprise, it opened just a crack.

"What was that?" one of the two men asked.

"It's nothing," Randolph assured him. "Just noise from the party. It has been a resounding success."

"And it's a fresh start without Herman," the first man said. "I wish I could get back the payments I'd already made him."

"We're not getting any of that money back," the second man said.

"It's unlikely," Randolph agreed. "It is nice to know that all that trouble has come to an end."

"But has it?" the second man asked. He was at least six inches taller than his counterpart. "How do we know that he was working alone?"

Randolph laughed, as if that was the most ridiculous question he'd ever heard. "Herman never worked with anyone. Maybe if he had, he wouldn't be dead."

I clapped a hand over my mouth to stifle a gasp. Was I hearing Randolph confess to murder? Had he killed Herman just to keep him from taking over the club? Was the club really that important to him? It sounded to me as if all three of them had been making payments to Herman for a long while. He had to have been blackmailing them. How many other club members had he extorted? There had to be over one hundred members of the club. Did this make every last one of them a suspect? I felt I finally had the true motive for

Herman's murder, but it increased the number of suspects exponentially.

A cold wind brushed my cheek and ruffled the drapes on the other side of the open window.

"Why on earth is there a window open in the middle of December?" Randolph asked.

"I'll shut it," one of the men said.

I jumped away from the window and pressed my body back against the cold stone of the building. I turned my head away, wincing as I waited to be found out. Maybe in my mind I thought that if I couldn't see them, they couldn't see me.

The window slammed closed, and I heard the lock slide home. I would not be getting back into the building through that route, not that it had worked for me before.

I waited there in the cold for a few more minutes, and then I lifted my skirts, which were soaked up to my knees by this point, and continued making my way around the building.

I sighed. I did have a knack for making things more difficult for myself. It was also safe to say that Agnes's dress was done for.

As I made the last turn around the building, I saw a small form running toward the entrance, then banging over and over again on the door.

"Please! Let me in! I have to speak to Mr. Shaw!" a woman's voice cried.

The footman opened the door just a crack. "This is a private club and event. Nonmembers and guests are not permitted without a written invitation." He slammed the door shut.

I walked up to the door and was astonished to see that it was Maggie Courtier, the Shaws' maid, who was knocking on the door with such ferocity.

"Maggie?" I asked.

She turned and looked at me. "You again? Must you be everywhere?"

"I could be asking you the same question. What's wrong?"

"Mrs. Shaw isn't well. She's seeing things. I ran for the doctor, but his wife said he was on an emergency call on the other side of the city. I don't know what to do, and Mr. Shaw must come home to help her."

I stepped around her and tried the door. It was locked, just like every other exterior door of the building that I had tried. It certainly made me wonder why security at the club was so tight.

However, when I knocked on the door, I did so politely, and the footman, not Samuel this time, thank heavens, opened it wide. "May I help you?"

"Yes, you may," I said. "I came out one of the side doors of the club for some fresh air and was not able to get back inside. I'd like to come in."

The footman looked me up and down. "You can't be a guest."

"I can assure you that I am. I just happened to fall on a Christmas tree a little while ago."

"Oh!" he said. "I heard that some clumsy young woman tripped and fell into the tree. Nearly caught herself on fire."

I held up my singed skirts. "As you can see from the state of my appearance, that woman was me."

"You can come back in to collect your things. The staff has been advised to escort you out if we see you."

"Whyever for?"

"I don't ask questions like that."

"Who told you this?"

"The order came from Mr. Shaw himself."

That didn't surprise me in the least.

At the mention of Randolph, Maggie bolted forward through the open door and into the hall.

"Stop!" the footman yelled, but it was far too late.

She stood in the middle of the dance floor in her long black dress, white apron, and worn navy coat, looking around the room. "I'm trying to find Mr. Shaw! Where is Mr. Shaw?"

Randolph appeared at the edge of the dance floor. "What is this all about? Tonight was supposed to be a happy celebration of the Christmas season, but we've had one disruption after another." He turned and glared at me standing by the door. "I blame you for that, Miss Wright. Are you the one who asked my maid to come here?"

I stepped forward. "I had nothing to do with her arrival, but I do believe you should hear her out."

"Very well." He turned to Maggie. "Maggie, come here and stop making a scene. We can discuss this in the library." He started to walk away.

When Maggie didn't follow him, he turned and snapped, "Come with me!"

As Maggie walked past me, she stared at me. There was something in her look that said she wanted me to follow her. I had been planning to do it regardless.

Randolph stepped into the wide hallway with the photographs of club members. I noted that one of the photographs was gone. It was that of Herman. The club was making a conscious effort to erase any memory of him.

He went into the first room off the hallway. Maggie followed him, and just before the door closed, I slipped my shoe into the opening and stopped it.

I hadn't anticipated how heavy the door was, and it pinched my toes. I bit down on my lip to stop from crying out. A doorstop sat by the wall. I reached for it and wedged it in place to hold the door open a crack in place of my foot.

I peeked inside. It was a gorgeous library, with floor-to-ceiling bookshelves and even more stacks of bookshelves in the middle of the room. If I'd had more time to explore the rows and rows of books, I would have. Every surface and every placard and award was free of any sign of dust. The books stood on the shelves with straight spines pointed at the ceiling.

Randolph folded his arms. "What is this about?"

"It's Mrs. Shaw. She is so upset. She's wailing and crying. I can't calm her down. She's making herself sick. You need to come back home to help her."

"Isn't Benjamin home with her? He can tend to her."

"No," Maggie said and held her small hands in front of herself, as if she was trying to stop the tremors that racked her body.

"He is supposed to be at home. It was one of the stipulations for his bail. Does he want to cause me more trouble than he already has?" Randolph slapped his hand on the top of a desk.

Maggie jumped. "Please go to her. I was afraid to leave her. I went for the doctor, but he is away on another emergency. She is distraught. I am afraid of what she might do."

"You should have run for an ambulance instead of coming to me. If she's not well, there is nothing I can do about it. She needs to be in a facility. I have been saying that for years."

"But she is your wife."

"A legality only, I can assure you." He stood a little straighter. "Go back to the house and sit with her until I come home. I will be there in a few hours. This event is important for the club, and I can't leave."

"Someone needs to come to the house. Mrs. Shaw is not well. I am worried about her."

"The doctor said she might have hallucinations from the medicine, but there is nothing to be concerned about. Over time, the side effects will lessen. The doctor has told me this."

"But, sir," Maggie said, "she needs help now."

"Maggie, I will not say this to you again. Go back to the house. This is not the place for you. They shouldn't have even let you in here."

By this point, I had heard enough and barged into the room. "Maggie, I will go with you to the Shaw mansion and check on Lenora."

Randolph glared at me. "Do you just make it a point to show up where you aren't wanted?"

"Sometimes, yes," I said. "I will go check on your wife, as you are too busy to bother."

"What do I care? It will give you crazy women a chance to commiserate."

"Even if you aren't worried about Lenora, what about Benny? He will be terrified to come home and find his mother in such a state."

"He is not my son." He narrowed his eyes at me. "But I am sure you already know that, don't you?"

I said nothing in return.

CHAPTER 38

When Maggie and I were alone, I asked, "How did you get here?"

"I hitched a ride with one of the stablemen who was headed home," she said softly.

I raised my brow. "And how were you planning to get back to the mansion?"

Her shoulders sagged. "I didn't think that far ahead. I just knew that I needed help. Mr. Shaw was the only person I could think of to ask. I should have known better than to come to him."

"There is a line of hansom cabs waiting for the ladies and gentlemen to leave the dance. We will take one of them."

"I don't have the money for that."

"I do, but before we leave, I have to tell my friend. I need to make sure she can get home safely."

She nodded. "I understand, but please hurry. I am truly concerned about Mrs. Shaw."

I nodded and went back into the great hall. I spotted Agnes on the dance floor, enjoying a slow waltz with Arthur. I didn't know what it was about the man I didn't like. He was polite, poised, professional, and certainly good looking, but there was just something about him that put me off. The feeling had only grown worse when Randolph said that Arthur had been close to Herman. *Protégé* was his exact word. *Protégé in what*? I wondered.

I tapped Agnes on the shoulder.

She turned. "Katie, are you all right?"

"I'm fine." I cleared my throat. "I'm going to take a hansom cab and leave with Maggie, the Shaws' maid." Then I explained why Maggie had come to the club.

"And you want to check on Mrs. Shaw?"

I nodded.

Arthur frowned at me. "She's probably just fine. I don't see her husband going."

"I wouldn't base my choices on the ones Randolph Shaw makes," I said.

"Yes, you should go," Agnes said. "I'll get a cab home. There should be many outside at the end of the dance."

"I will make sure Agnes gets home safely," Arthur said.

"Please do that." I left them on the floor before he could answer me.

It took me some time to track down a servant to retrieve my coat.

Maggie waited for me outside the club. It seemed that she preferred the frigid cold outside to the warm hall with the wealthy of Dayton society.

"There you are," she said. "We should hurry."

I nodded and tripped down the steps to the cab in my sodden skirts. I wished that I could go home and change my dress. I was uncomfortable and was certain that I looked a fright too. But there was no time for any detours. We had to go straight to Lenora.

"Please take us to the Shaw mansion as quick as you can," I told the driver and rattled off the address. "If you can make the trip in less than twenty minutes, I will double the fare."

Just as Maggie and I sat down on the bench seat, the driver shook the reins hard, and the carriage jerked forward. We fell back in the seat.

"Are you all right?" Maggie asked.

I rubbed my back. "I'm fine. The corset kept me upright. I suppose they are good for something."

The driver must have been very excited about the chance of double payment, because we crossed through the estate's highly polished gates in record time.

He stopped in front of the grand house, leapt from his seat, and threw open the cab door. "We arrived in eleven minutes, miss."

"Well done," I replied. I paid him what I'd promised, gave him an extra quarter, and asked him to wait for my return. I hoped very much that my stay at the Shaw home would be brief, just long enough to reassure myself that Lenora was well and safe.

The driver promised he would wait.

I followed Maggie toward the house. Instead of going in the front door, as I expected she would, she skirted around the Tudor-style home. As if she could read my mind, she said, "The front door is always locked this time of night, and the back door is closer to the conservatory, where Mrs. Shaw is."

"She's still in the conservatory at night, when it's so cold? It has to be chilly in there."

"She's there all the time, no matter the season. She told me once that it was the only room in the house that she ever thought was truly hers. Mr. Shaw has no interest in plants and never goes there."

"If he never goes in there and she rarely leaves, how do they spend time together?" I asked.

She looked over her shoulder at me. "They don't. They never have in all the time I have worked for them."

"And how long has that been?"

"Two years now. Two years in January, I should say. I have loved my position with the Shaws until recently."

I wanted to ask her what she meant by that, but we came upon a door, and she opened it. We stepped inside, and I found that we were inside a kitchen that was as big as the main floor of my home. It held every cooking utensil a person could imagine, and the room was spotless. There was nary a crumb on the floor.

As if she could read my thoughts, Maggie said, "The cook takes great pride in running the kitchen well. She and the staff always clean it top to bottom at the end of each day. She is great friends with the baker Mrs. Appleton. They remind me of each other."

I raised my brow. Perhaps it was through the cook that Mrs. Appleton was able to gather so much gossip about the Shaws.

"The conservatory is just down the hall."

I followed Maggie through the kitchen, down the hall, and into the conservatory. There was no way I could have prepared myself for what I saw when we stepped into the grand room.

CHAPTER 39

Popular, smart-aleck Benny Shaw sat at his mother's feet, in tears. "I don't blame you. None of this is your fault."

His mother, who was equally upset, shook her head. "It is. It is my fault you're here. I did this to you." She looked up.

"Maggie? You came back. Did you bring Randolph with you?" Lenora's eyes were dilated again, and I wondered if her doctor had given her yet another shot. How much medication could this poor woman be given before it had an ill effect on her?

Maggie winced. "I tried, ma'am, but as you know, he has many responsibilities at the club, and he said he had to stay."

Lenora frowned. "In truth, that was what I anticipated." She turned to me. "I didn't expect to see you here, Miss Wright."

Despite the dilated eyes, she was speaking like the Lenora I remembered from our PTA meetings. Her face was more relaxed, and she appeared to have more control of the direction in which she was looking. She certainly wasn't in the stupor of the past few days.

"When your husband couldn't get away, I offered to come with Maggie to make sure you were all right."

"That was kind of you."

"You seem well," I said. "I'm happy to see that."

"Yes, when the doctor came to give me my nighttime shot, Benny chased him away. When Randolph hears about this, he won't be pleased. But I feel more like myself than I have in days."

"I'm so glad to hear that, Mrs. Shaw," Maggie said. "I was very concerned for you."

"You have always been a kind young woman. Perhaps too trusting at times."

Maggie wrinkled her brow. "Ma'am?"

"You see, I remember that night now as clearly as if it was this morning. I remember seeing you run from the billiard room. I was on my way to the conservatory. I knew it was the only place I could escape the noise and the only place Randolph would not come to fetch me."

Benny stood up. "It was you? It was you I saw running away?"

Maggie backed up. "I—I don't know what you are talking about. It could have been any one of the female servants. We were all wearing the same uniform that night."

"I know what you look like, Maggie. You have been our maid for these past two years," Lenora said.

"I wouldn't kill anyone. I have no reason to."

Benny pointed his finger at her. "You do have a reason. I saw the two of you together."

"What?" Maggie asked, in shock.

"It was in the hallway. He was touching your face."

Maggie put a hand to her cheek, as if to cover the spot where Herman had touched her. She began to shiver. "He was forward with me, but nothing happened. I wouldn't allow it to."

"Maggie, was Herman bothering you?" I asked.

She turned to me. "He made me uncomfortable and had been making inappropriate comments to me for weeks."

She didn't say what those comments were, and we didn't

ask her to elaborate. We all could imagine what a man like Herman would be capable of saying to a young maid like Maggie.

Maggie took a breath. "Then he became more aggressive. He would touch my arm, my face, and my side any chance he got. Sometimes he would do it with Mr. and Mrs. Shaw in the room. He knew I couldn't complain. If I did, he would just deny it, and I would be the disgraced maid who was out of work."

I wished I could say to Maggie that this wouldn't have been the case, but I knew her description of how everything would unfold was most likely the truth.

She took a breath. "Finally, it got to the point that I couldn't take it any longer, and I asked him to leave me alone. It was at the Christmas party. He was becoming increasingly bold, trying to corner me in the mansion. When I cleaned a room anywhere in the house, I closed and locked the door, so that I could be sure Herman couldn't get in while I was working and catch me off guard. He began following me on errands. Every time Mrs. Shaw sent me to Mrs. Appleton's bakery, I had to take another way there because he would follow me."

I shivered as I remembered being shocked at seeing Herman Wheeler in my neighborhood the day the boys sent home their telegram. I knew now he must have been there because he was following and tormenting Maggie.

"And?" I asked. "What did he say when you asked him to leave you alone?"

"He said he would if I did one thing for him."

"And what was that?" Benny asked.

She looked me in the eye. "It was to bring him your brother's jacket."

"You were the one who picked up Orville's jacket that night?" I asked.

She nodded and glanced at Lenora, who seemed to be watching Maggie's every move.

"Did he tell you what he wanted it for?" I asked.

She shook her head. "I'm sorry I took it. I saw the two of you looking frantically around the house for it, and I felt awful. But please, you have to understand the situation I was in. I really thought that was the only way he would leave me alone. However, I soon learned that he was lying."

"Did he want the jacket itself or something in it?"

"He gave me no reason at all. He told me to get the jacket and bring it to the billiard room. And if I did that, he would leave me alone. He promised never to come near me again. What choice did I have? I worked for the Shaw family, and Herman was a fixture there. I knew I would never truly get away from him until he became bored with me."

"The screwdriver was my brother's, and it was in the jacket pocket at the beginning of the night."

"I—I found it in the pocket just before Herman came into the room. I felt something heavy in the pocket, and I didn't know what it was, so I looked. There was a screwdriver. When Herman walked into the room, I could tell that he had had too much to drink, and I knew this encounter was going to be the worst of all." She shuddered. "I held up the screwdriver. I thought the sight of it would show him I wouldn't back down. I don't think he even said anything when he entered the room. He ran toward me, and I don't believe he saw the screwdriver at all." She shuddered. "It went into him. He slumped over me, and I had to push him off. It was at that point that he landed on the billiard table. I ran from the room, but I swear to you, when I left, he was alive. He was alive."

Benny, Lenora, and I all stared at her.

Benny spoke first. "You killed him, and you let me go to jail for your crime? How could you do that? If you don't care about me, that's fine. But I thought you cared about my mother. You always spent extra time with her and would walk to her favorite bakery and get her sweets that my father forbade her to eat. Did you even think about what you've put her through the past few days?"

"I do care about Mrs. Shaw." Maggie was close to tears. "That is why I am confessing now. I can see how much pain this has caused her, and I am sorry for that."

"Benny," Lenora said, "I believe we should ring the police."

Maggie's eyes went wide, and she started to back away from the door.

Benny jumped at her. "You're not going to get away."

That was all he had to say to make her spring into action. She bolted toward the door. Benny was fast and almost caught the edge of her black skirt, but she pushed over a huge potted plant before fleeing the room. Benny tripped over the pot and flopped on top of it. Dirt spilled all over the pristine floor.

By the time Benny scrambled to his feet, Maggie was gone. A small part of me was happy she'd gotten away. Maybe it was wrong of me to feel that way. She'd taken a man's life, but I shivered to think what would happen to a poor girl like her in prison. She was only defending herself when she stabbed Herman, but would the police and the prosecutor believe her story?

Benny stood and brushed dirt from his clothes. "I thought you wanted to help me," he shouted at me. "You let the killer go."

"I didn't let her go," I said.

"You didn't try to stop her. You just stood there."

That was true.

Lenora lay back down against her chaise lounge. "Benny, go ring the police and the club. Your father will want to be here when they arrive."

To me, it sounded like this was the perfect time to make my exit. I didn't want to be here when the police or Randolph Shaw arrived.

Benny went out the conservatory door, and I moved to follow him. "Oh no, Miss Wright, you won't be leaving now. We need you here to corroborate our story to the police."

I glanced longingly at the door, but it wouldn't be right to leave now. I sat on a chair not far from Lenora, and her cat jumped on my lap. She then promptly curled up and went to sleep.

"The fact that Moonlight likes you is telling, but it is not the whole picture," Lenora said.

Before I could ask her what she meant by that, she closed her eyes and leaned back. I didn't know if she was simply resting or actually asleep. It seemed all the emotion of the past few minutes had worn her down.

The time sitting with Lenora and waiting for the police to arrive was excruciating. I was almost relieved when Officer Bertie Fallon walked through the door with two other officers and the detective. If Bertie was surprised to see me there in a ruined ball gown, with Lenora's large silver Persian cat on my lap, he gave no indication.

"Mrs. Shaw," Detective Gaylen said. "Are you all right?"

Lenora opened her eyes. "I'll be fine, but I want to hear from you once and for all that you have dropped the charges against my son. The murderess has confessed, and my son had nothing to do with it. Just as he told you the night of his arrest, he was trying to save Herman by removing the weapon from his chest. You were too quick to arrest him."

"And who is this murderess, Mrs. Shaw?" Detective Gaylen asked.

"My maid, Maggie Courtier. She confessed to all of us that she stabbed the man. That should be all you need to know to clear my son!"

"Who is all of you?" he asked in a quiet tone. It made me believe he was trying to speak calmly in order to keep Lenora equally calm.

"Benny, Miss Wright, and myself."

"Where is Benny now?" the detective asked.

"He went to call you. He will return shortly. In any case, that is not important. What is important is a woman confessed to murder and the four of you are just standing there staring at me like I'm a hysterical woman. Believe me, I know the look you are giving me all too well. My husband looks at me that way all the time."

The detective turned to me. "I must say I'm surprised to see you here tonight, Miss Wright." He looked at the hem of my dress. "It seems you have had some type of mishap."

I straightened my spine. "I had a run-in with a Christmas tree."

The detective looked as if he wanted to ask more about that, but continued with the topic at hand. "Is what Mrs. Shaw says true? Did this maid confess to stabbing Mr. Wheeler?"

"She did confess to stabbing Herman," I said. "But . . ."

"There are no buts!" Lenora snapped. "My son is innocent."

"We will take everything we learn here into account, but we can't immediately clear Benjamin. If what you say is proven to be true, your son has nothing to worry about. But it may take longer than usual to tie up the loose ends, as it is Christmas."

The time hit me. In all the excitement of Maggie's confession, I had forgotten that as soon as the clock chimed midnight, it was Christmas. This was not at all how I'd expected to spend my Christmas holiday. It was hard for me to believe just days ago all I was looking forward to was Orville and Wilbur's return home. We were going to celebrate Christmas and their historic flight. All of that changed when Orville and I walked into the Shaws' home for the first time.

"I would like to hear what the maid said from Miss Wright," the detective went on. "Verbatim."

I was surprised that he was more interested in my description of the events than Lenora's.

As if he could tell I was surprised, he said, "I believe, Miss Wright, that you will be able to tell us what happened in a factual manner with little emotion."

I nodded and recounted Maggie's confession. I ended by saying, "She did kill him. She admitted that, but it was in self-defense. There was no doubt that after weeks of tormenting her, Herman had plans to harm her. Alone with her in the billiard room, he had his best opportunity. If she had not had my brother's jacket with her and found his screwdriver, we would be talking about a very different crime right now."

The detective studied me. "On the night of the murder, you and Orville never said your brother's jacket might have been stolen. Why would anyone have interest in your brother's jacket?"

I rocked back on my feet, which were beginning to be sore from walking in Agnes's satin shoes, which pinched my toes. If I ever got home, I would have to soak my feet in hot salt water for nearly an hour to alleviate the pain and swelling.

"Miss Wright?" the detective asked.

"My brother had some important papers in his jacket that have to do with Wilbur and Orville's first flight. They are very important to my brothers. Orville suspected that the jacket was taken for those papers."

"And were the papers in the jacket?" the detective asked.

"No, not when we finally found it in the billiard room."

"And why didn't you tell us this in the first place?"

"Orville and I were hoping that the papers were misplaced, and that we would find them on our own."

"And have you?"

I pressed my lips together. "No."

He scowled at me. "It seems to me that one person after another in this case has been withholding information from the police. I very much hope that if there is anything else that any one of you has to share, you will do so now."

Lenora and I said nothing.

Benny came into the room. "Mother. Father's car just pulled in."

She nodded and turned to the detective. "Is Benny cleared?"

"I will have to talk with the captain, but I believe if the confession from the maid is confirmed, it will absolve Benny of any wrongdoing."

Lenora held her arms out to her son. He sat beside her on the chaise lounge, and she hugged him tightly. Tears ran down her face. "Thank you. Thank you. It will be proven true. It will."

The ache in my heart eased just a little. It was good to know that Benny would be all right. I hoped he would return to school when classes resumed in January, but I knew it was far too early to bring up the topic of school.

Randolph Shaw stomped into the room. "Lenora, what are you doing up? Why are the police here? What is going on?" He spotted me. "You! Is there no way to rid myself of you? You're every place I turn."

As carefully as I could, I picked up the sleeping cat and set him on the edge of Lenora's chaise lounge, next to Benny. The fluffy creature didn't seem to be the least bit disturbed at being moved. She curled up in a ball and buried her face under her paws. I wished I could do the same. Randolph Shaw was the last person I wanted to see. Yes, it was true that Maggie had confessed to the murder, but I still didn't trust him, considering all that I knew. I was certain he had wanted Herman dead. Had Maggie taken care of Herman before Randolph had the chance?

I brushed silver cat fur from my lap the best I could, but it was no use. The dress was a lost cause. At this point, I would have to use half my school wages to pay Agnes for a replacement.

Lenora looked her husband up and down. "Should I have been confined to my sickbed, where you wanted to keep me?"

"How dare you speak to me this way?"

"I will dare," she said. "I have kept quiet for too long, but when you turned your back on our son, that was the end of it."

"He's not my son."

She narrowed her eyes. "You raised him as such. It is what we have told him all these years. You were his parent. I want you out of my home, and I want a divorce."

"You lied to me," Randolph accused. "Don't be ridiculous. I'm never leaving my home."

"It's not your home," Lenora said with a small smile on her lips. "Did you not put the mansion in my name?"

"Is it true what your wife says about the mansion?" the detective wanted to know.

"It's merely a technicality for tax purposes. This is my home."

"If Mrs. Shaw is the sole owner, she can have you removed from the premises," Detective Gaylen said. "Officer Fallon, please escort him out. I'm concerned that he will take out his anger on Mrs. Shaw after we leave. I don't want to come back here to find another murder."

Randolph opened and closed his mouth. "I have never been so offended in all my life. How dare you speak that way to me? I'll have your job. Your captain is a member of my club."

The detective stepped toward him. "I know all about that. He was the one who told me to watch out for you."

Randolph was stricken, and Bertie took him by the arm and led him out of the conservatory. I believed the only reason he let Bertie lead him away was his state of shock.

CHAPTER 40

After I was interviewed again by Detective Gaylen and his officers, they finally released me. Bertie offered to take me home, and I gratefully accepted, as the hansom cab driver was long gone. I didn't blame him.

While the other officers and the detective drove away in automobiles, Bertie walked me to a horse and wagon. The wagon was painted navy blue, and POLICE was stenciled on the side in foot-high letters.

"You're the only one in a horse and wagon?"

"The police department is in transition. We have half automobiles and half wagons. Because I have been on the force for over a decade, I was offered one of the first automobiles, but I passed on it. I have cleaned up too many auto accidents to want to be behind the wheel in one of those. But I'm not going to be able to put it off forever. The department has a plan to replace all the horses and wagons in two years." He gave me his arm to help me into the wagon and then climbed in himself. "I will miss Malcolm here," he said, nodding at the horse. "Isn't that right, boy?"

The horse flicked his black mane.

Bertie shook the reins. "If I had a place to keep him and

the money to do it, I would buy him from the force when the time comes."

"I hope it comes later than that, for your sake, but as my brothers say, there is no stopping innovation."

"They said that when they were just lads. I remember when we were all in school together, they were always tinkering with something. I loved going to your house when I was a child. Your mother, God rest her soul, always had a project going herself. I never met such an industrious woman."

There was a small pang in my heart when he said that. My mother had been gone a long time now, but I still missed her every day. She had a special relationship with each one of us, and she was far less strict than our father. With Wilbur and Orville, she had a unique bond because they all liked to fiddle with objects and make things with their hands. I was always more drawn to books and languages. My mother would not have been surprised to learn I was now a Latin teacher.

"I don't think you should arrest Maggie Courtier," I said.

He glanced at me. "Are you kidding? You, Mrs. Shaw, and her son all told the same story—that she confessed to stabbing Herman."

"Yes, but it was in self-defense. He was planning to attack her. He did attack her, and she defended herself," I argued.

"Even if her claim is proven to be true, we have to bring her in for questioning. We can't just drop the whole thing. Herman Wheeler was becoming a very prominent man in Dayton. People are going to want answers. They will lose complete trust in the force if we just drop the case. There is due process."

"I'm afraid that she won't receive a fair hearing," I said. "She's a poor working-class girl, with no family that I know of and not much education. The odds are stacked against her."

"You need to know something," he said. "It might change your mind about Maggie."

"I doubt it, but I will hear you out."

"Herman was stabbed twice. Once in the stomach and once in the chest. The chest wound was the one that bled out."

"So the chest stabbing was the death blow."

"Katie, I wish you wouldn't be so blunt at times."

"But that is what you're telling me," I said.

I wrinkled my brow. "This new information doesn't fit with Maggie's story at all," I said. "She told us that Herman charged her, as if he was going to attack her, and he ran into the screwdriver. She pushed him off and then fled. She left the screwdriver and the jacket behind."

"So she lied to you. She removed the screwdriver and stabbed him a second time to make sure she finished the job. Does that sound like self-defense?" he replied.

"No, it sounds to me as if someone else came into that room after Herman was stabbed."

Bertie laughed. "Katie, you have always had a great imagination."

"What if two different people stabbed Herman? One was Maggie. We know how and why, but then a second person came into the billiard room and . . ."

"And what? Finished the job? My land, Katie, what have you been reading? We have no reason to believe that two people were involved in this crime. If we go with this theory, think of the repercussions."

"The only repercussion I can think of is that Maggie will no longer be blamed for the murder. She was terrified and would not have had the strength to stab him twice."

"You're not thinking how this will look for Benjamin Shaw. He will be a suspect again. He could very well have been that second person. The secret about his birth, which Herman was threatening to tell, could pull his family apart. In fact, even with Herman dead, it did pull them apart. Look at them now."

"Even if she stabbed him twice, which I don't believe she

did, it is still self-defense. Herman had been making unwelcome advances on her for weeks. She was terrified. He was good friends with her employer, or so it seemed to her. She couldn't go to Randolph for help."

"She could always have come to the police," Bertie said.

"Oh really? And you would believe a young maid over a successful businessman, one who was poised to be president of the most exclusive gentlemen's club in the city?"

"Maybe not, if you put it that way. Let me ask you this. If Maggie didn't stab Herman twice, who gave him the death blow, as you like to call it?"

"Bertie, that is the most important question of all. Herman had more enemies in life than I can count, and they were all at the Shaws' Christmas party. He was up to something at the club that allowed him to grab the power there. Randolph Shaw hated him for it. He knew secrets about the Shaws, but I believe that was just the tip of the iceberg. He could have been blackmailing other club members."

"And you want us to interrogate every man at the Gem City Club?"

"That's not a bad idea," I agreed.

"Our captain would never agree to that. He might dislike Randolph Shaw, but he's not going to allow us to make a mockery of his club."

"Even if it's the only way to get to the truth?" I asked.

He pulled the wagon up in front of my home. "Katie, I told you these things only so that you could see how difficult it will be to defend Maggie Courtier. You did what you set out to do. You cleared Benjamin Shaw's name. Now be done with it."

I climbed out of the wagon and looked up at Bertie. "I know I'm right, and deep down, you know I'm right too. If I have to prove it myself, I will."

CHAPTER 41

"No, no, a little that way," I said. "Nope, back the other way."

Wilbur and Orville were balancing the Christmas tree, which we had brought home from the fundraiser, in its stand while I directed them. It was going as well as could be expected with three stubborn siblings working on the same project.

"Sterchens!" Orville cried. "You have made us move this back and forth five times already."

"It is fine where it is," Wilbur said. He kneeled on the floor and tightened the base's screws into the tree trunk.

When the boys stepped back, the tree was mostly straight.

"We will compensate with the star on top," I said.

Father came into the room. "Is it safe to enter now? The three of you have been squabbling for close to an hour over the best way to put up the tree."

"It was Sterchens who was making the most fuss," Orville said, but his smile took the bite out of his words.

Wilbur chuckled.

I was happy to see the two of them were getting along. Wilbur was still upset about the lost drawings—they both were—but they had agreed to work harder on the next model of their flying machine, so they would make faster progress than the person who had taken the drawings. That was assuming the person who had them even knew how to read them.

We began decorating the tree with dried cranberries and orange slices, porcelain dolls from my childhood, and pinecones that we had collected at the park. After my mishap with the lit Christmas tree at the Gem City Club, we abstained from candles of any sort. I wasn't going to risk being set on fire again.

Carrie stepped into the room. She wore a long wool skirt, a blouse with puffed sleeves, and a blue and green vest. Her hair was pulled back in a tight bun. "Dinner is on the table for when the family arrives. The roast and potatoes are in the oven, being kept warm. Everything else is out and ready. I made the children each a mini pie."

"Lorin and his family will appreciate that so much," I said. "Thank you, Carrie."

"Are you sure you won't stay and have Christmas dinner with us?" Father asked. "You are part of the family."

Carrie shook her head. "My family is waiting for me. We're all going to church together, and then we'll have late Christmas snacks. It is our tradition."

"Then you must go," Father said. "It's important to keep family traditions alive."

She nodded and went back into the kitchen to leave by the back door, even though we'd told her often that she was free to use the front. I didn't imagine that was the case for the servants at the Shaws' home.

I left my father to supervise the boys as they decorated the tree, and went into the kitchen after her. She was just putting on her coat when I stepped into the room. She jumped when I said her name.

"Oh, Miss Katharine, you startled me."

"I didn't mean to do that."

"Is there something else you need me to do before I leave?" she asked.

"Have you seen Maggie today?"

All the color drained from her face. "Maggie?"

"Yes, your friend Maggie."

"No, no, I have not seen her."

"How much do you know about her life at the Shaws' home?"

Her eyes were wide. "I don't know what you mean."

She glanced at the door. It was clear to me that she wanted to escape.

"I think you knew that Herman Wheeler was pestering her. She was upset about it and came to visit you more than once to talk about what she should do. I also think you knew that she had to defend herself against him."

Tears sprang to Carrie's eyes. "She didn't mean to kill him. She is broken up over it. She is devastated."

"I imagine she is," I said. "But the truth is I don't think she killed him. I think someone else stabbed him a second time, delivering the killing blow, after she left."

Carrie covered her mouth with her hand.

"Where is she? I need to talk to her. The longer she hides from the police, the worse it will look to them. They will be even more likely to believe she stabbed Herman twice."

She lowered a shaking hand. "I promised that I wouldn't tell."

"I can help her. I have a friend who is a police officer. You've met him before. It's Bertie Fallon."

"I know you have been kind to her. She said you were," Carrie said quietly. "I knew you would be. I told her she could trust you. I promise I did."

"I believe you," I said. "And I'm trying to help. I don't want anyone to be blamed unjustly. I want to help clear her name."

She nodded. "I can't tell you where she is, but I can arrange a meeting. At your high school at ten o'clock tonight? Maybe you can convince her."

"Yes, of course."

"You have to come alone."

"Katie, there you are!" Agnes cried as she came into the room. "Your father said we would find you in the kitchen."

She was standing next to Arthur Bacon. I blinked. I had never expected to see Arthur in my home, let alone my kitchen.

Agnes beamed at me. "Arthur and I had to stop by because we have news!"

"News? What news?" I asked.

She held out her left hand to me, and there was a platinum band on her finger. "We are getting married! Can you believe it! Will you be my witness at the wedding?"

I stared at her, stunned.

When I didn't answer right away, she dropped her hand. "Will you?"

I shook myself from my stupor. "Yes, yes, of course!"

"I'm so happy!" She let go of Arthur's hand and crushed me in a hug.

I looked behind me; Carrie was gone.

CHAPTER 42

Usually, I loved spending time with my family on holidays. Lorin's children were endearing, and they loved their gifts. They truly embraced the joy of Christmas. But throughout the evening, I found myself watching the grandfather clock in the corner of the room. The minutes dragged by as its hands made their way to ten o'clock. At times, I thought the clock was going backward.

Lorin and his family finally left for home at the stroke of nine, and my father retired shortly after that. Wilbur and Orville began speaking about their flying machine next to the fire, and I wished them a Merry Christmas and said I was going to bed too.

However, instead of going upstairs to my room, I grabbed my coat, hat, and scarf, which I had stashed in the kitchen pantry, and went out the back door.

There was nothing my father or the boys could have said that would have kept me from going to meet Carrie and Maggie that night, but I didn't want them to worry, and I didn't want the boys to run and tell Bertie Fallon what I was up to. If there were any police around, I knew Maggie would not speak to me.

The remaining Christmas trees from the sale stood sad and lonely on the high school lawn. Some had fallen over, and the red ribbons that had been woven around the trees flapped in the cold wind.

The school loomed overhead, standing forbiddingly above the river. The sky was clear that night, which made the temperature drop well below zero. I almost turned around right then and there. What did I hope to gain by speaking to Maggie? I hoped to convince her to turn herself in to the police, because running would only make it worse for her. If she ran, she would always have to run.

"Miss Katharine," a voice whispered from the middle of the trees.

"Carrie?"

"Yes," the whisper came back.

I took a breath and walked into the middle of the unsold Christmas trees. Langston had told me the trees that weren't sold would be taken by wagon to a goat farm on the outskirts of Dayton, and the goats would feast on them for weeks. It seemed like an anticlimactic fate for the trees.

Inside the ring of spruces, I found Carrie and Maggie. Both were bundled head to toe in winter coats and scarves. Carrie had tears in her eyes, and even more tears were frozen on her pink cheeks. Maggie's pale face was resolute, as if she had come to some sort of monumental decision, and I knew what that decision was. A small suitcase sat at her feet. She was leaving Dayton for good.

"Where are you going?" I asked.

Maggie didn't answer my question. Instead, she said, "I'm here for Carrie's sake. She has been a good friend to me all our lives. She said you wanted to see me."

"I do."

"Why?"

"I think you need to go to the police station."

She shook her head. "I can't do that."

"You have to tell them your story. I told them what you told Benny, Lenora, and me, but they need to hear it from you."

"Why would I do that? I killed a man," she said. "They will put me in prison and rightly so. I was only trying to protect myself, but another person is dead because of what I have done. It's something I have to live with, but I won't go to prison for it when he was the one trying to hurt me first." Maggie squeezed her eyes shut. "He was so cruel to me. He said the most horrible things when I passed him in the hallways of the mansion."

Carrie gasped.

Maggie opened her eyes, and tears ran down her face. "He started squeezing my shoulder and arm or side when he got the chance, but I knew the bolder he became, the worse it would get. When you are a young woman in my position, you're used to wealthy men treating you so now and again. But I had never had anyone as focused on me as Mr. Wheeler was." She closed her eyes again.

"I don't believe you killed him," I said.

"How can you say that?" she snapped. "You weren't there. I saw that screwdriver go into his body. I was holding it when he ran into it. I was trying to defend myself."

"Where did the screwdriver enter his body?" I asked.

"I—I don't know," she said. "Does it matter? The ending is the same. The man is dead."

"It matters very much. It is what we need to know to prove that you are innocent of killing him."

"But I told you I killed him." She wrung her hands. "Why are you tormenting me? Don't you think I am in enough pain because of what I have done?"

"Maggie." Carrie put her hand on her friend's arm. "Miss Katharine is only trying to help. I know her. She would not be asking these questions if it wasn't important."

Maggie's chest heaved up and down, but she no longer tried to argue with me. When she spoke again, she said, "It was in his middle."

"His stomach?"

She nodded. "Yes, I think so. That is what I remember."

"And how many times did you stab him?"

She sucked in a sharp breath as she digested my blunt question. "He ran into the screwdriver only once."

"Then you didn't kill him. He was stabbed twice. The second time he was stabbed in the chest, in the heart," I explained.

She dropped her hands at her sides. "But that's not possible. I didn't do that."

"I know you didn't, but it's very possible. It happened when you left the room."

"Benny?" She covered her mouth as if she might be ill.

"I don't believe it was Benny."

There was the beep of an automobile horn.

"I will go see if it's your ride," Carrie said and melted into the trees.

"Your ride?" I asked.

"A friend has agreed to drive me to the Indiana state line. From there, I will find my way forward."

It terrified me that she was willing to put herself in such danger to escape Dayton. There was no telling what she would face out on the road alone. However, I now knew that she hadn't been safe in the Shaws' mansion either.

"I really think you should stay," I said. "I'll do everything I can to convince the police you're telling the truth. You're innocent of this crime."

"If what you're saying is true, it does not absolve me. If it hadn't been for me, that man would still be alive. Whoever stabbed him in the chest that night wouldn't have had the opportunity to do it if not for my actions. That is something I have to live with."

"And I have to live with finishing the job," a dark voice said behind us.

We spun around to find Arthur Bacon coming toward us with a pistol in his hand.

CHAPTER 43

"Arthur!" I gasped. "What are you doing here?"
"I'm trying to fix a problem that has me plaguing me since last Saturday night. You."

I pushed Maggie behind me. I prayed that Carrie was running for help or at least for safety. The fewer people I had to worry about getting out of this mess, the better.

"What is your problem with me?" I snapped. It was better to appear angry than scared, I decided.

"First of all, I know you're not keen on the idea of me marrying Agnes. She looks up to you. All I ever hear from her is, 'Katie this, Katie that. Do you know what Katie did at school today?' It's infuriating. Part of me believes that she's more in love with you than she is with me."

"Don't be ridiculous. Agnes loves you. There's nothing I can say or do to change her mind, much as I would like to. Because I can assure you if there was, I would have done it by now."

He laughed. "I've never met a woman who is so sure of herself. It's both impressive and annoying. Most women I know are more pliable than you."

"You're just meeting the wrong women then." I squeezed

Maggie's arm behind me and whispered, "Run. Run when you can. Don't wait."

I heard her swallow.

"Like Agnes?" he asked. "Is she the wrong woman for me?"

"Just like Agnes. She needs someone kind and even-tempered. You're neither of those things."

Behind Arthur, I saw movement through the trees. It was Carrie. In her hands, she held one of the wooden stakes that were used to hold up the trees.

"Did you kill Herman because of your own greed? You were his protégé after all, weren't you? You were helping him gather the information to blackmail the members of the club for money and for stature. Did you finally realize that he was never going to make you an equal and you would always be second?" I asked.

He shook the pistol at me. "Be quiet! You don't know anything."

"Of course I do," I said. "Essentially, you and Herman were cut from the same cloth. It made you great allies until jealousy blinded you. Neither one of you was going to share with the other. You would always be second, and just as Herman could not be second to Randolph, you couldn't be second to him, so you took the chance you were given that night. You came upon him hurt in the billiard room and killed him. You're studying to be a doctor. You would know just where the death blow should land."

All the while I spoke, Arthur was becoming increasingly unhinged. His whole body was shaking, but not from the cold. It was from rage, rage at me.

"Maybe it would be best if you just left," I said. "This is your chance."

He took a step forward and leveled the pistol at me. "Not without removing you first."

That was the moment Carrie burst forward and hit him in the back with the wooden stake.

"What?" he cried as he stumbled forward.

As he was bent over, I pushed a Christmas tree on top of him. And he cried out as the pistol was knocked from his hand.

A large cloud of fur flew through the trees, and Mae Bear landed on top of the tree, crushing him in place.

I scooped up the pistol.

When Langston appeared, I handed the pistol to him for fear I would set it off by accident.

"Don't you worry, ladies. I got him in place." He pointed the pistol at Arthur. "I heard the whole thing, and the police are on their way. I used the school's telephone to call for help."

Maggie and Carrie disappeared into the trees, and seeing that Langston had Arthur well in hand, I went after them. I found Maggie and Carrie standing in front of the school. They were locked in an embrace, as if they knew they would never see each other again. An automobile was a few feet away with its engine running. The driver wore his hat low, so I couldn't see his face.

"What are you going to do now?" Maggie asked me as she let Carrie go. "Are you going to tell the police?"

Telling the police was what I knew I should do. Maggie ought to tell her side of the story. The entire truth needed to come out, but would that be fair to her?

Would she really be absolved of any wrongdoing? I couldn't guarantee it. She was a woman and a maid. There was no telling what Arthur would say to the police. And would the police want to protect Herman? Herman had been an awful person, but there was a chance they would not want to paint him as a man who stalked and preyed upon women. And what about the Gem City Club? A club that donated hundreds of dollars to the police department every year would need to be protected.

I remembered the small bloody handprint on the wall in

the billiard room. Maggie must have been so frightened. That print had been hers. She had to be just as frightened now.

I stared at her. The sirens were growing closer.

"Go," I whispered.

"Go?" Maggie stared at me with frightened eyes.

I nodded. "Just go. I can't guarantee that your story will be believed. Indiana is not far, and I hear there is work in Chicago, especially for a domestic."

"I don't know if I'll be able to get work if I don't have a letter of reference, especially for the better houses in the city."

"When you're settled, write to me. I will send you a letter of reference as your teacher."

"But you weren't my teacher. I told you I was never good in school," she protested.

"Perhaps, but you have taught me so much more than I could teach you. What you taught me has been more valuable than any Latin lessons."

"What did I teach you?" she asked in a hushed voice.

I paused. "That sometimes doing the right thing is the wrong thing in the eyes of the law. That sometimes justice and mercy don't coincide. That sometimes mercy is the better choice."

Tears filled her hazel eyes. "Thank you," she whispered. She gave Carrie one final hug and climbed into the car.

It wasn't until the automobile drove away that I saw Benny's face.

Epilogue

Benny said very little in class when school resumed in January. He didn't make eye contact with any of the other students. He knew they were all talking about him. I found myself longing for Benny to make a rude comment. I wished he would distract his classmates with his antics, but he did none of these things. He sat quietly, looking straight ahead at the chalkboard, apparently completely focused on the lesson. Maybe I should just be happy that he'd come back to class.

The final bell rang at the end of the period, and as the students were filing out of my room, I called, "Benny, may I speak to you for a moment?"

His classmates whispered amongst themselves while they left.

After the last student had exited the room, I leaned against my desk and folded my arms. "How are you?"

He wouldn't look me in the eye.

I sighed. "I just want to say that I'm proud of you for being here today. It must have been very difficult to come back to school with everything that you've gone through in the past couple of weeks and are going through today."

The morning paper headline stated that Lenora Shaw had

filed for divorce from her husband and was keeping the mansion, whose deed had her name. The announcement was just below the headline stating that Herman Wheeler's blackmailing scheme was unraveling and that Arthur Bacon, one of his underlings, would be undergoing trial for Herman's murder. Because now Arthur had changed his tune and was proclaiming his innocence.

"I know what you did for me," Benny said finally. "It's something I didn't deserve. Not after the way I treated you all year in class. Why did you help me?"

I thought about my answer for a moment. "Because you're my student, and I believe in my students. I care about my students. I'm a teacher. It is what I'm supposed to do."

"Thank you," he whispered.

It was more than I'd ever expected to hear from him on the matter.

"I don't think it anymore, you know."

I wrinkled my brow.

He glanced at the chalkboard, and I followed his line of sight. "That you're a witch."

"I'm glad to hear that."

He nodded and started toward the door.

"Benny?"

He looked over his shoulder.

"Thank you for helping Maggie that night."

His eyes were wide, and then his shoulders relaxed. "It was the right thing to do."

"Yes, it was," I agreed.

He left the room.

I sighed and sat at my desk. Instead of rushing home as I usually did after school, I decided to stay behind for a few hours and work on some lesson plans for the coming weeks.

I was deep in verb conjugation, when there was a knock on the frame of my classroom door. To my surprise, I found

Carrie Kayler standing in the doorway. She held out an envelope. "Miss Katharine, there is a letter for you."

I took the envelope. "A letter that could not wait until I got home to read?"

"You mentioned at breakfast that you planned to stay late at school, and I thought I would bring it to you as I walked home."

Neither of us mentioned that her home was in the opposite direction from Steele High School.

Looking at the swooping handwriting and the lack of a return address, I had a feeling I knew who'd sent this letter.

Carrie turned to go.

"Carrie, wait a moment while I read this."

She shook her head. "No, miss. I know her handwriting. It would hurt me too much to hear what she has to say. It would be better for her and myself if I didn't know what she is doing or where she is. I can continue to pray for her without that knowledge."

"All right," I said and watched her go.

After Carrie was gone, I opened the envelope. There was a trifold sheaf of papers inside, with a handwritten letter on top.

Dear Miss Wright,

I hope this letter finds you well. I am well and safe. Please tell C. Tell her, too, that I think about our friendship fondly and will never forget her.

I thank you for your kindness and for letting me go. I stayed at first only because I could not stand the idea of Benny going to prison for what I had done. Your compassion and determination to help him touched me.

Enclosed you will find your brothers' drawings. I knew they were what Herman wanted that night, and I hid them in the kitchen before I met with him in the billiard room. I never intended to give them to him. I knew he would use them only to hurt someone else. I could not be part of that.

I'm sorry I didn't return them to you earlier. You will have to forgive me for that. I had a feeling that I needed them to protect myself in case I was to be arrested or worse. Please give my apologies to your brothers as well.

There are so many reasons to admire your family. Your father is a man of God, your brothers are changing our very world with their discoveries, and you are a good person, Miss Wright, and that is most valuable of all. Had you been my teacher, I never would have left school.

Yours,

M.C.

I unfolded the sheaf of papers. As Maggie had promised, the drawings were all there. My brothers would be pleased with their return. If they asked how I'd found them, I wouldn't tell. Every woman had her secrets, including me.

Author Note

When I learned of Wilbur and Orville Wright's younger sister, Katharine, I knew that I had to write about her. She was a teacher, feminist, scholar, and extrovert, and she was incredibly loyal. She was the kind of woman whom I would have wanted as a friend; and I like to think, as I am a fellow Ohioan, that had we been born in the same century, we would have met and been fast friends. As much as I admire Wilbur and Orville for their amazing accomplishment of manned flight, I admire her even more for the person she was.

Katharine Wright lost her mother when she fifteen years old, so from a very young age she shouldered the weight of running a household. She did an excellent job of it. As her mother was gone, her father made it very clear that he expected Katharine, his only surviving daughter, to take care of him in his old age.

Even though her father, Bishop Milton Wright, was very traditional in his beliefs about the roles of women in the home, he also believed in educating women and sent his daughter to Oberlin College, where she studied Greek and Latin. She was the only Wright sibling to attend college.

She graduated in 1898 and returned to Dayton, where she began teaching Latin at Steele High School, along the Great Miami River. She did very much want to teach advanced Greek, as ancient Greek was her specialty, but she was passed over again and again for male teachers who may have been less qualified but wanted the position.

While she was at Oberlin, her brothers Wilbur and Orville Wright became increasingly determined to build a flying machine; they had been studying the problem of flight for many years. The brothers began making trips to Kitty Hawk, on the Outer Banks of North Carolina, where they had the consistent wind they needed for takeoffs and soft dunes for landings.

While they were away, Katharine and their machinist Charlie Taylor, whom Katharine did not like, ran the brothers' bicycle shop. It was important for the shop to do well as the brothers would not take money from any donors for their project. They paid for their flying machine with their own money.

Because she was so busy with the bicycle shop and teaching, Katharine used her own money to hire Carrie Kayler to help care for the Wright family home when Carrie was only fourteen. Years later, Carrie married Charles Grumbach. She and her husband both worked in the Wright home until Orville, the last surviving member of the family, died in 1948.

The Wright brothers finally flew on December 17, 1903, and Orville sent a telegram as soon as he could to tell his father and sister. The telegram is copied verbatim in this novel. Yes, the telegram operator misspelled Orville's name.

The boys had already applied for a patent for their flying machine in the spring of 1903, but it can take years for patents to be approved. In fact, their patent was not approved until 1908, and by that time they would be world recognized as the first in flight.

They were not the only ones trying to fly, so they had good reason to want to protect their innovations with a legal patent. It was certainly a race to make it into the air first, and the loss of the secret of wing warping, which was the final discovery that allowed them to fly, to another inventor before the patent was secure was a constant fear.

Reading of the Wrights' anxiety about the patent, I knew it would make a great basis for a mystery, and Katharine, the sister whom they had always relied on, would be the one to solve it.

Discussion Questions

1. Before reading this book, did you know the Wright brothers had a sister?

2. What do you admire about the Wright family? About Katharine Wright?

3. Herman Wheeler was not a good man, but do you find anything tragic about his death?

4. How do you feel about Randolph and Lenora Shaw's marriage?

5. Gentlemen's clubs were very popular at the turn of the twentieth century. Such clubs existed in Dayton, Ohio, where the Wrights lived. The Gem City Club is fictional, but how is it like other clubs? How is it different?

6. Many people wanted Herman dead. What ultimately led to his death?

7. In the novel, Katharine alludes to a lost love who is an actual historical character. Do you know how that story ends?